COLORLESS
TSUKURU
TAZAKI

AND HIS YEARS
OF PILGRIMAGE

Also by Haruki Murakami

FICTION

After Dark

After the Quake

Blind Willow, Sleeping Woman

Dance Dance Dance

The Elephant Vanishes

Hard-Boiled Wonderland and the End of the World

Kafka on the Shore

Norwegian Wood

South of the Border, West of the Sun

Sputnik Sweetheart

A Wild Sheep Chase

The Wind-Up Bird Chronicle

1Q84

NON-FICTION

Underground: The Tokyo Gas Attack and the Japanese Psyche

What I Talk About When I Talk About Running

Haruki Murakami

COLORLESS TSUKURU TAZAKI

AND HIS YEARS OF PILGRIMAGE

Translated from the Japanese by
Philip Gabriel

Harvill Secker

LONDON

Published by Harvill Secker 2014

2 4 6 8 10 9 7 5 3 1

First published with the title *Shikisai o Motanai Tazaki Tsukuru to,
Kare no Junrei no Toshi* in 2013 by Bungeishunjū Ltd., Tokyo

First published in Great Britain in 2014 by
HARVILL SECKER
Random House
20 Vauxhall Bridge Road
London SW1V 2SA

www.vintage-books.co.uk

Addresses for companies within The Random House Group Limited
can be found at: www.randomhouse.co.uk/offices.htm

The Random House Group Limited Reg. No. 954009

A CIP catalog record for this book is available from the British Library

ISBN 9781846558337 (hardback)

The Random House Group Limited supports the Forest Stewardship Council® (FSC®), the
leading international forest-certification organisation. Our books carrying the FSC label are
printed on FSC®-certified paper. FSC is the only forest-certification scheme supported by the
leading environmental organisations, including Greenpeace. Our paper procurement
policy can be found at www.randomhouse.co.uk/environment

Typeset by Palimpsest Book Production Ltd, Falkirk, Stirlingshire
Printed and bound in Great Britain by Clays Ltd, St Ives plc

From July of his sophomore year in college until the following January, all Tsukuru Tazaki could think about was dying. He turned twenty during this time, but this special watershed – becoming an adult – meant nothing. Taking his own life seemed the most natural solution, and even now he couldn't say why he hadn't taken this final step. Crossing that threshold between life and death would have been easier than swallowing down a slick, raw egg.

Perhaps he didn't commit suicide then because he couldn't conceive of a method that fit the pure and intense feelings he had toward death. But method was beside the point. If there had been a door within reach that led straight to death, he wouldn't have hesitated to push it open, without a second thought, as if it were just a part of ordinary life. For better or for worse, though, there was no such door nearby.

I really should have died then, Tsukuru often told himself. Then this world, the one in the here and now, wouldn't exist. It was a captivating, bewitching thought. The present world wouldn't exist, and reality would no longer be real. As far as this world was concerned, he would simply no longer exist – just as this world would no longer exist for him.

At the same time, Tsukuru couldn't fathom why he had reached this point, where he was teetering over the precipice. There was an actual event that had led him to this place – this he knew all too well – but why should death have such a hold over him, enveloping him in its embrace for nearly half a year? *Envelop* – the word expressed it precisely. Like Jonah in the belly of the whale, Tsukuru had fallen into the bowels of death, one untold day after another, lost in a dark, stagnant void.

It was as if he were sleepwalking through life, as if he had already died but not yet noticed it. When the sun rose, so would Tsukuru – he'd brush his teeth, throw on whatever clothes were at hand, ride the train to college, and take notes in class. Like a person in a storm desperately grasping at a lamppost, he clung to this daily routine. He only spoke to people when necessary, and after school, he would return to his solitary apartment, sit on the floor, lean back against the wall, and ponder death and the failures of his life. Before him lay a huge, dark abyss that ran straight through to the earth's core. All he could see was a thick cloud of nothingness swirling around him; all he could hear was a profound silence squeezing his eardrums.

When he wasn't thinking about death, his mind was blank. It wasn't hard to keep from thinking. He didn't read any newspapers, didn't listen to music, and had no sexual desire to speak of. Events occurring in the outside world were, to him, inconsequential. When he grew tired of his room, he wandered aimlessly around the neighborhood or went to the station, where he sat on a bench and watched the trains arriving and departing, over and over again.

He took a shower every morning, shampooed his hair well, and did the laundry twice a week. Cleanliness was another one of his pillars: laundry, bathing, and teeth brushing. He barely noticed what he ate. He had lunch at the college cafeteria, but other than that, he hardly consumed a decent meal. When he felt hungry he stopped by the local supermarket and bought an apple or some vegetables. Sometimes he ate plain bread, washing it down with milk straight from the carton. When it was time to sleep, he'd gulp down a glass of whiskey as if it were a dose of medicine. Luckily he wasn't much of a drinker, and a small dose of alcohol was all it took to send him off to sleep. He never dreamed. But even if he had dreamed, even if dreamlike images arose from the edges of his mind, they would have found nowhere to perch on the slippery slopes of his consciousness, instead quickly sliding off, down into the void.

The reason why death had such a hold on Tsukuru Tazaki was clear. One day his four closest friends, the friends he'd known for a long time, announced that they did not want to see him, or talk with him, ever again. It was a sudden, decisive declaration, with no room for compromise. They gave no explanation, not a word, for this harsh pronouncement. And Tsukuru didn't dare ask.

He'd been friends with the four of them since high school, though when they cut him off, Tsukuru had already left his hometown and was attending college in Tokyo. So being banished didn't have any immediate negative effects on his daily routine – it wasn't like there would be awkward moments when he'd run into them on the street. But that was just quibbling. The pain he felt was, if anything, more intense, and weighed down on him even more greatly because of the physical distance. Alienation and loneliness became a cable that stretched hundreds of miles long, pulled to the breaking point by a gigantic winch. And through that taut line, day and night, he received indecipherable messages. Like a gale blowing between trees, those messages varied in strength as they reached him in fragments, stinging his ears.

The five of them had been classmates at a public high school in the suburbs of Nagoya. Three boys, and two girls. During summer vacation of their freshman year, they all did some volunteer work together and became friends. Even after freshman year, when they were in different classes, they remained a close-knit group. The volunteer work that had brought them together had been part of a social studies summer assignment, but even after it ended, they chose to volunteer as a group.

Besides the volunteer work, they went hiking together on holidays, played tennis, swam at the Chita Peninsula, or got together at one of their houses to study for tests. Or else – and this was what they did most often – they just hung out someplace, and talked for hours. It wasn't like they showed up with a topic in mind – they just never ran out of things to talk about.

Pure chance had brought them together. There were several volunteer opportunities they could have chosen from, but the one they all chose, independently, was an after-school tutoring program for elementary school kids (most of whom were children who refused to go to school). The program was run by a Catholic church, and of the thirty-five students in their high school class, the five of them were the only ones who selected it. To start, they participated in a three-day summer camp outside Nagoya, and got to be good friends with the children.

Whenever they took a break, the five of them gathered to talk. They got to know each other better, sharing their ideas and opening up about their dreams, as well as their problems. And when the summer camp was over, each one of them felt they were in the

4

right place, where they needed to be, with the perfect companions. A unique sense of harmony developed between them – each one needed the other four and, in turn, shared the sense that they too were needed. The whole convergence was like a lucky but entirely accidental chemical fusion, something that could only happen once. You might gather the same materials and make identical preparations, but you would never be able to duplicate the result.

After the initial volunteer period, they spent about two weekends a month at the after-school program, teaching the kids, reading to them, playing with them. They mowed the lawn, painted the building, and repaired playground equipment. They continued this work for the next two years, until they graduated from high school.

The only source of tension among them was the uneven number – the fact that their group was comprised of three boys and two girls. If two of the boys and two of the girls became couples, the remaining boy would be left out. That possibility must have always been hanging over their heads like a small, thick, lenticular cloud. But it never happened, nor did it even seem a likely possibility.

Perhaps coincidentally, all five of them were from suburban, upper-middle-class families. Their parents were baby boomers; their fathers were all professionals. Their parents spared no expense when it came to their children's education. On the surface, at least, their families were peaceful, and stable. None of their parents got divorced, and most of them had stay-at-home mothers. Their high school emphasized academics, and their grades were uniformly good. Overall there were far more similarities than differences in their everyday environments.

And aside from Tsukuru Tazaki, they had another small, co-incidental point in common: their last names all contained a color. The two boys' last names were Akamatsu – which means 'red pine' – and Oumi – 'blue sea'; the girls' family names were Shirane – 'white root' – and Kurono – 'black field.' Tazaki was the only last name that did not have a color in its meaning. From the very beginning this fact made him feel a little bit left out. Of course, whether or not you had a color as part of your name had nothing to do with your personality. Tsukuru under-stood this. But still, it disappointed him, and he surprised himself by feeling hurt. Soon, the other four friends began to use nicknames: the boys were called Aka (red) and Ao (blue); and the girls were Shiro (white) and Kuro (black). But he just remained Tsukuru. How great it would be, he often thought, if I had a color in my name too. Then everything would be perfect.

Aka was the one with the best grades. He never seemed to study hard, yet was at the top of his class in every subject. He never bragged about his grades, however, and preferred to cautiously stay in the background, almost as if he were embar-rassed to be so smart. But as often is the case with short people – he never grew past five foot three – once he made up his mind about something, no matter how trivial it might be, he never backed down. And he was bothered by illogical rules and by teachers who couldn't meet his exacting standards. He hated to lose; whenever he lost a tennis match, it put him in a bad mood. He didn't act out, or pout – instead, he just became unusually quiet. The other four friends found his short temper amusing and often teased him about it. Eventually Aka would always break down and laugh along with them. His father was a professor of economics at Nagoya University.

Ao was impressively built, with wide shoulders and a barrel chest, as well as a broad forehead, a generous mouth, and an imposing nose. He was a forward on the rugby team, and in his senior year he was elected team captain. He really hustled on the field and was constantly getting cuts and bruises. He wasn't good at buckling down and studying, but he was a cheerful person and enormously popular among his classmates. He always looked people straight in the eye, spoke in a clear, strong voice, and had an amazing appetite, seeming to enjoy everything set down in front of him. He also had a quick recall of people's names and faces, and seldom said anything bad about anyone else. He was a good listener and a born leader. Tsukuru could never forget the way he'd gather his team around him before a match to give them a pep talk.

'Listen up!' Ao would bellow. 'We're going to win. The only question is *how* and *by how much*. Losing is not an option for us. You hear me? *Losing is not an option!*'

'*Not an option!*' the team would shout, before rushing out onto the field.

Not that their high school rugby team was all that good. Ao was clever and extremely athletic, but the team itself was mediocre. When they went up against teams from private schools, where players had been recruited from all over the country on athletic scholarships, Ao's team usually lost. 'What's important,' he'd tell his friends, 'is the will to win. In the real world we can't always win. Sometimes you win, sometimes you lose.'

'And sometimes you get rained out,' Kuro remarked, with typical sarcasm.

Ao shook his head sadly. 'You're confusing rugby with baseball or tennis. Rugby's never postponed on account of rain.'

'You play even when it's raining?' Shiro asked, surprised. Shiro knew next to nothing about sports, and had zero interest in them.

'That's right,' Aka said seriously. 'Rugby matches are never canceled. No matter how hard it rains. That's why every year you get a lot of players who drown during matches.'

'My God, that's awful!' Shiro said.

'Don't be silly. He's joking,' Kuro said, in a slightly disgusted tone.

'If you don't mind,' Ao went on, 'my point is that if you're an athlete you have to learn how to be a good loser.'

'You certainly get a lot of practice with that every day,' Kuro said.

Shiro was tall and slim, with a model's body and the graceful features of a traditional Japanese doll. Her long hair was a silky, lustrous black. Most people who passed her on the street would turn around for a second look, but she seemed to find her beauty embarrassing. She was a serious person, who above all else disliked drawing attention to herself. She was also a wonderful, skilled pianist, though she would never play for someone she didn't know. She seemed happiest while teaching piano to children in an after-school program. During these lessons, Shiro looked completely relaxed, more relaxed than Tsukuru saw her at any other time. Several of the children, Shiro said, might not be good at regular schoolwork, but they had a natural talent for music and it would be a shame to not develop it. The school only had an old upright piano, almost an antique, so the five of them started a fund-raising drive to buy a new one. They worked part-time during summer vacation, and persuaded a company that made musical instruments to help them out. In the spring of their senior year, their hard work finally paid off, resulting in the purchase of a grand piano for the school. Their campaign caught people's attention and was even featured in a newspaper.

Shiro was usually quiet, but she loved animals so much that when a conversation turned to dogs and cats, her face lit up and the words would cascade out from her. Her dream was to become a veterinarian, though Tsukuru couldn't picture her with a scalpel, slicing open the belly of a Labrador retriever, or sticking her hand up the anus of a horse. If she went to vet school, that's exactly the kind of training she'd have to do. Her father ran an ob-gyn clinic in Nagoya.

Kuro wasn't beautiful, but she was eager and charming and always curious. She was large-boned and full-bodied, and already had a well-developed bust by the time she was sixteen. She was independent and tough, with a mind as quick as her tongue. She did well in humanities subjects, but was hopeless at math and physics. Her father ran an accounting firm in Nagoya, but there was no way she would ever be able to help out. Tsukuru often helped her with her math homework. She could be sarcastic but had a unique, refreshing sense of humor, and he found talking with her fun and stimulating. She was a great reader, too, and always had a book under her arm.

Shiro and Kuro had been in the same class in junior high and knew each other well, even before the five of them became friends. To see them together was a wonderful sight: a unique and captivating combination of a beautiful, shy artist and a clever, sarcastic comedian.

Tsukuru Tazaki was the only one in the group without anything special about him. His grades were slightly above average. He wasn't especially interested in academics, though he did pay close attention during class and always made sure to do the minimum amount of practice and review needed to get by. From the time he was little, that was his habit, no different from washing your hands before you eat and brushing your teeth after a meal. So although his grades were never stellar, he always passed his classes with ease. As long as he kept his grades up, his parents were never inclined to pester him to attend cram school or study with a tutor.

He didn't mind sports but never was interested enough to join a team. He'd play the occasional game of tennis with his family or friends, and go skiing or swimming every once in a while. That was about it. He was pretty good-looking, and sometimes people even told him so, but what they really meant was that he had *no particular defects to speak of.* Sometimes, when he looked at his face in the mirror, he detected an incurable boredom. He had no deep interest in the arts, no hobby or special skill. He was, if anything, a bit taciturn; he blushed easily, wasn't especially outgoing, and could never relax around people he'd just met.

If pressed to identify something special about him, one might notice that his family was the most affluent of the five friends, or that an aunt on his mother's side was an actress – not a star by any means, but still fairly well known. But when it came to Tsukuru himself, there was not one single quality he possessed that was worth bragging about or showing off to others. At least that was how he viewed himself. Everything about him was middling, pallid, lacking in color.

The only real interest he had was train stations. He wasn't sure why, but for as long as he could remember, he had loved to observe train stations – they had always appealed to him. Huge bullet-train stations; tiny, one-track stations out in the countryside; rudimentary freight-collection stations – it didn't matter what kind, because as long as it was a railway station, he loved it. Everything about stations moved him deeply.

Like most little boys he enjoyed assembling model trains, but what really fascinated him weren't the elaborate locomotives or cars, the intricately intersecting rail tracks, or the cleverly designed dioramas. No, it was the models of ordinary stations set down among the other parts, like an afterthought. He loved to watch as the trains passed by the station, or slowed down as they pulled up to the platform. He could picture the passengers coming and going, the announcements on the speaker system, the ringing of the signal as a train was about to depart, the station employees briskly going about their duties. What was real and what was imaginary mingled in his mind, and he'd tremble sometimes with the excitement of it all. But he could never adequately explain to people why he was so attracted to the stations. Even if he could, he knew they would think he was one weird kid. And sometimes Tsukuru himself wondered if something wasn't exactly right with him.

Though he lacked a striking personality, or any qualities that made him stand out, and despite always aiming for what was average, the middle of the road, there was (or *seemed* to be) something about him that wasn't exactly normal, something that set him apart. And this contradiction continued to perplex and confuse him, from his boyhood all the way to the present, when he was thirty-six years old. Sometimes the confusion was momentary and insubstantial, at other times deep and profound.

Sometimes Tsukuru couldn't understand why he was included in their group of five. Did the others really *need* him? Wouldn't they be able to relax and have a better time if he weren't there?

Maybe they just hadn't realized it yet, and it was only a matter of time before they did? The more he pondered this dilemma, the less he understood. Trying to sort out his value to the group was like trying to weigh something that had no unit value. The needle on the scale wouldn't settle on a number.

But none of these concerns seemed to bother the other four. Tsukuru could see that they genuinely loved it when all five of them got together as a group. Like an equilateral pentagon, where all sides are the same length, their group's formation had to be composed of five people exactly – any more or any less wouldn't do. They believed that this was true.

And naturally Tsukuru was happy, and proud, to be included as one indispensable side of the pentagon. He loved his four friends, loved the sense of belonging he felt when he was with them. Like a young tree absorbing nutrition from the soil, Tsukuru got the sustenance he needed as an adolescent from this group, using it as necessary food to grow, storing what was left as an emergency heat source inside him. Still, he had a constant, nagging fear that someday he would fall away from this intimate community, or be forced out and left on his own. Anxiety raised its head, like a jagged, ominous rock exposed by the receding tide, the fear that he would be separated from the group and end up entirely alone.

—

'So you really liked railroad stations that much, ever since you were little?' Sara Kimoto asked. She sounded impressed.

Tsukuru nodded cautiously. The last thing he wanted was for her to think he was one of those *otaku* nerds he knew from the engineering department at work, the kind who were so wrapped up in their jobs that work became their whole world. The way the conversation was going, though, she might end up thinking just that. 'That's right,' he admitted. 'Since I was a kid, I've always liked stations.'

'You've certainly led a very consistent life,' she said. She seemed amused by it, but he couldn't detect any negativity in her tone.

'Why it had to be stations, I can't say.'

Sara smiled. 'It must be your calling.'

'Maybe so,' Tsukuru said.

How did we wind up talking about this? Tsukuru wondered. *That* had happened so long ago, and he'd much prefer to wipe it from memory. But Sara, for whatever reason, wanted to hear about his high school days. What kind of student was he, what did he do back then? And before he knew it, he'd segued into talking about his close group of five friends. The four colorful people – and colorless Tsukuru Tazaki.

Sara and Tsukuru were at a bar on the outskirts of Ebisu. They'd had a dinner reservation at a small Japanese-style restaurant that Sara knew, but since she had eaten a late lunch and wasn't hungry, they canceled the reservation and went out for cocktails instead. Tsukuru wasn't hungry either and didn't mind skipping dinner. He wasn't such a big eater to begin with. He could get by on cheese and nuts at the bar.

Sara was two years older than Tsukuru and worked in a large travel agency. She specialized in package tours abroad and took a lot of business trips overseas. Tsukuru (in his 'calling') worked for a railway company, in a department that oversaw the design of railroad stations in the western part of the Kanto region around Tokyo. So although there was no direct connection between their jobs, in a way they both involved aspects of the transportation industry. He and Sara had met at a party to celebrate his boss's newly constructed house, where they had exchanged email addresses. This was their fourth date. After dinner on their third date, in what seemed like a natural progression of events, they had gone back to his apartment and made love. Today was one week later, a delicate stage in their burgeoning relationship. If they continued to see each other after this, things would surely get more serious. Tsukuru was thirty-six, Sara thirty-eight. This wasn't, of course, some high school crush.

From the first time he saw her, Tsukuru had liked Sara's looks. She wasn't typically beautiful. Her prominent cheekbones gave her an obstinate look, and her nose was narrow and pointed, but there was something indefinably vital and alive about her face that caught his eye. Her eyes were narrow, but when she really looked at something they suddenly opened wide: two dark eyes, never timid, brimming with curiosity.

He wasn't normally conscious of it, but there was one part of his body that was extremely sensitive, somewhere along his back. This soft, subtle spot he couldn't reach was usually covered by something, so that it was invisible to the naked eye. But when, for whatever reason, that spot became exposed and someone's finger pressed down on it, something inside him would stir. A special substance would be secreted, swiftly carried by his bloodstream to every corner of his body. That special stimulus was both a physical sensation and a mental one, creating vivid images in his mind.

The first time he met Sara, he felt an anonymous finger reach out and push down forcefully on that trigger on his back. The day they met they talked for a long time, though he couldn't recall much of what they said. What he did recall was the special feeling on his back, and the indefinably thrilling sensation it brought to his mind and body. One part of him relaxed, another part tightened up. That sort of feeling. But what did it mean? Tsukuru thought about this for days, but he was not, by nature, adept at abstract thinking. So Tsukuru emailed Sara and invited her to dinner. He was determined to find out the meaning of that feeling, of that sensation.

Just as he appreciated Sara's appearance, he also enjoyed the way she dressed. Her clothes were always simple and subdued, but they were lovely and fit her perfectly. Tsukuru could easily imagine, though, that what appeared to be simple outfits had taken much time to choose, and also hadn't come cheap. Her accessories and makeup, too, were low-key yet refined. Tsukuru himself wasn't particular about clothes, but he'd always loved seeing a well-dressed woman. Just like he enjoyed listening to beautiful music.

His two older sisters loved clothes, and when they were young, before they went out on a date, they had grabbed Tsukuru first to get his opinion of their outfit. He wasn't sure why, but they were very serious about it. What do you think? they'd ask. Do these go well together? And he would give his honest opinion, from a male perspective. His sisters respected his opinion, which made him happy, and before long, this became a habit.

As he sipped his weak highball, Tsukuru mentally undressed Sara. Unhooking the back of her dress, quietly unzipping her. He'd only slept with her once, but it had been wonderful, and fulfilling. Dressed or undressed, she looked five years younger than she was, with pure white skin and beautifully rounded, modestly sized breasts. Leisurely foreplay, caressing her, had been amazing, and after he came, he had felt at peace as he held her close. But that wasn't all there was to it. He was well aware that there was something more. Making love was a joining, a connection between one person and another. You receive something, and you also have to give.

'What were *your* high school days like?' Tsukuru asked.

Sara shook her head. 'I don't want to talk about that. It was pretty boring. I'll tell you about it sometime, but right now, I want to hear about you. What happened to your group of five friends?'

Tsukuru picked up a handful of nuts and tossed a few in his mouth.

'We had several unspoken rules among us, one of them being *As much as we possibly can, we do things together, all five of us.* We tried to avoid having just two of us, for instance, going off somewhere. Otherwise, we were worried that the group might fall apart. We had to be a centripetal unit. I'm not sure how to put it – we were trying our best to maintain the group as an orderly, harmonious community.'

'An orderly, harmonious community?' Genuine surprise showed in her voice.

Tsukuru blushed a little. 'We were in high school, and had all kinds of weird ideas.'

Sara looked intently at Tsukuru, cocking her head a degree or two. 'I don't find it weird. But what was the purpose of that community?'

'The original purpose, like I said, was to help out at an after-school program. This was where we all met and we all felt strongly about it – it remained an important collective goal. But as time passed, simply being a community ourselves became one of our goals, too.'

'You mean maintaining the group itself, and keeping it going, became one of your aims.'

'I guess so.'

Sara narrowed her eyes in a tight line. 'Just like the universe.'

'I don't know much about the universe,' Tsukuru said. 'But for us it was very important. We had to protect the special chemistry that had developed among us. Like protecting a lit match, keeping it from blowing out in the wind.'

'Chemistry?'

'The power that happened to arise at that point. Something that could never be reproduced.'

'Like the Big Bang?'

'I'm not sure about that,' Tsukuru said.

Sara took a sip of her mojito and examined the mint leaf from several angles.

'I went to private girls' schools,' she said, 'so I really don't understand those kind of co-ed groups at public schools. I can't picture what they're like. In order for the five of you to maintain that community, so it wouldn't fall apart, you tried to be as abstinent as you could. Is that how it worked?'

'Abstinent? I'm not sure that's the right word. It wasn't something that dramatic. It's true, though, we were careful to keep relations with the opposite sex out of the group.'

'But you never put that into words,' Sara said.

Tsukuru nodded. 'We didn't verbalize it. It wasn't like we had rules or anything.'

'What about you? You were with them all the time, so weren't you attracted at all to Shiro or Kuro? From what you told me, they sound pretty appealing.'

'Both of the girls were appealing in their own way. I'd be lying if I said I wasn't attracted to them. But I tried as much as possible not to think of them that way.'

'*As much as possible?*'

'As much as possible,' Tsukuru said. He felt his cheeks reddening again. 'When I couldn't help thinking of them, I always tried to think of them as a pair.'

'The two of them as a pair?'

Tsukuru paused, searching for the right words. 'I can't really explain it. I thought of them like they were a fictitious being. Like a formless, abstract being.'

'Hmm.' Sara appeared impressed. She thought about it. She seemed to want to say something, but then thought better of it. After a while she spoke.

'So after you graduated from high school you went to college in Tokyo, and left Nagoya. Is that right?'

'That's right,' Tsukuru said. 'I've lived in Tokyo ever since.'

'What about the other four?'

'They went to colleges in the Nagoya area. Aka studied in the economics department of Nagoya University, the department where his father taught. Kuro attended a private women's college famous for its English department. Ao got into business school at a private college that had a well-known rugby team, on the strength of his athletic abilities. Shiro finally was persuaded to give up on being a veterinarian and instead she studied piano in a music school. All four schools were close enough for them to commute from home. I was the only one who went to Tokyo, in my case to an engineering college.'

'Why did you want to go to Tokyo?'

'It's simple, really. There was a professor at my university who was an expert on railroad station construction. Constructing stations is a specialized field – they have a different structure from other buildings – so even if I went to an ordinary engineering school and studied construction and engineering, it wouldn't have been of much practical use. I needed to study with a specialist.'

'Having set, specific goals makes life easier,' Sara said.

Tsukuru agreed.

'So the other four stayed in Nagoya because they didn't want that beautiful community to break up?'

'When we were seniors in high school, we talked about where we were going to go to college. Except for me, they all planned to stay in Nagoya and go to college there. They didn't come out and say it exactly, but it was obvious they were doing that because they wanted to keep the group together.'

With his GPA, Aka could have easily gotten into a top school like Tokyo University, and his parents and teachers urged him to try. And Ao's athletic skills could have won him a place in a well-known university too. Kuro's personality was well suited to the more sophisticated, intellectually stimulating life she might have found in a cosmopolitan environment, and she should have gone on to one of the private universities in Tokyo. Nagoya, of course, is a large city, but culturally it was much more provincial. In the end, all four of them decided to stay in Nagoya, settling for much less prestigious schools than they could have attended. Shiro was the only one who never would have left Nagoya, even if the group hadn't existed. She wasn't the type to venture out on her own in search of a more stimulating environment.

'When they asked me what my plans were,' Tsukuru said, 'I told them I hadn't decided yet. But I'd actually made up my mind to go to school in Tokyo. I mean, if I could have managed to stay back in Nagoya, and half-heartedly study at some so-so college, I would have done it, if it meant I got to stay close to them. In a lot of ways that would have been easier, and that's actually what my family was hoping I'd do. They sort of expected that after I graduated from college, I'd eventually take over my father's company. But I knew that if I didn't go to Tokyo, I'd regret it. I just felt that I had to study with that professor.'

'That makes sense,' Sara said. 'So after you decided you'd go to Tokyo, how did the others take it?'

'I don't know how they *really* felt about it, of course. But I'm pretty sure they were disappointed. Without me in the equation, part of that sense of unity we always had was inevitably going to vanish.'

'The chemistry, too.'

'It would have changed into something different. To some extent.'

Yet when his friends realized how determined Tsukuru was to go, they didn't try to stop him. In fact, they encouraged him. Tokyo was only an hour and a half away by bullet train. He could come back any time he wanted, right? And there's no guarantee you'll get into your first-choice school anyway, they said, half kidding him. Passing the entrance exam for that university meant Tsukuru had to buckle down and study like never before.

'So what happened to your group after you all graduated from high school?' Sara asked.

'At first everything went fine. I went back to Nagoya whenever there was a school vacation – spring and fall break, summer vacation and New Year's – and spent as much time as I could with the others. We were as close as always, and got along well.'

Whenever he was back home, Tsukuru and his friends had

lots to catch up on. After he left Nagoya, the other four continued to spend time together, but once he was back in town, they'd revert to their five-person unit (though of course there were times when some of them were busy and only three or four of them could get together). The other four brought him back into the fold, as if there had been no gap in time. Or at least, Tsukuru detected no subtle shift in mood, no invisible distance between them, and that made him very happy. That's why he didn't care that he hadn't made a single friend in Tokyo.

Sara narrowed her eyes and looked at him. 'You never made even one friend in Tokyo?'

'I don't know why, but I just couldn't,' Tsukuru said. 'I guess I'm basically not very outgoing. But don't get the wrong idea – I wasn't a shut-in or anything. This was the first time I was living on my own, free to do whatever I liked. I enjoyed my days. The railroad lines in Tokyo are like a web spread out over the city, with countless stations. Just seeing them took a lot of time. I'd go to different stations, check out how they were designed, pencil out some rough sketches, jot down anything special I noticed.'

'It sounds like fun,' Sara said.

The university itself, though, wasn't very exciting. Most of his courses in the beginning were general education classes, uninspiring and numbingly boring. Still, he'd worked hard to get into college, so he tried not to cut class. He studied German and French; he even went to the language lab to practice English. He discovered, to his surprise, that he had a knack for learning languages. Yet he didn't meet anyone he was drawn to. Compared to his colorful, stimulating group of friends from high school, everyone else seemed spiritless, dull, insipid. He never met anyone he felt like getting to know better, so he spent most of his time in Tokyo alone. On the plus side, he read constantly, more than he ever had before.

'But didn't you feel lonely?' Sara asked.

'I felt alone, but not especially lonely. I guess I just took that for granted.'

He was young, and there was so much about the world he still didn't know. And Tokyo was a brand-new place for him, so very different from the environment he'd grown up in, and those differences were greater than he'd ever anticipated. The scale of the city was overwhelming, the diversity of life there extraordinary. There were too many choices of things to do, the way people talked struck him as odd, and the pace of life was too fast. He couldn't strike a good balance between himself and the world around him. But there was still a place for him to return. He knew this. Get on the bullet train at the Tokyo station and in an hour and a half he'd arrive at an *orderly, harmonious, intimate place.* Where time flowed by peacefully, where friends he could confide in eagerly awaited him.

'What about now?' Sara asked. 'Do you feel like you're maintaining a good balance between yourself and the world around you?'

'I've been with this company for fourteen years. The job's fine, and I enjoy the work. I get along with my colleagues. And I've been in relationships with a few women. Nothing ever came of it, but there were lots of reasons for that. It wasn't entirely my fault.'

'And you're alone, but not lonely.'

It was still early, and they were the only customers in the bar. Music from a jazz trio played softly in the background.

'I suppose,' Tsukuru said after some hesitation.

'But you can't go back now? To that orderly, harmonious, intimate place?'

He thought about this, though there was no need to. 'That place doesn't exist anymore,' he said quietly.

It was in the summer of his sophomore year in college when that place vanished forever.

2.

This drastic change took place during summer vacation of his sophomore year, between the first and second semesters. Afterward, Tsukuru Tazaki's life was changed forever, as if a sheer ridge had divided the original vegetation into two distinct biomes.

As always, when vacation rolled around he packed his belongings (though he did not have very many to begin with) and rode the bullet train back home. After a short visit with his family in Nagoya, he called up his four friends, but he couldn't get in touch with any of them. All four of them were out, he was told. He figured they must have gone out together somewhere. He left a message with each of their families, went downtown to a movie theater in the shopping district, and killed time watching a movie he didn't particularly want to see. Back at home, he ate dinner with his family, then phoned each of his friends again. No one had returned.

The next morning he called them again, with the same result: they were all still out. He left another message with each family member who answered the phone. Please have them call me when they get back, he said, and they promised to pass the message along. But something in their voices bothered him. He hadn't noticed it the first time he called, but now he sensed something subtly different, as if, for some reason, they were trying to keep him at arm's length. As if they wanted to hang up on him as soon as possible. Shiro's older sister, in particular, was curt and abrupt. Tsukuru had always gotten along very well with her – she was two years older than Shiro, and though not as stunning as Shiro, still a beautiful woman. They often joked around when he called – or if not a joke, at least they exchanged a friendly greeting. But now she hurriedly said goodbye, as if she could barely wait to end the conversation. After he had called all four homes, Tsukuru was left feeling like an outcast, as if he were carrying some virulent pathogen that the others were desperately trying to avoid.

Something must have happened, *something* had taken place while he was away to make them create this distance. Something inappropriate, and offensive. But what it was – what it could possibly be – he simply had no clue.

He was left feeling like he'd swallowed a lump of something he shouldn't have, something he couldn't spit out, or digest. He stayed home the whole day waiting for the phone to ring. His mind was unfocused, and he was unable to concentrate. He'd left repeated messages with his friends' families, telling them he was in Nagoya. Usually his friends would call right away and cheerfully welcome him back, but this time the phone remained implacably silent.

Tsukuru thought about calling them again in the evening, but then decided not to. Maybe all of them really were at home. Maybe they didn't want to come to the phone and instead were pretending to be out. Maybe they had told their families, 'If Tsukuru Tazaki calls, tell him I'm not here.' Which would explain why their family members sounded so ill at ease.

But why?

He couldn't imagine a reason. The last time the five of them had been together was in early May, during the Golden Week holidays. When Tsukuru had taken the train back to Tokyo, his four friends had come to the station to see him off, giving him big, hearty, exaggerated waves through the window as the train pulled away, like he was a soldier being shipped off to the ends of the earth.

After that point, Tsukuru had written a couple of letters to Ao. Shiro was hopeless with computers, so they normally relied on letters, and Ao was their contact person. Tsukuru always addressed the letter to Ao, who made sure that the letters circulated among the others. That way Tsukuru could avoid writing individual letters to everyone. He mainly wrote about his life in Tokyo, what he saw there, what experiences he had, what he was feeling. But always, no matter what he saw or did, he knew he would be having a much better time if the four of them were there to share the experience with him. That's how he really felt. Other than that, he didn't write anything much.

The other four wrote letters to him, jointly signed, but there was never anything negative in them. They just reported in detail on what they'd been up to in Nagoya. They'd all been born and raised there, but they seemed to be enjoying their college lives. Ao had bought a used Honda Accord (with a stain on the backseat that looked like a dog had peed there, he reported, the kind of car five people could easily ride in, as long as none of them was too fat), and all of them piled into the car to take a trip to Lake Biwa. Too bad you couldn't go with us, Tsukuru, they wrote. Looking forward to seeing you during the summer, they added. To Tsukuru, it sounded like they meant it.

That night, after he still hadn't heard from his friends, Tsukuru had trouble sleeping. He felt agitated. Random, senseless thoughts flitted around in his head. But all these thoughts were just variations on one theme. Like a man who has lost his sense of direction, Tsukuru's thoughts endlessly circled the same place. By the time he became aware of what his mind was doing, he found himself back where he'd started. Finally, his thinking process got stuck, as if the folds of his brain were a broken screw.

He remained awake in bed until 4 a.m. Then he fell asleep, but he woke up again shortly after six. He didn't feel like eating, and drank a glass of orange juice, but even that made him nauseous. His lack of appetite worried his family, but he told them it was nothing. My stomach's just a little tired out, he explained.

Tsukuru stayed at home that day, too. He lay next to the phone, reading a book, or at least trying to. In the afternoon he called his friends' homes again. He didn't feel like it, but he couldn't just sit around with this baffling, disconcerting feeling, praying for the phone to ring.

The result was the same. The family members who answered the phone told Tsukuru – curtly, or apologetically, or in an overly neutral tone of voice – that his friends weren't at home. Tsukuru thanked them, politely but briefly, and hung up. This time he didn't leave a message. Probably they were as tired of pretending to be out as he was tired of trying to contact them. He assumed that eventually the family members who were screening his calls might give up. If he kept on calling, there had to be a reaction.

And eventually there was. Just past eight that night, a call came from Ao.

'I'm sorry, but I have to ask you not to call any of us anymore,' Ao said abruptly and without preface. No 'Hey!' or 'How've you been?' or 'It's been a while.' *I'm sorry* was his only concession to social niceties.

Tsukuru took a breath, and silently repeated Ao's words, quickly assessing them. He tried to read the emotions behind them, but the words were like the formal recitation of an announcement. There had been no room for feelings.

'If everybody's telling me not to call them, then of course I won't,' Tsukuru replied. The words slipped out, almost automatically. He had tried to speak normally, calmly, but his voice sounded like a stranger's. The voice of someone living in a distant town, someone he had never met (and probably never would).

'Then don't,' Ao said.

'I don't plan on doing anything people don't want me to do,' Tsukuru said.

Ao let out a sound, neither a sigh or a groan of agreement.

'But if possible, I do want to know the reason for this,' Tsukuru said.

'That's not something I can tell you,' Ao replied.

'Then who can?'

A thick stone wall rose. There was silence on the other end. Tsukuru could faintly hear Ao breathing through his nostrils. He pictured Ao's flat, fleshy nose.

'Think about it, and you'll figure it out,' Ao said, finally.

Tsukuru was speechless. What was he talking about? *Think about it?* Think about *what*? If I think any harder about anything, I won't know who I am anymore.

'It's too bad it turned out like this,' Ao said.

'All of you feel this way?'

'Yeah. Everyone feels it's too bad.'

'Tell me – what happened?' Tsukuru asked.

'You'd better ask yourself that,' Ao said. Tsukuru detected a quaver of sadness and anger in his voice, but it was just for an instant. Before Tsukuru could think of how to respond, Ao had hung up.

—

'That's all he told you?' Sara asked.

'It was a short conversation, minimalist. That's the very best I can reproduce it.'

The two of them were face-to-face across a small table in the bar.

'After that, did you ever talk with him, or any of the other three about it?'

Tsukuru shook his head. 'No, I haven't talked to any of them since then.'

Sara's eyes narrowed as she gazed at him, as if she were inspecting a scene that violated the laws of physics. 'None of them?'

'I never saw any of them again. And we've never spoken.'

'But didn't you want to know why they suddenly kicked you out of the group?'

'I don't know how to put it, but at the time nothing seemed to matter. The door was slammed in my face, and they wouldn't let me back inside. And they wouldn't tell me why. But if that's what all of them wanted, I figured there was nothing I could do about it.'

'I don't get it,' Sara said, as if she really didn't. 'It could have been a complete misunderstanding. I mean, you couldn't think of any reason why it happened? Didn't you find the whole thing deplorable? That some stupid mistake might have led you to lose such close friends? Why wouldn't you try to clear up a misunderstanding that might have been easily rectified?'

Her mojito glass was empty. She signaled the bartender and asked for a wine list, and, after some deliberation, she chose a glass of Napa Cabernet Sauvignon. Tsukuru had only drunk half his highball. The ice had melted, forming droplets on the outside of his glass. The paper coaster was wet and swollen.

'That was the first time in my life that anyone had rejected me so completely,' Tsukuru said. 'And the ones who did it were the people I trusted the most, my four best friends in the world. I was so close to them that they had been like an extension of my own body. Searching for the reason, or correcting a misunderstanding, was beyond me. I was simply, and utterly, in shock. So much so that I thought I might never recover. It felt like something inside me had snapped.'

The bartender brought over the glass of wine and replenished the bowl of nuts. Once he'd left, Sara turned to Tsukuru.

'I've never experienced that myself, but I think I can imagine how *stunned* you must have been. I understand that you couldn't recover from it quickly. But still, after time had passed and the shock had worn off, wasn't there something you could have done? I mean, it was so unfair. Why didn't you challenge it? I don't see how you could stand it.'

Tsukuru shook his head slightly. 'The next morning I made up some excuse to tell my family and took the bullet train back to Tokyo. I couldn't stand being in Nagoya for one more day. All I could think of was getting away from there.'

'If it had been me, I would have stayed there and not left until I got to the bottom of it,' Sara said.

'I wasn't strong enough for that,' Tsukuru said.

'You didn't want to find out the truth?'

Tsukuru stared at his hands on the tabletop, carefully choosing his words. 'I think I was afraid of pursuing it, of whatever facts might come to light. Of actually coming face-to-face with them. Whatever the truth was, I didn't think it would save me. I'm not sure why, but I was certain of it.'

'And you're certain of it now?'

'I don't know,' Tsukuru said. 'But I was then.'

'So you went back to Tokyo, stayed holed up in your apartment, closed your eyes, and covered up your ears.'

'You could say that, yes.'

Sara reached out and rested her hand on top of his. 'Poor Tsukuru,' she said. The softness of her touch slowly spread through him. After a moment she took her hand away and lifted the wineglass to her mouth.

'After that I went to Nagoya as seldom as possible,' Tsukuru said. 'When I did return, I tried not to leave my house, and once I was done with whatever I had to do, I came back to Tokyo as quickly as I could. My mother and older sisters were worried and asked me if something had happened, but I never said anything. There was no way I could tell them.'

'Do you know where the four of them are now, and what they're doing?'

'No, I don't. Nobody ever told me, and I never really wanted to know.'

Sara swirled the wine in her glass and gazed at the ripples, as if reading someone's fortune.

'I find this very strange,' she said. 'That incident was obviously a huge shock, and in a way, it changed your life. Don't you think?'

Tsukuru gave a small nod. 'In a lot of ways I've become a different person.'

'How so?'

'Well, I feel more often how dull and insignificant I am for other people. And for myself.'

Sara gazed into his eyes for a time, her voice serious. 'I don't think you're either dull or insignificant.'

'I appreciate that,' Tsukuru said. He gently pressed his fingers against his temple. 'But that's an issue I have to figure out on my own.'

'I still don't follow,' Sara said. 'The pain caused by that incident is still in your mind, or your heart. Or maybe both. But I think it's very clearly there. Yet for the last fifteen or sixteen years you've never tried to trace the reason why you had to suffer like that.'

'I'm not saying I didn't feel like knowing the truth. But after all these years, I think it's better just to forget about it. It was a long time ago, and it's all sunk within the past.'

Sara's thin lips came together, and then she spoke. 'I think that's dangerous.'

'Dangerous? How so?'

'You can hide memories, suppress them, but you can't erase the history that produced them.' Sara looked directly into his eyes. 'If nothing else, you need to remember that. You can't erase history, or change it. It would be like destroying yourself.'

'Why are we talking about this?' Tsukuru said, half to himself, trying to sound upbeat. 'I've never talked to anybody about this before, and never planned to.'

Sara smiled faintly. 'Maybe you needed to talk with somebody. More than you ever imagined.'

That summer, after he returned to Tokyo from Nagoya, Tsukuru was transfixed by the odd sensation that, physically, he was being completely transformed. Colors he'd once seen appeared completely different, as if they'd been covered by a special filter. He heard sounds that he'd never heard before, and couldn't make out other noises that had always been familiar. When he moved, he felt clumsy and awkward, as if gravity were shifting around him.

For the five months after he returned to Tokyo, Tsukuru lived at death's door. He set up a tiny place to dwell, all by himself, on the rim of a dark abyss. A perilous spot, teetering on the edge, where, if he rolled over in his sleep, he might plunge into the depth of the void. Yet he wasn't afraid. All he thought about was how easy it would be to fall in.

All around him, for as far as he could see, lay a rough land strewn with rocks, with not a drop of water, nor a blade of grass. Colorless, with no light to speak of. No sun, no moon or stars. No sense of direction, either. At a set time, a mysterious twilight and a bottomless darkness merely exchanged places. A remote border on the edges of consciousness. At the same time, it was a place of strange abundance. At twilight birds with razor-sharp beaks came to relentlessly scoop out his flesh. But as darkness covered the land, the birds would fly off somewhere, and that land would silently fill in the gaps in his flesh with something else, some other indeterminate material.

Tsukuru couldn't fathom what this substance was. He couldn't accept or reject it. It merely settled on his body as a shadowy swarm, laying an ample amount of shadowy eggs. Then darkness would withdraw and twilight would return, bringing with it the birds, who once again slashed away at his body.

He was himself then, but at the same time, he was not. He

was Tsukuru Tazaki, and not Tsukuru Tazaki. When he couldn't stand the pain, he distanced himself from his body and, from a nearby, painless spot, observed Tsukuru Tazaki enduring the agony. If he concentrated really hard, it wasn't impossible.

Even now that feeling would sometimes spring up. The sense of leaving himself. Of observing his own pain as if it were not his own.

After they left the bar Tsukuru invited Sara to dinner again. Maybe we could just have a bite nearby? he asked. Grab a pizza? I'm still not hungry, Sara replied. Okay, Tsukuru said, then how about going back to my place?

'Sorry, but I'm not in the mood today,' she said, reluctantly but firmly.

'Because I went on about all that stupid stuff?' Tsukuru asked.

She gave a small sigh. 'No, that's not it. I've just got some thinking to do. About all kinds of things. So I'd like to go home alone.'

'Of course,' Tsukuru said. 'You know, I'm really glad I could see you again, and talk with you. I just wish we'd had a more pleasant topic to talk about.'

She pursed her lips tightly for a moment and then, as if coming to a decision, spoke. 'Would you ask me out again? As long as you don't mind, I mean.'

'Of course. If it's okay with you.'

'It is.'

'I'm glad,' Tsukuru said. 'I'll email you.'

They said goodbye at the subway entrance. Sara took the escalator up to the Yamanote line and Tsukuru took the stairs down to the Hibiya line. Each of them back to their homes. Each lost in their own thoughts.

Tsukuru, of course, had no idea what Sara was thinking about. And he didn't want to reveal to her what was on his mind. There are certain thoughts that, no matter what, you have to keep inside. And it was those kinds of thoughts that ran through Tsukuru's head as he rode the train home.

3.

In the half year when he wandered on the verge of death, Tsukuru lost fifteen pounds. It was only to be expected, as he barely ate. Since childhood his face had been full, if anything, but now he became wasted and gaunt. Tightening his belt wasn't enough; he had to buy smaller trousers. When he undressed, his ribs stuck out like a cheap birdcage. His posture grew visibly worse, his shoulders slumped forward. With all the weight loss his legs grew spindly, like a stork's. As he stared at his naked self in the mirror, a thought hit him: This is an old man's body. Or that of someone near death.

But even if I do look like someone who is nearly dead, there's not much I can do about it, he told himself, as he stared at the mirror. Because I really am on the brink of death. I've survived, but barely – I've been clinging to this world like the discarded shell of an insect stuck to a branch, about to be blown off forever by a gust of wind. But that fact – that he looked like someone about to die – struck him again, forcefully. He stared fixedly at the image of his naked body for the longest time, like someone unable to stop watching a TV news report of a huge earthquake or terrible flood in a faraway land.

A sudden thought struck him – maybe I really *did* die. When the four of them rejected me, perhaps the young man named Tsukuru Tazaki really did pass away. Only his exterior remained, but just barely, and then over the course of the next half year, even that shell was replaced, as his body and face underwent a drastic change. The feeling of the wind, the sound of rushing water, the sense of sunlight breaking through the clouds, the colors of flowers as the seasons changed – everything around him felt changed, as if they had all been recast. The person here now, the one he saw in the mirror, might at first glance resemble Tsukuru Tazaki, but it wasn't actually him. It was merely a container that, for the sake of convenience, was labeled with the same name – but its contents had been replaced. He was called by that name simply because there was, for the time being, no other name to call him.

That night he had a strange dream, one in which he was tormented by strong feelings of jealousy. He hadn't had such a vivid, graphic dream in a long time.

Tsukuru had never understood the feeling of jealousy. He understood the concept, of course – the sensation you could have toward a person who possesses – or could easily acquire – the talents or gifts or position you covet. The feeling of being deeply in love with a woman only to find her in the arms of another man. Envy, resentment, regret, a frustration and anger for which there is no outlet.

But he had never once personally experienced those emotions. He'd never seriously wished for talents and gifts he didn't have, or been passionately in love. Never had he longed for, or envied, anyone. Not to say there weren't things he was dissatisfied with, things about himself he found lacking. If he had to, he could have listed them. It wouldn't have been a massive list, but not just a couple of lines, either. But those dissatisfactions and deficiencies stayed inside him – they weren't the type of emotions that motivated him to go out, somewhere else, in search of answers. At least until then.

In this dream, though, he burned with desire for a woman. It wasn't clear who she was. She was just *there*. And she had a special ability to separate her body and her heart. I will give you one of them, she told Tsukuru. My body or my heart. But you can't have both. You need to choose one or the other, right now. I'll give the other part to someone else, she said. But Tsukuru wanted *all* of her. He wasn't about to hand over one half to another man. He couldn't stand that. If that's how it is, he wanted to tell her, I don't need either one. But he couldn't say it. He was stymied, unable to go forward, unable to go back.

A horrendous pain lashed out at him, as if his entire body were being wrung out by enormous hands. His muscles snapped, his bones shrieked in agony, and he felt a horrendous thirst, as if every cell in his body were drying up, sapped of moisture. His body shook with rage at the thought of giving half of her to someone else. That rage became a thick, sloppy ooze that squeezed out from his marrow; his lungs were a pair of crazed bellows, while his heart raced like an engine with the accelerator slammed to the floor. Darkish, agitated blood pulsed to all his extremities.

He woke up, his body quaking. It took a while before he understood that it had been a dream. He tore off his sweat-soaked pajamas and dried himself with a towel, but no matter how hard he wiped the sweat away, he couldn't rid himself of that slimy feeling. And he came to a realization. Or maybe felt it intuitively. *So this was jealousy.* The body or the heart of the woman he loved, or maybe even both, were being wrested from him by someone else.

Jealousy — at least as far as he understood it from his dream — was the most hopeless prison in the world. Jealousy was not a place he was forced into by someone else, but a jail in which the inmate entered voluntarily, locked the door, and threw away the key. And not another soul in the world knew he was locked inside. Of course if he wanted to escape, he could do so. The prison was, after all, his own heart. But he couldn't make that decision. His heart was as hard as a stone wall. This was the very essence of jealousy.

Tsukuru grabbed a carton of orange juice from the fridge and drank glass after glass. His throat was bone dry. He sat down at the table and, watching through the window as the day slowly dawned, willed himself to calm down. This surge of overpowering emotion that had struck him had his heart and body trembling. What in the world could this dream mean? he wondered. Was it a prophecy? A symbolic message? Was it trying to tell him something? Or was this his true self, unknown to him until now, breaking out of its shell, struggling to emerge? Some ugly creature that had hatched, desperate to reach the air outside.

Tsukuru Tazaki only understood this later, but it was at this point that he stopped wanting to die. Having stared at his naked form in the mirror, he now saw someone else reflected there. That same night was when, in his dreams, he experienced jealousy (or what he took for jealousy) for the first time in his life. And by the time dawn came, he'd put behind him the dark days of the previous five months, days spent face-to-face with the utter void of extinction.

He speculated that, just as a powerful west wind blows away thick banks of clouds, the graphic, scorching emotion that passed through his soul in the form of a dream must have canceled and negated the longing for death, a longing that had reached out and grabbed him around the neck.

All that remained now was a sort of quiet resignation. A colorless, neutral, empty feeling. He was sitting alone in a huge, old, vacant house, listening as a massive grandfather clock hollowly ticked away time. His mouth was closed, his eyes fixed on the clock as he watched the hands move forward. His feelings were wrapped in layer upon layer of thin membrane and his heart was still a blank, as he aged, one hour at a time.

Tsukuru gradually began to eat again. He bought fresh ingredients and prepared simple, decent meals. Still, he regained only a little of the weight he'd lost. Over nearly a half year's time his stomach had drastically shrunk, and now, if he ate more than a fixed amount, he threw up afterward. He started swimming again early in the mornings at the university pool. He'd lost a lot of muscle, got out of breath when he went up stairs, and needed to regain his strength. He bought new swim trunks and goggles, and swam the crawl every day, between 1,000 and 1,500 meters. Afterward he'd stop by the gym and silently use the machines to train.

After a few months of decent meals and regular workouts, he'd mostly recovered. He had the muscles he needed (though he was muscular in a very different way from before). His posture became erect, not slouched, and the color returned to his face. For the first time in a long while, he even had stiff erections again when he woke up in the morning.

Around this time his mother paid a rare visit to Tokyo. She found that Tsukuru had started to act and speak a little oddly, and, after he hadn't been home for New Year's, she decided to go to check up on him. When she saw how much her son had changed in the space of a few months, she was speechless. But Tsukuru attributed it to 'normal changes you go through when you're my age.' What he really needed, he told her, were clothes that actually fit him now, and his mother totally accepted his explanation. She'd grown up with a sister and, after her own marriage, was more familiar with how to raise her daughters. She had no idea how to raise a boy, and so Tsukuru convinced her that his changes were normal developments. She happily took him to a department store to buy new clothes, mostly Brooks Brothers and Polo, the brands she preferred. His old clothes they either threw away or donated.

His face had changed as well. The mirror no longer showed a soft, decent-looking, though unthreatening and unfocused boy's face. What stared out at him now was the face of a young man with cheekbones so prominent they looked as if they'd been chiseled by a trowel. There was a new light in his eyes, a glint he'd never seen before, a lonely, isolated light with limited range. His beard suddenly grew thicker, and he had to shave every morning. He grew his hair out, too.

Tsukuru didn't particularly like his new looks. Nor did he hate them. They were, after all, just a convenient, makeshift mask. Though he was grateful, for the time being, that it wasn't the face he'd worn before.

In any case, the boy named Tsukuru Tazaki had died. In the savage darkness he'd breathed his last and was buried in a small clearing in the forest. Quietly, secretly, in the predawn while everyone was still fast asleep. There was no grave marker. And what stood here now, breathing, was a brand-new Tsukuru Tazaki, one whose substance had been totally replaced. But he was the only one who knew this. And he didn't plan to tell.

Just as before, he made the rounds sketching railroad stations and never missed a lecture at college. When he got up, he'd take a shower, wash his hair, and always brush his teeth after eating. He made his bed every morning, and ironed his own shirts. He did his best to keep busy. At night he read for two hours or so, mostly history or biographies. A long-standing habit. Habit, in fact, was what propelled his life forward. Though he no longer believed in a perfect community, nor felt the warmth of chemistry between people.

Every morning he'd stand at the bathroom sink and study his face in the mirror. And slowly he grew used to this new self, with all its changes. It was like acquiring a new language, memorizing the grammar.

Eventually he made a new friend. In June, nearly a year after his four friends in Nagoya abandoned him. This new friend went to the same college and was two years younger. He met the man at the college pool.

4.

He met the man at the college pool.

Like Tsukuru, the man swam by himself early every morning. They began to have a nodding acquaintance, and eventually, they started to talk. After changing in the locker room, they went out for breakfast together in the school cafeteria. The man was two years behind Tsukuru in college, and was majoring in physics. They were in the same engineering college, but students in the physics department and civil engineering department were like beings from different planets.

'What exactly do you do in the civil engineering department?' the student asked him.

'I build stations,' Tsukuru replied.

'Stations?'

'Railroad stations. Not TV stations or anything.'

'But why railroad stations?'

'The world needs them, that's why,' Tsukuru said, as if it were obvious.

'Interesting,' the man said, as if he truly felt that way. 'I've never really given much thought to the necessity of stations.'

'But you use stations yourself, I imagine. If there weren't any, you'd be in trouble when you ride the train.'

'I do ride the train, and I see your point . . . It's just that I – well – never imagined there were people in the world who had a passion for building them.'

'Some people write string quartets, some grow lettuce and tomatoes. There have to be a few who build railroad stations, too,' Tsukuru said. 'And I wouldn't say I have a *passion* for it, exactly. I just have an interest in one specific thing.'

'This might sound rude, but I think it's an amazing achievement to find even one specific thing that you're interested in.'

Tsukuru thought the younger man was poking fun at him, and gazed intently at his handsome face. But he seemed serious, his expression open and straightforward.

'You like making things, just as your name implies,' the man said, referring to the fact that *tsukuru* meant 'to make or build.'

'I've always liked making things that you can actually see,' Tsukuru admitted.

'Not me,' the man said. 'I've always been terrible at making things. Ever since I was in grade school I've been hopeless with my hands. Couldn't even put together a plastic model. I prefer thinking about abstract ideas, and I never get tired of it. But when it comes to actually using my hands to make something real, forget about it. I do like cooking, though, but that's because it's more like *deconstructing* things than constructing them . . . I guess it must seem a little disturbing for someone like me, who can't make anything, to go to engineering school.'

'What do you want to focus on here?'

The man gave it some thought. 'I don't really know. I don't have any set, clear goal like you. I just want to think deeply about things. Contemplate ideas in a pure, free sort of way. That's all. If you think about it, that's kind of like constructing a vacuum.'

'Well, the world needs a few people who create a vacuum.'

The other man laughed happily. 'Yeah, but it's different from people growing lettuce or tomatoes. If everybody in the world worked their hardest to create a vacuum, we'd be in big trouble.'

'Ideas are like beards. Men don't have them until they grow up. Somebody said that, but I can't remember who.'

'Voltaire,' the younger man said. He rubbed his chin and smiled, a cheerful, unaffected smile. 'Voltaire might be off the mark, though, when it comes to me. I have hardly any beard at all, but have loved thinking about things since I was a kid.'

His face was indeed smooth, with no hint of a beard. His eyebrows were narrow, but thick, his ears nicely formed, like lovely seashells.

'I wonder if what Voltaire meant wasn't ideas as much as meditation,' Tsukuru said.

The man inclined his head a fraction. 'Pain is what gives rise to meditation. It has nothing to do with age, let alone beards.'

The young man's name was Haida, which meant, literally, 'gray field.' Fumiaki Haida. Another person with a color, Tsukuru mused. Mister Gray. Though gray, of course, was a fairly subdued color.

Neither of them was very sociable, but as they continued to meet, a natural friendliness grew between them and they began to open up to each other. They decided to meet every morning and swim laps together. They both swam long distances, freestyle, though Haida was a little faster. He'd gone to a swim school since he was a child, and his swimming form was beautiful, without a single wasted motion. His shoulder blades moved smoothly, like the wings of a butterfly, barely skimming the surface. After Haida gave Tsukuru some detailed pointers, and after Tsukuru had done more strength training, he was finally able to match Haida's speed. At first they mainly talked about swimming techniques, but later branched out into other topics.

Haida was a short but handsome young man. His face was small and narrow, like an ancient Greek statue, but his facial features were, if anything, classical, with a kind of intelligent and reserved look. He wasn't the type of pretty young boy who immediately grabbed people's attention, but one whose graceful beauty only became apparent over time.

Haida's hair was short and slightly curly, and he always dressed casually in the same chinos and light-colored shirts. But despite his simple, ordinary outfit, he knew how to wear his clothes well. He loved reading above all else, and, like Tsukuru, he seldom read novels. His preferences ran to philosophy and the classics. He enjoyed reading plays, too, and was a big fan of Greek tragedies and Shakespeare. He also knew Noh and bunraku well. Haida was from Akita Prefecture in the far north of Japan. He had very white skin and long fingers. Like Tsukuru, he couldn't hold his liquor well, but unlike Tsukuru, he was able to distinguish between the music of Mendelssohn and the music of Schumann. Haida was extremely shy, and when he was together with more than three people, he did his best to stay invisible. There was an old, deep scar, about an inch and a half long, on his neck, like he'd been cut by a knife, but this scar added a strange accent to this otherwise serene young man's appearance.

Haida had come from Akita to Tokyo that spring and was living in a student dorm near campus, but had not yet made any friends. When the two of them discovered that they got along so well, they started to spend time together, and Haida began dropping by Tsukuru's apartment.

46

'How can a student afford such an expensive condo?' Haida asked in wonder the first time he visited Tsukuru's place.

'My father runs a real estate business in Nagoya and owns some properties in Tokyo,' Tsukuru explained. 'This one happened to be vacant, so they let me live here. My second sister used to live here, but after she graduated from college she moved out and I moved in. The place is in the company's name.'

'Your family must be pretty well off?'

'You know, I'm not really sure. Maybe – I have no idea. I don't think even my father would know unless he assembled his accountant, lawyer, tax consultant, and investment consultant together in one room. It seems like we're not so badly off now, which is why I can live in this kind of place. Believe me, I'm grateful.'

'But you're not interested in the sort of business your father does?'

'No, not at all. In his line of work you're constantly shifting capital around – from one side to another and back again. The whole thing's way too restless for me. I'm not like him. I much prefer plugging away at building stations, even if it isn't very profitable.'

'Your one set interest,' Haida commented, a big smile on his face.

—

Tsukuru ended up staying in that one-bedroom condo in Jiyu-gaoka even after he graduated from college and began working for a railway company headquartered in Shinjuku. When he was thirty, his father died and the condo officially became his. His father had apparently intended to give it to Tsukuru all along and unbeknownst to him had previously transferred the deed to his name. Tsukuru's eldest sister's husband took over his father's company, and Tsukuru continued his work in Tokyo building railroad stations, without much contact with his family. His visits to Nagoya remained few and far between.

When he was back in his hometown for his father's funeral, he half expected his four friends to show up to pay their condolences. He wondered how he should greet them if they did. But none of them showed up. Tsukuru felt relieved, but at the same time a little sad, and it hit him all over again: what they had had really *was* over. They could never go back again. All five of them were already, at this point, thirty years old – no longer the age when one dreamed of an ordered, harmonious community of friends.

About half the people in the world dislike their own name. Tsukuru happened to run across this statistic in a newspaper or magazine. He himself was in the other half – or, at least, he didn't dislike his name. Perhaps it was more accurate to say he couldn't imagine having a different name, or the kind of life he'd lead if he did.

The first name 'Tsukuru' was officially written with a single Chinese character, though usually he spelled it out phonetically in hiragana, and his friends all thought that was how his name was written. His mother and two sisters used an alternate reading of the same character for Tsukuru, calling him Saku or Saku-chan, which they found easier.

His father had been the one who named him. Well before Tsukuru was born, his father had already decided on his name. Why was unclear. Maybe it was because his father had spent many years of his own life far removed from anything having to do with making things. Or maybe at some point he'd received something akin to a revelation – a bolt of unseen lightning, accompanied by soundless thunder, searing the name Tsukuru in his brain. But his father never spoke of where he'd gotten the idea for the name. Not to Tsukuru, and not to anybody else.

When it came to which Chinese character he would choose to write out Tsukuru, however – the character that meant 'create,' or the simpler one that meant 'make' or 'build' – his father couldn't make up his mind for the longest time. The characters might read the same way, but the nuances were very different. His mother had assumed it would be written with the character that meant 'create,' but in the end his father had opted for the more basic meaning.

After his father's funeral, Tsukuru's mother recalled the discussion that had taken place when her husband had chosen the name. 'Your father felt that giving you the character for "create" would be a burden to you,' she told Tsukuru. 'The simpler character was also read as Tsukuru, and he thought it was a more easygoing, comfortable sort of name. You should know, at least, that your father thought long and hard about it. You were his first son, after all.'

Tsukuru had almost no memories of being close to his father, but when it came to his father's choice of name, Tsukuru had to agree. The plainer, simpler form of *tsukuru* indeed fit him better, for he barely had a creative or original bone in his body. But did any of this lighten the *burdens* of his life? Maybe because of his name, these burdens took on a different form. But whether that made them lighter, Tsukuru couldn't say.

That's how he became the person known as Tsukuru Tazaki. Before that, he'd been nothing – dark, nameless chaos and nothing more. A less-than-seven-pound pink lump of flesh barely able to breathe in the darkness, or cry out. First he was given a name. Then consciousness and memory developed, and, finally, ego. But everything began with his name.

His father's name was Toshio Tazaki – Toshio spelled out in characters that meant 'man who profits,' Tazaki literally meaning 'many peninsulas.' The perfect name for a man who indeed profited handsomely in many fields. He'd gone from poverty to a distinguished career, had devoted himself to the real estate business and ridden the era of high growth in Japan to brilliant success, then suffered from lung cancer and died at age sixty-four. But this came later. When Tsukuru met Haida, his father was still in good health, tirelessly and aggressively buying and selling high-end Tokyo residential properties as he puffed his way through fifty unfiltered cigarettes a day. The real estate bubble had already burst, but he had anticipated this risk and had diversified his holdings to lessen the financial effects on his bottom line. And the ominous shadow on his lungs still lay hidden away, yet to be discovered.

'My father teaches philosophy at a public university in Akita,' Haida told Tsukuru. 'Like me, his favorite thing is mulling over abstract ideas. He's always listening to classical music, and devouring books that no one else ever reads. He has zero ability to earn money, and any money he does earn goes to pay for books or records. He rarely thinks about his family, or savings. His mind is always off in the clouds. I was only able to study in Tokyo because my college has pretty low tuition, and I'm in a dorm so I can keep my living expenses down.'

'Is it better, financially, to go to the physics department than the philosophy department?' Tsukuru asked.

'When it comes to their graduates not earning anything, they're about even. Unless you win the Nobel Prize or something,' Haida said, flashing his usual winning smile.

Haida was an only child. He'd never had many friends, and relied on his dog and classical music to keep him company. The dorm he lived in wasn't exactly the best place to listen to classical music (and of course you couldn't keep a dog there), so he'd come over to Tsukuru's apartment with a few CDs and listen to them there. Most of them he'd borrowed from the university library. Occasionally he'd bring over some old LPs of his own. Tsukuru had a fairly decent stereo system in his apartment, but the only records his sister had left behind were of the Barry Manilow and Pet Shop Boys variety, so Tsukuru had hardly ever touched the record player.

Haida preferred to listen to instrumental music, chamber music, and vocal recordings. Music where the orchestral component was loud and prominent wasn't to his liking. Tsukuru wasn't very interested in classical music (or any other music, for that matter), but he did enjoy listening to it with Haida.

As they listened to one piano recording, Tsukuru realized that he'd heard the composition many times in the past. He didn't know the title, however, or the composer. It was a quiet, sorrowful piece that began with a slow, memorable theme played out as single notes, then proceeded into a series of tranquil variations. Tsukuru looked up from the book he was reading and asked Haida what it was.

'Franz Liszt's "Le mal du pays." It's from his *Years of Pilgrimage* suite, "Year 1: Switzerland."'

'"Le mal du . . . "?'

'"Le mal du pays." It's French. Usually it's translated as "home-sickness," or "melancholy." If you put a finer point on it, it's more like "a groundless sadness called forth in a person's heart by a pastoral landscape." It's a hard expression to translate accurately.'

'A girl I know used to play that piece a lot. A classmate of mine in high school.'

'I've always liked this piece. It's not very well known, though,' Haida said. 'Was your friend a good pianist?'

'Hard to say. I don't know much about music. But every time I heard it I thought it was beautiful. How should I put it? It had a calm sadness, but wasn't sentimental.'

'Then she must have played it well,' Haida said. 'The piece seems simple technically, but it's hard to get the expression right. Play it just as it's written on the score, and it winds up pretty boring. But go the opposite route and interpret it too intensely, and it sounds cheap. Just the way you use the pedal makes all the difference, and can change the entire character of the piece.'

'Who's the pianist here?'

'A Russian, Lazar Berman. When he plays Liszt it's like he's painting a delicately imagined landscape. Most people see Liszt's piano music as more superficial, and technical. Of course, he has some tricky pieces, but if you listen very carefully to his music you discover a depth to it that you don't notice at first. Most of the time it's hidden behind all the embellishments. This is particularly true of the *Years of Pilgrimage* suite. There aren't many living pianists who can play this piece accurately and with such beauty. Among more contemporary pianists, Berman gets it right, and with the older pianists I'd have to go with Claudio Arrau.'

Haida got quite talkative when it came to music. He went

on, delineating the special characteristics of Berman's perform-ance of Liszt, but Tsukuru barely listened. Instead, a picture of Shiro performing the piece, a mental image, vivid and three-dimensional, welled up in his mind. As if those beautiful moments were steadily swimming back, through a waterway, against the legitimate pressure of time.

The Yamaha grand piano in the living room of her house. Reflecting Shiro's conscientiousness, it was always perfectly tuned. The lustrous exterior without a single smudge or finger-print to mar its luster. The afternoon light filtering in through the window. Shadows cast in the garden by the cypress trees. The lace curtain wavering in the breeze. Teacups on the table. Her black hair, neatly tied back, her expression intent as she gazed at the score. Her ten long, lovely fingers on the keyboard. Her legs, as they precisely depressed the pedals, possessed a hidden strength that seemed unimaginable in other situations. Her calves were like glazed porcelain, white and smooth. When-ever she was asked to play something, this piece was the one she most often chose. 'Le mal du pays.' The groundless sadness called forth in a person heart's by a pastoral landscape. Home-sickness. Melancholy.

As he lightly shut his eyes and gave himself up to the music, Tsukuru felt his chest tighten with a disconsolate, stifling feeling, as if, before he'd realized it, he'd swallowed a hard lump of cloud. The piece ended and went on to the next track, but he said nothing, simply allowing those scenes to wash over him. Haida shot him an occasional glance.

'If you don't mind, I'd like to leave this record here. I can't listen to it in my dorm room anyway,' Haida said as he slipped the LP back in its jacket.

Even now this three-disc boxed set was still in Tsukuru's apartment. Nestled right next to Barry Manilow and the Pet Shop Boys.

Haida was a wonderful cook. To thank Tsukuru for letting him listen to music, he would go shopping and prepare a meal in Tsukuru's kitchen. Tsukuru's sister had left behind a set of pots and pans, as well as a set of dishes. These were his inheritance – as well as most of his furniture, and the occasional phone call from one of her ex-boyfriends ('Sorry, my sister doesn't live here anymore'). He and Haida had dinner together two or three times a week. They'd listen to music, talk, and eat the meal Haida had prepared. The meals he made were mostly simple, everyday dishes, though on holidays when he had more time, he'd try more elaborate recipes. Everything he made was delicious. Haida seemed to have a gift as a cook. Whatever he made – a plain omelet, miso soup, cream sauce, or paella – was done skillfully and intelligently.

'It's too bad you're in the physics department. You should open a restaurant,' Tsukuru said, half joking.

Haida laughed. 'That sounds good. But I don't like to be tied down in one place. I want to be free – to go where I want, when I want, and be able to think about whatever I want.'

'Sure, but that can't be easy to actually do.'

'It isn't. But I've made up my mind. I always want to be free. I like cooking, but I don't want to be holed up in a kitchen doing it as a job. If that happened, I'd end up hating somebody.'

'Hating somebody?'

'*The cook hates the waiter, and they both hate the customer,*' Haida said. 'A line from the Arnold Wesker play *The Kitchen*. People whose freedom is taken away always end up hating somebody. Right? I know I don't want to live like that.'

54

'Never being constrained, thinking about things freely – that's what you're hoping for?'

'Exactly.'

'But it seems to me that thinking about things freely can't be easy.'

'It means leaving behind your physical body. Leaving the cage of your physical flesh, breaking free of the chains, and letting pure logic soar. Giving a natural life to logic. That's the core of free thought.'

'It doesn't sound easy.'

Haida shook his head. 'No, depending on how you look at it, it's not that hard. Most people do it at times, without even realizing it. That's how they manage to stay sane. They're just not aware that's what they're doing.'

Tsukuru considered this. He liked talking with Haida about these kinds of abstract, speculative ideas. Usually he wasn't much of a talker, but something about talking with this younger man stimulated his mind, and sometimes the words just flowed. He'd never experienced this before. Back in Nagoya, in his group of five, he'd more often than not played the listener.

'But unless you can do that intentionally,' Tsukuru said, 'you can't achieve the real *freedom of thought* you're talking about, right?'

Haida nodded. 'Exactly. But it's as difficult as intentionally dreaming. It's way beyond your average person.'

'Yet you want to be able to do it intentionally.'

'You could say that.'

'I don't imagine they teach that technique in the physics department.'

Haida laughed. 'I never expected they would. What I'm looking for here is a free environment, and time. That's all. In an academic setting if you want to discuss what it means to think, you first need to agree on a theoretical definition. And that's where things get sticky. Originality is nothing but judicious *imitation*. So said Voltaire, the realist.'

'You agree with that?'

'Everything has boundaries. The same holds true with thought. You shouldn't fear boundaries, but you also should not be afraid of destroying them. That's what is most important if you want to be free: respect for and exasperation with boundaries. What's really important in life is always the things that are secondary. That's about all I can say.'

'Can I ask you a question?' Tsukuru said.

'Sure.'

'In different religions prophets fall into a kind of ecstasy and receive a message from an absolute being.'

'Correct.'

'And this takes place somewhere that transcends free will, right? Always passively.'

'That's correct.'

'And that message surpasses the boundaries of the individual prophet and functions in a broader, universal way.'

'Correct again.'

'And in that message there is neither contradiction nor equivocation.'

Haida nodded silently.

'I don't get it,' Tsukuru said. 'If that's true, then what's the value of human free will?'

'That's a great question,' Haida said, and smiled quietly. The kind of smile a cat gives as it stretches out, napping in the sun. 'I wish I had an answer for you, but I don't. Not yet.'

Haida began staying over at Tsukuru's apartment on the weekends. They would talk until late at night, at which point Haida would make up the fold-out sofa in the living room and go to sleep. In the morning he would make coffee and cook them omelets. Haida was very particular about coffee, always using special aromatic beans, which he ground with a small electric mill that he brought along. His devotion to coffee beans was the one luxury in his otherwise poor, meager lifestyle.

To this new friend and confidant, Tsukuru opened up about all sorts of personal things. Still, he carefully avoided ever mentioning his four friends in Nagoya. It wasn't something he could easily talk about. The wounds were still too fresh, too deep.

Yet when he was with this younger friend he could, by and large, forget those four people. No, *forget* wasn't the right word. The pain of having been so openly rejected was always with him. But now, like the tide, it ebbed and flowed. At times it flowed up to his feet, at other times it withdrew far away, so far away he could barely detect it. Tsukuru could feel, little by little, that he was setting down roots in the new soil of Tokyo, building a new life there, albeit one that was small and lonely. His days in Nagoya felt more like something in the past, almost foreign. This was, unmistakably, a step forward that Haida, his new friend, had brought to his life.

Haida had an opinion on everything, and was always able to logically argue his perspective. The more time Tsukuru spent with this younger friend, the deeper his respect grew. Yet Tsukuru couldn't understand why Haida was drawn to him, or was even

57

interested in him. But they enjoyed each other's company so much that time spent bantering just flew by.

When he was alone, though, sometimes Tsukuru longed for a girlfriend. He wanted to hold a woman close, caress her body, inhale the scent of her skin. It was an entirely natural desire for a healthy young man. But when he tried to conjure up the image of a woman, and when he thought about embracing one, for some reason what automatically came to mind was an image of Shiro and Kuro. They always appeared, in this imaginary world, as an inseparable pair. And that always gave Tsukuru an inexplicably gloomy feeling. Why, *even now*, does it always have to be these two? he thought. They flatly rejected me. Said they never wanted to see me anymore, or talk to me ever again. Why can't they just make a quiet exit and leave me alone? Tsukuru Tazaki was twenty years old at this point, but had never held a woman in his arms. Or kissed a woman, or held someone's hand, or even gone on a date.

Something must be fundamentally wrong with me, Tsukuru often thought. Something must be blocking the normal flow of emotions, warping my personality. But Tsukuru couldn't tell whether this blockage came about when he was rejected by his four friends, or whether it was something innate, a structural issue unrelated to the trauma he'd gone through.

One Saturday night, he and Haida were up talking late as usual when they turned to the subject of death. They talked about the significance of dying, about having to live with the knowledge that you were going to die. They discussed it mainly in theoretical terms. Tsukuru wanted to explain how close to death he had been very recently, and the profound changes that experience had brought about, both physically and mentally. He wanted to tell Haida about the strange things he'd seen. But he knew that if he mentioned it, he'd have to explain the whole sequence of events, from start to finish. So as always, Haida did most of the talking, while Tsukuru sat back and listened.

A little past 11 p.m. their conversation petered out and silence descended on the room. At this point they would normally have called it a night and gotten ready for bed. Both of them tended to wake up early. But Haida remained seated, cross-legged, on the sofa, deep in thought. Then, in a hesitant tone, something unusual for him, he spoke up.

'I have a kind of weird story related to death. Something my father told me. He said it was an actual experience he had when he was in his early twenties. Just the age I am now. I've heard the story so many times I can remember every detail. It's a really strange story – it's hard even now for me to believe it actually happened – but my father isn't the type to lie about something like that. Or the type who would concoct such a story. I'm sure you know this, but when you make up a story the details change each time you retell it. You tend to embellish things, and forget what you said before . . . But my father's story, from start to finish, was always exactly the same, each time he told it. So I think it must be something he actually experienced. I'm his son, and I know him really well, so the only thing I can do is believe what he said. But you don't know my father, Tsukuru, so feel free to believe it or not. Just understand that this is what he told me. You can take it as folklore, or a tale of the supernatural, I don't mind. It's a long story, and it's already late, but do you mind if I tell it?'

Sure, Tsukuru said, that would be fine. I'm not sleepy yet.

59

5.

'When my father was young, he spent a year wandering around Japan,' Haida began. 'This was at the end of the 1960s, the peak of the counterculture era, when the student movement was upending universities. I don't know all the details, but when he was in college in Tokyo, a lot of stupid things happened, and he got fed up with politics and left the movement. He took a leave of absence from school and wandered around the country. He did odd jobs to earn a living, read books when he had the time, met all sorts of people, and gained a lot of real-life, practical experience. My father says this was the happiest time of his life, when he learned some important lessons. When I was a kid, he used to tell me stories from those days, like an old soldier reminiscing about long-ago battles in some far-off place. After those bohemian days, he went back to college, and returned to academic life. He never went on a long trip ever again. As far as I know, he's spent his time since just shuttling back and forth between home and his office. It's strange, isn't it? No matter how quiet and conformist a person's life seems, there's always a time in the past when they reached an impasse. A time when they went a little crazy. I guess people need that sort of stage in their lives.'

That winter Haida's father worked as general handyman at a

small hot springs resort in the mountains of Oita Prefecture in southern Japan. He really liked the place and decided to stay put for a while. As long as he completed his daily tasks, and any other miscellaneous jobs they asked him to undertake, the rest of the time he could do as he pleased. The pay was minimal, but he got a free room plus three meals a day, and he could bathe in the hot springs as often as he liked. When he had time off he lay around in his tiny room and read. The other people there were kind to this taciturn, eccentric Tokyo student, and the meals were simple but tasty, made with fresh, local ingredients. The place was, above all, isolated from the outside world – there was no TV reception, and the newspapers were a day late. The nearest bus stop was three kilometers down the mountain, and the only vehicle that could make it from there and back on the awful road was a battered old jeep owned by the inn. They'd only just recently gotten electricity installed.

In front of the inn was a beautiful mountain stream where one could catch lots of firm, colorful fish. Noisy birds were always skimming over the surface of the stream, their calls piercing, and it wasn't unusual to spot wild boar or monkeys roaming around nearby. The mountains were a treasure trove of edible wild plants. In this isolated environment, young Haida was able to indulge himself in reading and contemplation. He no longer cared what was happening in the real world.

Two months into his stay at the inn, he began to chat with a guest who was staying there. The man appeared to be in his mid-forties. He was tall, with lanky arms and legs, and short hair. He wore gold-framed glasses, and he had a receding hairline, which made the top of his head as smooth as a freshly laid egg. He had walked up the mountain road alone, a plastic travel bag hanging from one shoulder, and had been staying at the inn for a week. Whenever he went out, he invariably dressed in a leather jacket, jeans, and work boots. On cold days he would add a wool cap and a navy-blue muffler. The man's name was Midorikawa. At least that was the name he signed in the guest book at the inn, along with an address in Koganei City in Tokyo. He meticulously paid in cash every morning for the previous night's stay.

(Midorikawa? 'Green river.' Another person with a color, Tsukuru thought, but said nothing and listened to the rest of the story.)

Midorikawa didn't do anything special. He spent time soaking in the open-air bath, took walks in the nearby hills, or lay in the *kotatsu* – the foot-warmer table – reading the paperbacks he'd brought with him (mostly mindless mysteries). In the evening he'd enjoy two small bottles of hot sake – no more, no less. He was as taciturn as Haida's father, and never spoke unless absolutely necessary, though it didn't seem to bother the people at the inn. They were used to these sorts of guests. All of the people who came to these remote, backwoods hot springs were odd, those who stayed long term even more so.

One morning, just before dawn, Haida was soaking in the open-air hot spring next to the river when Midorikawa came to bathe and started talking to him. For some reason Midorikawa seemed to have taken a deep interest in this young odd-job worker. It might have stemmed, in part, from the time he saw Haida on the porch reading a book by Georges Bataille.

I'm a jazz pianist from Tokyo, Midorikawa said. I had some personal disappointments, and the daily grind was wearing me down, so I came alone to this quiet place deep in the mountains, hoping to rest up. Actually, I set out without any plan, and just happened to land here. I like it, everything's stripped to the bare essentials. I hear you're from Tokyo too?

As he soaked in the hot water in the dim light, Haida explained, as briefly as he could, his own situation. How he'd taken a leave of absence from college and was traveling around the country. Besides, the campus was blockaded, he added, so there was no reason to stay in Tokyo.

Aren't you interested in what's going on now in Tokyo? Midorikawa asked. It's quite a spectacle. One uproar after another, every day. Like the whole world's turned upside down. Don't you feel bad that you're missing out?

The world isn't that easily turned upside down, Haida replied. It's people who are turned upside down. I don't feel bad about missing that. Midorikawa seemed to appreciate the younger man's curt, direct way of speaking.

I wonder if there's anyplace around here where I might play the piano, Midorikawa asked Haida.

There's a junior high school on the other side of the mountain, Haida replied. After school's out for the day, they might let you play the piano in their music room. Midorikawa was happy to hear this. If it isn't any trouble, he said, could you take me there? Haida relayed this request to the inn's owner, who instructed him to escort Midorikawa to the school. The owner phoned the junior high to set it up. After lunch, the two of them hiked over the mountain. The rain had just stopped falling, so the path was slippery, but Midorikawa, shoulder bag slung diagonally across his shoulders, strode quickly, surefooted, down the path. Though outwardly a city person, he was much more robust than he appeared.

The keyboard of the old upright piano in the music room was uneven, and the tuning was off, but overall it was tolerable. Midorikawa sat down on the creaky chair, stretched out his fingers, ran through all eighty-eight keys, then began trying out a few chords. Fifths, sevenths, ninths, elevenths. He didn't seem too pleased with the sound, but appeared to get a certain physical satisfaction from the mere act of pressing down on the keys. As Haida watched the nimble, resilient way his fingers moved over the keyboard, he decided that Midorikawa must be a pretty well-known pianist.

After trying out the piano, Midorikawa took a small cloth bag from his shoulder bag and gingerly placed it on top of the piano. The bag was made of expensive cloth, the opening tied up with string. Somebody's funeral ashes, maybe? Haida thought. It seemed like placing the bag on top of the piano was his habit, whenever he played. You could tell by the practiced way he went about it.

Midorikawa hesitantly began playing "Round Midnight." At first he played each chord carefully, cautiously, like a person sticking his toes into a stream, testing the swiftness of the water and searching for a foothold. After playing the main theme, he started a long improvisation. As time went by, his fingers became more agile, more generous, in their movements, like fish swimming in clear water. The left hand inspired the right, the right hand spurred on the left. Haida's father didn't know much about jazz, but he did happen to be familiar with this Thelonious Monk composition, and Midorikawa's performance went straight to the heart of the piece. His playing was so soulful it made Haida forget about the piano's erratic tuning. As he listened to the music in this junior high music room deep in the mountains, as the sole audience for the performance, Haida felt all that was unclean inside him washed away. The straightforward beauty of the music overlapped with the fresh, oxygen-rich air and the cool, clear water of the stream, all of them acting in concert. Midorikawa, too, was lost in his playing, as if all the minutiae of reality had disappeared. Haida had never seen someone so thoroughly absorbed in what he was doing. He couldn't take his eyes off Midorikawa's ten fingers, which moved like independent, living creatures.

In fifteen minutes Midorikawa finished playing, took out a thick towel from his shoulder bag, and carefully wiped his perspiring face. He closed his eyes for a while as if he were meditating. 'Okay,' he finally said, 'that's enough. Let's go back.' He reached out, picked up the cloth bag on the piano, and gently returned it to his shoulder bag.

'What is that bag?' Haida's father ventured to ask.

'It's a good-luck charm,' Midorikawa said simply.

'Like the guardian god of pianos?'

'No, it's more like my alter ego,' Midorikawa replied, a weary smile rising to his lips. 'There's a strange story behind it. But it's pretty long, and I'm afraid I'm too worn out to tell it right now.'

Haida stopped and glanced at the clock on the wall. Then he looked at Tsukuru. He was, of course, Haida the son, but Haida the father had been his same age in this story, and so the two of them began to overlap in Tsukuru's mind. It was an odd sensation, as if the two distinct temporalities had blended into one. Maybe it wasn't the father who had experienced this, but the son. Maybe Haida was just relating it as if his father had experienced it, when in reality he was the one who had. Tsukuru couldn't shake this illusion.

'It's getting late. If you're sleepy I can finish this later.'

No, it's fine, Tsukuru said. I'm not sleepy. In fact, he'd gotten his second wind, and wanted to hear the rest of the story.

'Okay, then I'll continue,' Haida said. 'I'm not very sleepy either.'

—

That was the only time that Haida heard Midorikawa play the piano. Once he had played ''Round Midnight' in the junior high music room, Midorikawa seemed to lose all interest in playing again. 'Don't you want to play anymore?' Haida asked, trying to draw him out, but a silent shake of Midorikawa's head was his only response. Haida gave up asking. Midorikawa no longer planned to play the piano. Haida wished he could hear him perform just one more time.

Midorikawa had a genuine talent. Of that there was no doubt. His playing had the power to physically and viscerally move the listener, to transport you to another world. Not the sort of thing one could easily create.

But what did this unusual talent mean for Midorikawa himself? Haida couldn't quite grasp it. If you possessed a talent like Midorikawa did, was it amazingly blissful, or was it a burden? A blessing or a curse? Or something that simultaneously contained all of these components? Either way, Midorikawa didn't seem like a very happy person. His expression switched between gloom and apathy. A slight smile would occasionally rise to his lips, but it was always subdued and a little ironic.

One day as Haida was chopping and carrying firewood in the backyard, Midorikawa came over to him.

'Do you drink?' he asked.

'A little bit,' Haida replied.

'A little bit's fine,' Midorikawa said. 'Can you have some drinks with me tonight? I'm tired of drinking alone.'

'I have some chores to do in the evening, but I'll be free at seven thirty.'

'Okay. Come to my room then.'

When young Haida arrived at Midorikawa's room, dinner was already laid out for both of them, along with bottles of hot sake. They sat across from each other, eating and drinking. Midorikawa ate less than half of his dinner, mainly drinking the sake, serving himself. He didn't say anything about his own life, instead asking Haida about where he had grown up (in Akita) and about his college life in Tokyo. When he learned that Haida was studying philosophy, he asked a few technical questions. About Hegel's worldview. About Plato's writings. It became clear that he had systematically read those kinds of books. Mysteries weren't the only books he read.

'I see. So you believe in logic, do you?' Midorikawa said.

'I do. I believe in logic, and I rely on it. That's what philosophy's all about, after all,' Haida replied.

'So you don't much like anything that's at odds with logic?'

'Apart from whether I like it or not, I don't reject thinking about things that aren't logical. It's not like I have some deep faith in logic. I think it's important to find the point of intersection between what is logical and what is not.'

'Do you believe in the devil?'

'The devil? You mean the guy with horns?'

'That's right. Whether he actually has horns or not, I don't know.'

'If you mean the devil as a metaphor for evil, then of course I believe in him.'

'How about if this metaphor for evil takes on actual form?'

'I couldn't say, unless I actually saw him,' Haida said.

'But once you saw him, it might be too late.'

'Well, we're speaking in hypotheticals here. If we wanted to pursue this further, we'd need some concrete examples. Like a bridge needs girders. The further you go with a hypothesis, the more slippery it gets. Any conclusions you draw from it become more fallacious.'

'Examples?' Midorikawa said. He took a drink of sake and frowned. 'But sometimes when an actual example appears, it all comes down to a question of whether or not you accept it, or if you believe it. There's no middle ground. You have to make a mental leap. Logic can't really help you out.'

'Maybe it can't. Logic isn't some convenient manual you just consult. Later on, though, you should be able to apply logic to any given situation.'

'But by then it might be too late.'

'But that has nothing to do with logic.'

Midorikawa smiled. 'You're right, of course. Even if you find out, down the road, that it is too late, that's different from the logic of it. That's a sound argument. No room for debate.'

'Have you ever had that kind of experience, Mr. Midorikawa? Accepting something, believing it, taking a leap beyond logic?'

'No,' Midorikawa said. 'I don't believe in anything. Not in logic, or illogic. Not in God, or the devil. No extension of a hypothesis, nothing like a leap. I just silently accept everything as it is. That's my basic problem, really. I can't erect a decent barrier between subject and object.'

'But you're so gifted, musically.'

'You think so?'

'Your music can move people. I don't know much about jazz, but that much I can tell.'

Midorikawa grudgingly shook his head. 'Talent can be a nice thing to have sometimes. You look good, attract attention, and if you're lucky, you make some money. Women flock to you. In that sense, having talent's preferable to having none. But talent only functions when it's supported by a tough, unyielding physical and mental focus. All it takes is one screw in your brain to come loose and fall off, or some connection in your body to break down, and your concentration vanishes, like the dew at dawn. A simple toothache, or stiff shoulders, and you can't play the piano well. It's true. I've actually experienced it. A single cavity, one aching shoulder, and the beautiful vision and sound I hoped to convey goes out the window. The human body's that fragile. It's a complex system that can be damaged by something very trivial, and in most cases once it's damaged, it can't easily be restored. A cavity or stiff shoulder you can get over, but there are a lot of things you can't get past. If talent's the foundation you rely on, and yet it's so unreliable that you have no idea what's going to happen to it the next minute, what meaning does it have?'

'Talent might be ephemeral,' Haida replied, 'and there aren't many people who can sustain it their whole lives. But talent makes a huge spiritual leap possible. It's an almost universal, independent phenomenon that transcends the individual.'

Midorikawa pondered that for a while before replying. 'Mozart and Schubert died young, but their music lives on forever. Is that what you mean?'

'That would be one example.'

'That kind of talent is always the exception. Most people like that have to pay a price for their genius – through accepting foreshortened lives and untimely deaths. They strike a bargain, putting their lives on the line. Whether that bargain's with God or the devil, I wouldn't know.' Midorikawa sighed and was silent for a while. 'Changing the subject a little,' he went on, 'but actually – I'm dying. I have only a month left.'

It was Haida's turn now to be silent. No words came to him.

'I'm not battling a disease or anything,' Midorikawa said. 'I'm in good health. And I'm not contemplating suicide. If that's what you were thinking, you can rest easy.'

'Then how do you know you only have a month left?'

'Someone told me that. You have only two months left to live, he said. That was a month ago.'

'Who would ever say something like that?'

'It wasn't a doctor, or a fortune teller. Just an ordinary person. Though *at that point* he was dying, too.'

Young Haida turned this over in his mind, but a logical foothold eluded him. 'Then did you . . . come here looking for a place to die?'

'You could say that.'

'I can't totally follow you, but isn't there some way you can avoid death?'

'There is one way,' Midorikawa said. 'You take that capacity – a death token, if you will – and transfer it to somebody else. What I mean is, you find somebody else to die in your place. You pass them the baton, tell them, "Okay, your turn," and then leave. Do that, and you'll avoid death, for the time being. But I don't plan to. I've been thinking for a long time that I'd like to die as soon as possible. Maybe this is just what I need.'

'So you think it's okay to die, as you are now?'

70

'Life has gotten to be too much. I have no problem with dying as I am. I don't have the energy to go out and find a method to help me take my life. But quietly accepting death, that I can handle.'

'But how, exactly, do you hand over this *death token* to somebody else?'

Midorikawa shrugged, as if he didn't really care. 'It's easy. The other person just has to understand what I'm saying, accept it, give their complete consent, and agree to take on the token. Then the transfer is complete. It can be a verbal agreement. A handshake is fine. No need for a signed, sealed document or contract or anything. It isn't some kind of bureaucratic thing.'

Haida inclined his head. 'But it can't be easy to find somebody willing to take it over from you, if taking over means they're going to die soon.'

'That's a reasonable point,' Midorikawa said. 'You can't bring up this idea with just anybody. Can't just sidle up to somebody and whisper, *Excuse me, but would you die in my place?* You have to be very careful who you pick. Here's where things get a little tricky.'

Midorikawa slowly gazed around the room, and cleared his throat.

'Every person has their own color. Did you know that?' he said.

'No, I didn't.'

'Each individual has their own unique color, which shines faintly around the contours of their body. Like a halo. Or a backlight. I'm able to see those colors clearly.'

Midorikawa poured himself another cup of sake and sipped it, leisurely savoring the taste.

'Is this ability to detect colors something you were born with?' Haida asked, dubiously.

Midorikawa shook his head. 'No, it's not innate; it's a temporary ability. You get it in exchange for accepting imminent death. And it's passed along from one person to the next. Right now, I'm the one who's been entrusted with it.'

Young Haida was silent for a while. No words came to him.

'There are colors I really like in the world,' Midorikawa said, 'and ones I hate. Pleasant colors, sad colors. Some people have a very a deep color, while for others it's fainter. It can get really tiring, because you see all these colors even if you don't want to. I don't like to be in crowds much because of that. It's why I wound up in this remote place.'

Haida could barely follow along. 'So you're telling me you can see what color I'm giving off?'

'Yes, of course. Though I'm not about to tell you what color it is,' Midorikawa said. 'What I need to do is find people who have a certain type of color, with a certain glow. Those are the only ones I can transfer the death token to. I can't hand it over to just anybody.'

'Are there many people in the world with that color and glow?'

'Not so many. My guess would be one in a thousand, or maybe two thousand. They're not so easy to find, but not impossible, either. What's harder is finding the opportunity to sit down with them and discuss it seriously. As you can imagine, that's not easy.'

'But what sort of people would they be? People who would be willing to die in place of somebody they don't even know?'

Midorikawa smiled. 'What kind of people? I really can't say. All I know is, they have a certain color, a certain depth of glow

72

outlining their bodies. Those are only external qualities. If I were to venture a guess – and this is just my personal opinion, mind you – I'd say they're people who aren't afraid of taking a leap. I'm sure there are all sorts of reasons why.'

'Okay, granted they're unafraid of taking a leap, but why are they leaping?' Midorikawa didn't say anything for a while. In the silence, the flow of the mountain stream sounded more intense. Finally, he grinned.

'Now comes my sales pitch.'

'This I'd like to hear,' Haida said.

'At the point when you agree to take on death, you gain an extraordinary capacity. A special power, you could call it. Perceiving the colors that people emit is merely one function of that power, but at the root of it all is an ability to expand your consciousness. You're able to push open what Aldous Huxley calls 'the doors of perception.' Your perception becomes pure and unadulterated. Everything around you becomes clear, like the fog lifting. You have an omniscient view of the world and see things you've never seen before.'

'Is your performance the other day a result of that ability?'

Midorikawa gave a short shake of his head. 'No, that was just what I've always been capable of. I've played like that for years. Perception is complete in and of itself; it doesn't reveal itself in an outward, concrete manifestation. There are no tangible bene-fits to it, either. It's not easy to explain in words. You have to experience it to understand. One thing I can say, though, is that once you see that *true sight* with your own eyes, the world you've lived in up till now will look flat and insipid. There's no logic or illogic in that scene. No good or evil. Everything is merged into one. And you are one part of that merging. You leave the boundary of your physical body behind to become a metaphysical being. You become intuition. It's at once a wonderful sensation and a hopeless one, because, almost at the last minute, you realize how shallow and superficial your life has been. And you shudder at the fact that up to that point you've been able to stand such a life.'

'And you think it's worth experiencing this sensation, even if it means taking on death? And you only have it for a little while?'

Midorikawa nodded. 'Absolutely. It's that valuable. I guarantee it.'

Haida was quiet for a while.

'So what do you think?' Midorikawa said and smiled. 'Are you starting to get interested in accepting that token?'

'Could I ask a question?'

'Go right ahead.'

'Are you – possibly telling me that I'm one of those few people with that certain color and certain glow? One in a thousand, or two thousand?'

'You are. I knew it the minute I saw you.'

'So I'm one of those people who would want to take a leap?'

'That's hard to say. I don't really know. That's something you need to ask yourself, don't you think?'

'But you said you don't want to pass that token on to anyone else.'

'Sorry about that,' the pianist said. 'I plan on dying, and I don't feel like handing over that right. I'm like a salesman who doesn't want to sell anything.'

'If you die, though, what happens to the token?'

'You got me. Good question. Maybe it'll simply vanish along with me. Or maybe it'll remain, in some form, and be passed along again from one person to the next. Like Wagner's ring. I have no idea, and frankly, I don't care. I mean, I'm not responsible for what happens after I'm gone.'

Haida tried creating some sort of order in his mind for all these ideas, but they wouldn't line up neatly.

'So, what I told you isn't one bit logical, is it?' Midorikawa said.

'It's a fascinating story, but hard to believe,' Haida admitted.

'Because there's no logical explanation?'

'Exactly.'

'No way to prove it.'

'The only way you know if it's real or not, the only way to prove it, is by actually making the deal. Isn't that how it works?'

Midorikawa nodded. 'Exactly. Unless you take the leap, you can't prove it. And once you actually make the leap, there's no need to prove it anymore. There's no middle ground. You either take the leap, or you don't. One or the other.'

'Aren't you afraid of dying?'

'Not really. I've watched lots of good-for-nothing, worthless people die, and if people like that can do it, then I should be able to handle it.'

'Do you ever think about what comes after death?'

'The afterworld, and the afterlife? Those kinds of things?'

Haida nodded.

'I made up my mind not to think about them,' Midorikawa said as he rubbed his beard. 'It's a waste of time to think about things you can't know, and things you can't confirm even if you know them. In the final analysis, that's no different from the slippery slope of hypotheses you were talking about.'

Haida drew a deep breath. 'Why did you tell me all this?'

'I've never told anybody until now, and never planned to,' Midorikawa said, and took a drink. 'I was just going to quietly vanish by myself. But when I saw you, I thought, Now here's a man worth telling.'

'And you don't care whether or not I believe you?'

Midorikawa, his eyes looking sleepy, gave a slight yawn.

'I don't care if you believe it. Because sooner or later you will. Someday you will die. And when you're dying – I have no idea when or how that will happen, of course – you will definitely remember what I told you. And you will totally accept what I said, and understand every detail of the logic behind it. The real logic. All I did was sow the seeds.'

It had started raining again, a soft, quiet rain. The rushing stream drowned out the sound of the rain. Haida could tell it was raining only by the slight variation in the air against his skin.

Sitting in that small room across from Midorikawa suddenly felt strange to him, as if they were in the midst of something impossible, something at odds with the principles of nature. Haida grew dizzy. In the still air he'd caught a faint whiff of death, the smell of slowly rotting flesh. But it had to be an illusion. Nobody there was dead yet.

'You'll be going back to college in Tokyo before much longer,' Midorikawa quietly stated. 'And you'll return to real life. You need to live it to the fullest. No matter how shallow and dull things might get, this life is worth living. I guarantee it. And I'm not being either ironic or paradoxical. It's just that, for me, what's worthwhile in life has become a burden, something I can't shoulder anymore. Maybe I'm just not cut out for it. So, like a dying cat, I've crawled into a quiet, dark place, silently waiting

76

for my time to come. It's not so bad. But you're different. You should be able to handle what life sends your way. You need to use the thread of logic, as best you can, to skillfully sew onto yourself *everything that's worth living for.*'

'That's the end of the story,' Haida, the son, said. 'In the morning, two days after that conversation, while my father was out taking care of some business, Midorikawa left the inn. Just like when he arrived, with one bag slung over his shoulder, hiking the three kilometers down the mountain to the bus stop. My father never found out where he went. Midorikawa paid his bill for the previous day and took off without a word, or any message for my father. All he left behind was a stack of mystery novels. Not long after this, my father returned to Tokyo. He reentered college and concentrated on his studies. I don't know if meeting Midorikawa was the catalyst that ended his long journey, but hearing my father tell the story, I get the sense that it played a big part.'

Haida sat up on the sofa, reached out with his long fingers, and massaged his ankles.

'After my father got back to Tokyo, he checked to see if there were jazz pianists named Midorikawa, but he couldn't find anyone by that name. Maybe he'd used an alias. So he never found out, to this day, if the man really did die a month later.'

'But your father's alive and well, right?' Tsukuru asked.

Haida nodded. 'He still hasn't reached the end of his life.'

'Did your father believe that weird story Midorikawa told him? Didn't he think it was just a clever story designed to pull his leg?'

'You know, it's hard to say. I think for my father, at the time, it wasn't an issue of whether or not he believed it. I think he totally accepted it as the weird tale it was. Like the way a snake will swallow its prey and not chew it, but instead let it slowly digest.'

Haida stopped at this point and took a deep breath.

'I guess I am pretty sleepy now. How about we go to bed?'

It was nearly 1 a.m. Tsukuru went to his bedroom, and Haida got the sofa ready and turned off the light. As Tsukuru lay in bed in his pajamas, he heard water rushing by in a mountain stream. But that was impossible, of course. They were in the middle of Tokyo.

He soon fell into a deep sleep.

That night, several strange things happened.

6.

Five days after they'd talked in the bar in Ebisu, Tsukuru emailed Sara from his computer, inviting her to dinner. Her reply came from Singapore. 'I'll be back in Japan in two days,' she wrote, 'and I'm free Saturday evening, the day after I get back. I'm glad you got in touch. There's something I want to talk with you about.'

Something to talk about? Tsukuru had no idea what that might be. But the thought of seeing her again cheered him up, and made him realize once more how much he wanted her. When he didn't see her for a while it was as if something vital were missing from his life, and a dull ache settled in his chest. He hadn't felt this way in a long time.

The three days after this exchange, though, were hectic for Tsukuru, as a sudden, unexpected assignment came up. A plan for the joint use of a subway line ran into a snag when it was discovered that a difference in the shape of the train cars created a safety issue (why couldn't they have told us about such a critical issue beforehand? Tsukuru asked himself), and necessitated emergency repairs of platforms at several stations. Tsukuru's job was to create the repair schedule. He worked nearly around the clock, but still managed to free up his calendar so he could take off from Saturday evening to Sunday morning. On Saturday he set out from his office, still in his suit, to the place he and Sara were to meet in Aoyama. On the subway he fell sound asleep, nearly missing his transfer at Akasaka-Mitsuke.

'You look exhausted,' Sara said when she saw him.

Tsukuru explained – as concisely and simply as he could – the reason he had been so busy the last few days.

'I was planning to go home, shower, and change into something more comfortable, but I had to come straight from work,' he said.

Sara took a beautifully wrapped box, long, flat, and narrow, from her shopping bag and handed it to him. 'A present, from me to you.'

Tsukuru unwrapped the box and found a necktie inside, an elegant blue tie made of plain silk. Yves Saint Laurent.

'I saw it in the duty-free shop in Singapore and thought you'd look good in it.'

'Thank you. It's beautiful.'

'Some men don't like to get ties as gifts.'

'Not me,' Tsukuru said. 'I never get the urge to go out to buy a tie. And you have such good taste.'

'I'm glad,' Sara said.

Tsukuru removed the tie he'd been wearing, one with narrow stripes, and put on the one Sara had given him. He was wearing a dark blue summer suit and a plain white shirt, and the blue necktie went well with it. Sara reached over the table and, with a practiced hand, adjusted the knot. Tsukuru caught a pleasant hint of perfume.

'It looks very nice on you,' she said with a smile.

The old tie lying on the table looked more worn out than

he'd thought, like some unseemly habit he wasn't aware he had. The thought struck him that he should start paying more attention to his appearance. At the railroad company office there wasn't much call to worry about clothes. The workplace was almost entirely male, and as soon as he got to work he'd take off his tie and roll up his sleeves. Much of the time he was out at worksites, where what kind of suit or necktie he wore was irrelevant. And this was the first time in quite a while he'd had a regular girlfriend.

Sara had never given him a present before, and it made him happy. I need to find out when her birthday is, he thought. I should give her something. He thanked her again, then folded the old tie and stuffed it in his jacket pocket.

They were in a French restaurant in the basement level of a building in Aoyama, a restaurant that Sara had been to before. It was an unpretentious place, with reasonably priced wine and food. It was closer to a casual bistro, but the seating was generously spaced to allow for relaxed conversation. The service was friendly, too. They ordered a carafe of red wine and studied the menu.

Sara was wearing a dress with a delicate floral pattern and a thin white cardigan. Both looked like designer items. Tsukuru had no idea how much Sara earned, but she seemed used to spending a fair amount on her wardrobe.

As they ate she told him about her work in Singapore – negotiating hotel prices, selecting restaurants, securing ground transportation, setting up day trips, confirming the availability of medical facilities . . . There was a whole array of tasks to take care of in setting up a new tour. Preparing a long checklist, traveling to the destination, and checking each item off one by one. Going to each venue to make sure firsthand that each item was handled properly. The process sounded a lot like the one his company followed when they constructed a new station. As he listened to her, it became clear what a meticulous, competent specialist she was.

'I think I'll have to go there again sometime soon,' Sara said. 'Have you ever been to Singapore?'

'No, I haven't. Actually I've never been out of Japan. I haven't had any chance to go on an overseas business trip, and traveling abroad by myself always seemed like too much trouble.'

'Singapore's fascinating. The food is amazing, and there's a beautiful resort nearby. It'd be nice if I could show you around.'

He imagined how wonderful it would be to travel abroad with her, just the two of them.

Tsukuru had one glass of wine, as usual, while Sara finished the rest of the carafe. Alcohol didn't seem to affect her, and no matter how much she drank her face was never flushed. He had beef Bourguignon, while she ordered roast duck. After she finished her entrée, she agonized over whether or not to order dessert, and finally decided she'd do so. Tsukuru had a coffee.

'After I saw you last time I've really been thinking about things,' Sara said, sipping the tea that rounded out her meal. 'About your four friends in high school. About that beautiful community, and your affection for each other.'

Tsukuru gave a small nod, and waited for her to go on.

'I find the story of your group really intriguing. I guess because I've never experienced anything like that myself.'

'Maybe it would have been for the best if I never had, either,' Tsukuru said.

'Because you ended up getting hurt?'

He nodded.

'I understand how you feel,' Sara said, with her eyes narrowed. 'But even if it ended badly, and you were hurt, I think it was a good thing for you to have met them. It's not very often that people become that close. And when you think of five people having that sort of connection, well, it's nothing short of miraculous.'

'I agree. It was kind of a miracle. And I do think it was a good thing for me that it happened,' Tsukuru said. 'But that made the shock all the worse when the connection was gone – or snatched from me, I should say. The feeling of loss, the isolation . . . Those words don't come even close to expressing how awful it felt.'

'But more than sixteen years have passed. You're an adult now, in your late thirties. The pain might have been terrible back then, but isn't it time to finally get over it?'

'Get over it,' Tsukuru repeated. 'What exactly do you mean?'

Sara rested her hands on the table, spreading her ten fingers apart slightly. She wore a ring on the little finger of her left hand, with a small, almond-shaped jewel. She gazed at the ring for a while, then looked up.

'I get the feeling that the time has come for you to find out why you were cut off, or had to be cut off, so abruptly, by those friends of yours.'

Tsukuru was about to drink the rest of his coffee, but he noticed his cup was empty and laid it back down on the saucer. The cup struck the saucer with an unexpectedly loud clatter. The waiter, in response to the noise, hurried over and refilled their glasses with ice water.

Tsukuru waited until the waiter left before he spoke.

'Like I told you, I want to put it all out of my mind. I've managed to slowly close up the wound and, somehow, conquer the pain. It took a long time. Now that the wound is closed, why gouge it open again?'

'I understand, but maybe it only appears, from the outside, that the wound is closed.' Sara gazed into his eyes and spoke quietly. 'Maybe inside the wound, under the scab, the blood is still silently flowing. Haven't you ever thought that?'

Tsukuru pondered this, but he had no good reply.

'Can you tell me the full names of those four people? And the name of your high school, the year you graduated, the colleges they attended, and their addresses the last time you were in touch?'

'What are you planning to do with that information?'

'I want to find out as much as I can about where they are now, what they're doing.'

Tsukuru's breathing suddenly grew shallow. He picked up his glass and gulped down some water. 'What for?'

'So you can meet them, talk with them. So they can explain to you why they abandoned you.'

'But what if I say I don't want to?'

She turned her hands over on the table, palms up. She continued to look at Tsukuru directly. Her eyes never broke their gaze.

'Can I be totally candid?' Sara asked.

'Of course.'

'It's not easy to say this.'

'I want to know what you're thinking, so please, say what's on your mind.'

'The last time we met, I told you I didn't want to go back to your place. You remember that? Do you know why I said it?'

Tsukuru shook his head.

'I think you're a good person, and I really like you. Not just as a friend,' Sara said, and paused. 'But I think you have – some kind of unresolved emotional issues.'

Tsukuru looked at her silently.

'This part is a little hard to talk about. It's hard to express, is what I mean. If I put it into words, it sounds oversimplified. I can't explain it reasonably, or logically. It's more of an intuitive thing.'

'I trust your intuition,' Tsukuru said.

Sara bit her lip lightly and looked off, as if measuring a distance, and then spoke. 'When we made love, it felt like you were *somewhere* else. Somewhere apart from the two of us in bed. You were very gentle, and it was wonderful, but still . . .'

Tsukuru lifted the empty coffee cup again, wrapping it in both hands. He replaced it on the saucer, this time without making a sound.

'I don't understand,' he said. 'The *whole time* I was only thinking of you. I don't remember being elsewhere. Truthfully, I don't think there was any way I could have thought of anything but you.'

'Maybe. Maybe you were just thinking about me. If you say so, I believe you. But there was something else on your mind. At least I sensed a sort of distance between us. Maybe it's something only a woman can pick up on. Anyway, what I want you to know is that I can't continue a relationship like that for very long, even if I'm very fond of you. I'm more possessive, more straightforward than I might seem. If we're going to have a serious relationship, I don't want whatever it is to come between us. This unidentifiable *something*. Do you know what I'm saying?'

'That you don't want to see me anymore?'

'No, that's not it,' she said. 'I'm fine seeing you and talking like this. I enjoy it a lot. But I don't want to go back to your place.'

'You mean you can't make love with me?'

'I can't,' Sara said bluntly.

'Because I have some – emotional issues?'

'That's right. You have some problems you're carrying around, some things that might go much deeper than you realize. But I think they're the kind of problems you can overcome, if you really make up your mind to do so. Just like you'd set about repairing a defect in a station. To do that, though, you need to collect the necessary data, draw up an accurate blueprint, create a detailed work schedule. Above all, you need to identify your priorities.'

'And to do that, I need to see those four people again and talk with them. Is that what you're saying?'

She nodded. 'You need to come face-to-face with the past, not as some naive, easily wounded boy, but as a grown-up, independent professional. Not to see what you want to see, but what you *must* see. Otherwise you'll carry around that baggage for the rest of your life. That's why I want you to tell me the names of your four friends. I'll start by finding out where they are now.'

'How will you do that?'

Sara shook her head in amazement. 'You graduated from engineering school, but you don't use the Internet? Haven't you ever heard of Google or Facebook?'

'I use the Internet at work, sure. And I'm familiar with Google and Facebook. But I hardly ever use them. I'm just not interested.'

'Then leave it to me. That's what I'm good at,' Sara said.

After dinner they walked to Shibuya. It was a pleasant evening, near the end of spring, and the large, yellow moon was covered in mist. There was a hint of moisture in the air. The hem of Sara's dress fluttered prettily next to him in the breeze. As he walked, Tsukuru pictured the body underneath those clothes. He thought about making love to her again, and as he pictured this, he felt his penis start to stiffen. He had no problem with feeling those desires – they were, after all, the natural urges and cravings of a healthy adult male. But maybe at the core, at the very root – as Sara had suggested – lay something illogical, something twisted. He couldn't really say. The more he thought about the boundary between the conscious and the unconscious, the less certain he became of his own identity.

Tsukuru hesitated but then spoke. 'There's something I need to correct about what I told you the other day.'

As she walked along Sara shot him a look, her curiosity piqued. 'What's that?'

'I've had relationships with several women, but nothing ever really came of any of them, for various reasons. I told you it wasn't all my fault.'

'I remember.'

'During the last ten years, I've gone out with three or four women. All of them were fairly long-term, serious relationships. I wasn't just playing around. And the reason none of them worked out was because of me. Not because there was any problem with any of the women.'

'And what was the problem?'

'It was a little different depending on the person,' Tsukuru said. 'But one common factor was that I wasn't seriously attracted to any of them. I mean, I liked them, and enjoyed our time together. I have a lot of good memories. But I never felt – swept away, overpowered by desire for any of them.'

Sara was silent for a while. 'So for ten years,' she finally said, 'you had *fairly long-term, serious relationships* with women you weren't all that attracted to.'

'That's about right.'

'That doesn't strike me as very rational.'

'I'd have to agree.'

'Maybe you didn't want to get married, or get tied down?'

Tsukuru shook his head. 'No, I don't think that was it. I'm the sort of person who craves stability.'

'But still there was something holding you back psychologic-ally?'

'Maybe so.'

'You could only have a relationship with women you didn't have to totally open up to.'

'I might have been afraid that if I really loved someone and needed her, one day she might suddenly disappear without a word, and I'd be left all alone.'

'So consciously or unconsciously you always kept a distance between yourself and the women you dated. Or else you chose women you could keep that distance from. So you wouldn't get hurt. Does that sound about right?'

Tsukuru didn't reply, his silence an affirmation. At the same time, though, he knew that wasn't what was at the heart of the problem.

'And the same thing might happen with you and me,' Sara said.

'No, I don't think so. It's different with you. I really mean that. I want to open up my heart to you. I truly feel that way. That's why I'm telling you all this.'

'You want to see more of me?' Sara asked.

'Of course I do.'

'I'd like to see more of you, too, if I can,' Sara said. 'You're a good person, honest and sincere.'

'Thank you,' Tsukuru said.

'So tell me those four names. After that, you decide. Once I find out more about them, if you feel you don't want to see them, then you don't have to go ahead with it. That's entirely up to you. But apart from all that, personally, I'm curious about them. I want to find out more about these people who are still weighing you down.'

When he got back to his apartment Tsukuru took an old pocket notebook out of his desk drawer, opened it to the list of addresses, and typed the four names, addresses, and phone numbers from when he'd last seen his four friends into his laptop.

Kei Akamatsu
Yoshio Oumi
Yuzuki Shirane
Eri Kurono

As he gazed at the four names on the screen, and considered the memories those names brought back, he felt the past silently mingling with the present, as a time that should have been long gone hovered in the air around him. Like odorless, colorless smoke leaking into the room through a small crack in the door. Finally, at a certain point, he snapped back to the present, clicked the key on his laptop, and sent the email to Sara's address. He checked that it had been sent and switched off the computer. And waited for time to become real again.

Personally, I'm curious about them. I want to find out more about these people who are still weighing you down.

Sara is right, he thought as he lay down on his bed. Those four people are still stuck to me. Probably more tightly than Sara can ever imagine.

Mister Red

Mister Blue

Miss White

Miss Black

7.

The night that Haida told him the story from his father's youth, about meeting a jazz pianist named Midorikawa at a hot springs resort deep in the mountains of Kyushu, several strange things happened.

Tsukuru bolted awake in the darkness. A tapping sound had woken him, like the sound of a pebble striking a window. Maybe he'd only imagined it, but he wasn't sure. He wanted to check the alarm clock on his nightstand, but he couldn't turn his neck. His entire body was immobile. He wasn't numb, it was just that when he tried to make his body move, he couldn't. The connection between mind and muscles had been severed.

The room was swathed in darkness. Tsukuru had trouble sleeping when there was any light in the room, and always closed the curtains tightly when he went to bed, so there was no light filtering in from outside. Still, he felt the presence in the room of someone else, concealed in the darkness, watching him. Like a camouflaged animal, whoever it was held his breath, hid his scent, changed his color, and receded into the shadows. Still, for some reason Tsukuru knew who it was. Haida.

Mister Gray.

Gray is a mixture of white and black. Change its shade, and it can easily melt into various gradations of darkness.

Haida was standing in a corner of the dark room, staring down at Tsukuru, who lay faceup on the bed. As if he were a mime pretending to be a statue, Haida didn't move a muscle for a long time. The only thing that moved, possibly, were his long eyelashes. Therein lay a strange contrast: Haida chose to be completely still, while Tsukuru chose to move, but couldn't. I have to say something, Tsukuru thought, I need to speak and break down this illusory balance. But his voice wouldn't come. His lips wouldn't move, his tongue was frozen. The only thing slipping from his throat was dry, soundless breathing.

What is Haida doing here? Why is he standing here, staring so intently at me?

This isn't a dream, Tsukuru decided. Everything is too distinct to be a dream. But he couldn't say if the person standing there was the real Haida. The real Haida, his actual flesh and blood, was sound asleep on the sofa in the next room. The Haida standing here must be a kind of projection that had slipped free of the real Haida. That's the way it felt.

Tsukuru didn't feel that this presence was threatening, or evil. Haida would never hurt him – of this, Tsukuru felt certain. He'd known this, instinctively, from the moment they first met.

His high school friend Aka was very bright too, with a practical, even utilitarian intelligence. Compared to Aka, Haida's intelligence was more pure iteration, more theoretical, even self-contained. When they were together Tsukuru often couldn't grasp what Haida might be thinking. Something in Haida's brain surged forward, outpacing Tsukuru, but what sort of thing that *something* was, he couldn't say. When that happened he felt confused and left behind, alone. But he never felt anxiety or irritation toward his younger friend. Haida's mind was just too quick, his sphere of mental activity too broad, on a different level entirely. With this knowledge, Tsukuru ceased trying to keep up with Haida.

In Haida's brain there must have been a kind of high-speed circuit built to match the pace of his thoughts, requiring him to occasionally engage his gears, to let his mind race for fixed periods of time. If he didn't – if he kept on running in low gear to keep pace with Tsukuru's reduced speed – Haida's mental infrastructure would overheat and start to malfunction. Or at least, Tsukuru got that impression. After a while Haida would debark from this circuit and, as if nothing had happened, smile calmly and return to the place where Tsukuru lay waiting. He'd slow down, and keep pace with Tsukuru's mind.

How long did Haida's intense gaze continue? Tsukuru could no longer judge the length of time. Haida stood there, unmoving, in the middle of the night, staring wordlessly at him. Haida seemed to have something he wanted to say, a message he needed to convey, but for some reason he couldn't translate that message into words. And this made Tsukuru's younger, intelligent friend unusually irritated.

As he lay in bed, Tsukuru recalled Haida's story about Midorikawa. Before Midorikawa had played the piano in the junior high music room, he'd laid a small bag on top of the piano. He'd been on the verge of death – or so he'd said. What was in the bag? Haida's story had ended before he revealed the contents. Tsukuru was intensely curious about what had been inside, and wanted someone to tell him its significance. Why did Midorikawa so carefully place that bag on top of the piano? This had to be the missing key to the story.

But he wasn't given the answer. After a long silence Haida – or Haida's alter ego – quietly left. At the very end of his visit, Tsukuru felt like he caught the sound of Haida's light breathing, but he couldn't be sure. Like incense smoke swallowed up in the air, Haida's presence faded and vanished, and before Tsukuru knew it, he was alone again in the dark room. He still couldn't move his body. The cable between his will and his muscles remained disconnected, the bolt that linked them together having fallen off.

How much of this is real? he wondered. This wasn't a dream, or an illusion. It had to be real. But it lacked the weight you'd expect from reality.

Mister Gray.

Tsukuru must have fallen asleep again, but he woke up once more in a dream. Strictly speaking, it might not be a dream. It was reality, but a reality imbued with all the qualities of a dream. A different sphere of reality, where – at a special time and place – imagination had been set free.

The girls were in bed, as naked as the day they were born, snuggled up close on either side of him. Shiro and Kuro. They were sixteen or seventeen, invariably that age. Their breasts and thighs were pressed against him, their bodies smooth and warm, and Tsukuru could feel all this, clearly. Silently, greedily, they groped his body with their fingers and tongues. He was naked too.

This was not something Tsukuru was hoping for, not a scenario he wanted to imagine. It wasn't something that should be happening. But that image, against his will, grew more vivid, the feelings more graphic, more real.

The girls' fingers were gentle, slender, and delicate. Four hands, twenty fingers. Like some smooth, sightless creatures born in the darkness, they wandered over every inch of Tsukuru's body, arousing him completely. He felt his heart stir, intensely, in a way he'd never before experienced, as if he'd been living for a long time in a house only to discover a secret room he'd never known about. Like a kettledrum, his heart trembled, pounding out an audible beat. His arms and legs were still numb, and he couldn't lift a finger.

The girls entwined themselves lithely around Tsukuru. Kuro's breasts were full and soft. Shiro's were small, but her nipples were as hard as tiny round pebbles. Their pubic hair was as wet as a rain forest. Their breath mingled with his, becoming one, like currents from far away, secretly overlapping at the dark bottom of the sea.

These insistent caresses continued until Tsukuru was inside the vagina of one of the girls. It was Shiro. She straddled him, took hold of his rigid, erect penis, and deftly guided it inside her. His penis found its way with no resistance, as if swallowed up into an airless vacuum. She took a moment, gathering her breath, then began slowly rotating her torso, as if she were drawing a complex diagram in the air, all the while twisting her hips. Her long, straight black hair swung above him, sharply, like a whip. The movements were bold, so out of character with the everyday Shiro.

The entire time, both Shiro and Kuro treated it as a completely natural turn of events, nothing they had to think over. They never hesitated. The two of them caressed him together, but Shiro was the one he penetrated. *Why Shiro?* Tsukuru wondered in the midst of his deep confusion. Why does it have to be Shiro? They are supposed to be completely equal. They're supposed to be one being.

95

Beyond that, he couldn't think. Shiro's movements grew faster, more pronounced. And before he knew it, he was coming inside her. The time elapsed between penetration and orgasm was short. Too short, Tsukuru thought, way too short. But maybe he'd lost any sense of time. At any rate, the urge was unstoppable, and, like a huge wave crashing over him, this urge engulfed him without warning.

Now, though, he wasn't coming inside Shiro, but in Haida. The girls had suddenly disappeared, and Haida had taken their place. Just as Tsukuru came, Haida had quickly bent over, taken Tsukuru's penis in his mouth, and – careful not to get the sheets dirty – taken all the gushing semen inside his mouth. Tsukuru came violently, the semen copious. Haida patiently accepted all of it, and when Tsukuru had finished, Haida licked his penis clean with his tongue. He seemed used to it. At least it felt that way. Haida quietly rose from the bed and went to the bathroom. Tsukuru heard water running from the faucet. Haida was probably rinsing his mouth.

Even after he came, Tsukuru's penis remained erect. He could feel the warmth and softness of Shiro's vagina, as if it were the afterglow of actual sex. And he still couldn't grasp the boundary between dream and imagination, between what was imaginary and what was real.

In the darkness, Tsukuru searched for words. Not words directed at any particular person. He just felt he had to say something, had to find even one word to fill that mute, anonymous gap, before Haida came back from the bathroom. But he couldn't find anything. The whole time, a simple melody swirled around in his head. It was only later that he realized this was the theme of Liszt's 'Le mal du pays.' *Years of Pilgrimage*, 'First

96

Year: Switzerland.' A groundless sadness called forth in a person's heart by a pastoral landscape.

And then a deep sleep violently took hold of him.

It was just before 8 a.m. when he woke up.

He immediately checked his underwear for signs of semen. Whenever he had sexual dreams like this one, there was always evidence. But this time, nothing. Tsukuru was baffled. In his dream – or at least in a place that wasn't reality – he'd most definitely ejaculated. Intensely. The afterglow was still with him. A copious amount of *real* semen should have gushed out. But there was no trace of it.

And then he remembered how Haida had taken it all in his mouth.

He shut his eyes and grimaced. Did that really happen? No, that's impossible. It all took place in the dark interior of my mind. No matter how you look at it. So where did all that semen gush out to? Did it all vanish, too, in the inner recesses of my mind?

Confused, Tsukuru got out of bed and, still clad in pajamas, padded out to the kitchen. Haida was already dressed and sitting on the sofa, reading. He was lost in his thick book, off in another world, but as soon as Tsukuru appeared, he shut the book, smiled brightly, and went to the kitchen to make coffee, omelets, and toast. The fresh smell of coffee soon wafted through the apartment, the smell that separates night from day. They sat across the table from each other and ate breakfast while listening to music, set low. As usual, Haida had dark toast with a thin spread of honey.

Haida explained, excitedly, about the new coffee beans he'd discovered, and the quality of the roast, but after that, he was silently thoughtful. Probably contemplating the book he'd been reading. His eyes were fixed on an imaginary point. Clear, limpid eyes, and Tsukuru couldn't read anything behind them. The sort of gaze Haida had when he was mulling over some abstract proposition, eyes that always reminded Tsukuru of a mountain spring, glimpsed through a gap in the trees.

Nothing seemed out of the ordinary. It was a typical Sunday morning. A thin layer of clouds covered the sky, the sunlight soft. When they talked, Haida looked him right in the eye, and Tsukuru could read nothing in his look. Probably nothing had happened, *in reality*. It had to have been an illusion drawn by his unconscious, Tsukuru concluded. The thought embarrassed and confused him. He'd had any number of sexual dreams involving Shiro and Kuro together. This was nothing new. The dreams came fairly regularly, always involuntarily, and always made him orgasm. Yet this was the first time a sexual dream had been, from beginning to end, so startlingly vivid and real. But what really baffled him was Haida's presence.

Tsukuru decided not to pursue it further. He could think about it all he wanted and never find an answer. He placed this doubt inside a drawer in his mind labeled 'Pending' and post-poned any further consideration. He had many such drawers inside him, with numerous doubts and questions tucked away.

After breakfast they went to the college swimming pool and swam together for a half hour. It was Sunday morning and they nearly had the pool to themselves, and could enjoy going at their own pace. Tsukuru concentrated on moving the required muscles in a precise, controlled fashion – back muscles, hip muscles, abs. Breathing and kicking were already second nature.

Once he got into a rhythm, the rest happened on its own. As always Haida swam ahead and Tsukuru followed. Tsukuru watched as he swam, mesmerized by the subtle white foam rhythmically generated by Haida's gentle kicks. The scene always left him slightly hypnotized.

By the time they had showered and changed in the locker room, Haida's eyes no longer had that clear and penetrating light, but had regained their usual gentle look. Exercise had dulled Tsukuru's earlier confusion. The two of them left the gym and walked to the library. They hardly spoke, but that wasn't unusual. 'I have something I need to look up at the library,' Haida said. And this wasn't unusual either. Haida liked *looking things up* at the library. Generally this meant *I want to be alone for a while.* 'I'll go back and do some laundry,' Tsukuru said.

They came to the library entrance, gave a quick wave to each other, and went their separate ways.

He didn't hear from Haida for quite a while. Haida was absent from the pool and class. Tsukuru returned to a solitary life, eating alone, swimming alone, taking notes in class, memorizing foreign vocabulary and sentences. Time passed indifferently, barely leaving a trace. Occasionally he would put the record of 'Le mal du pays' on the turntable and listen to it.

After the first week with no word from Haida, the thought struck Tsukuru that his friend may have decided not to see him anymore. Without a word, giving no reason, he may have just gone away somewhere. Like his four friends had done back in his hometown.

Tsukuru began to think that his younger friend had left him because of the graphic sexual dream he'd experienced. Maybe something had made it possible for Haida to observe all that had taken place in Tsukuru's consciousness, and it had disgusted him. Or maybe it angered him.

No, that wasn't possible – the experience couldn't have slipped outside his consciousness. There's no way Haida could have known about it. Still, Tsukuru couldn't shake the feeling that Haida's clear eyes had homed in on the twisted aspects that lay buried in Tsukuru's mind, and the thought left him feeling ashamed.

Either way, after his friend disappeared, he realized anew how important Haida was to him, how Haida had transformed his daily life into something much richer and more colorful. He missed their conversations, and Haida's light, distinctive laugh. The music he liked, the books he sometimes read aloud from, his take on current events, his unique sense of humor, his spot-on quotations, the food he prepared, the coffee he brewed. Haida's absence left behind blank spaces throughout his life.

Haida had brought so much to Tsukuru's life, but, he wondered, what had *he* given to Haida? What memories had Tsukuru left him?

Maybe I am fated to always be alone, Tsukuru found himself thinking. People came to him, but in the end they always left. They came, seeking something, but either they couldn't find it, or were unhappy with what they found (or else they were disappointed or angry), and then they left. One day, without warning, they vanished, with no explanation, no word of farewell. Like a silent hatchet had sliced the ties between them, ties through which warm blood still flowed, along with a quiet pulse.

There must be something in him, something fundamental, that disenchanted people. 'Colorless Tsukuru Tazaki,' he said aloud. I basically have nothing to offer to others. If you think about it, I don't even have anything to offer myself.

On the morning ten days after they said goodbye in front of the library, Haida showed up at the college swimming pool. As Tsukuru was about to make another flip turn, someone tapped the back of his right hand as it touched the pool wall. He looked up and Haida was squatting there in his swim trunks, black goggles pushed up on his forehead, his usual pleasant smile gracing his face. Though they hadn't seen each other in a while, they didn't say anything, merely nodded and, as usual, started swimming in the same lane. The only communication between them in the water was the pliant movement of muscles and their gentle, rhythmic kicks. There was no need for words.

'I went back to Akita for a while,' Haida explained later. They'd finished swimming, had showered, and he was toweling off his hair. 'Some family matter suddenly came up.'

Tsukuru nodded and gave a noncommittal reply. It wasn't like Haida to take off ten days in the middle of a semester. Like Tsukuru, he tried never to skip class unless it was absolutely necessary. So it must have been something very important. But Haida said nothing more about his reason for having gone back home, and Tsukuru didn't push him on it. Yet his young friend's casual return made Tsukuru feel as if he were somehow able to spit out a hard lump of air that had been stuck in his chest. As if the pressure weighing on his chest were relieved. He hadn't been abandoned after all.

Haida continued to act the same as always toward Tsukuru. They talked and ate together. They'd sit on the sofa, listening to the classical CDs Haida borrowed from the library, discussing music, and books they'd read. Or else they'd simply be together, sharing an amiable silence. On the weekends Haida came to his apartment, they'd talk until late, and Haida would stay over on the sofa. Never again did Haida (or his alter ego) visit Tsukuru's bedroom and gaze at him in the dark – assuming, of course, that this had actually happened the first time. Tsukuru had many more sexual dreams involving Shiro and Kuro, but Haida never appeared.

Still, Tsukuru felt that Haida's clear eyes had seen right through him that night, to what lay in his unconscious. Traces of Haida's gaze still stung, like a mild burn. Haida had, at that time, observed Tsukuru's secret fantasies and desires, examining and dissecting them one by one, and yet he remained friends with Tsukuru. He had just needed some time apart from Tsukuru in order to accept what he'd seen, to get his feelings in order and compose himself. Which explained why he'd deliberately avoided Tsukuru for those ten days.

This was mere conjecture, of course. Baseless, unreasonable speculation. Delusion, you might even call it. But Tsukuru couldn't shake that thought, and it made him anxious. The idea that every fold in the depths of his mind had been laid bare left him feeling reduced to being a pathetic worm under a damp rock.

And yet Tsukuru Tazaki still needed this younger friend. More than anything.

8.

Haida left Tsukuru for good at the end of the following February, eight months after they'd first met. This time he never came back.

The end-of-year exams were over, the grades posted, when Haida went home to Akita. 'I should come back soon,' he told Tsukuru. 'Winters in Akita are freezing cold, and two weeks home is about as much as I can stand,' he said. 'Much easier to be in Tokyo. But I need to help get the snow off the roof, so I have to go there for a while.' But two weeks passed, then three, and Haida didn't return to Tokyo. He never once got in touch.

Tsukuru didn't worry too much in the beginning. He figured Haida was having a better time at home than he'd thought he might. Or maybe they'd had more snow than usual. Tsukuru himself went to Nagoya for three days in the middle of March. He didn't want to visit, but he couldn't stay away forever. No snow needed to be shoveled off the family roof in Nagoya, of course, but his mother had called him incessantly, wondering why, if school was out, he didn't want to come home. 'I have an important project I need to finish during the break,' Tsukuru lied. 'But you should still be able to come home for a couple of day at least,' his mother insisted. One of his older sisters called too, underscoring how much his mother missed him. 'You really should come home,' she said, 'even for a little while.' 'Okay, I get it,' he said. 'I will.'

Back in Nagoya, except for walking the dog in the park in the evening, he never went out. He was afraid of running into one of his four former friends, especially after he'd been having erotic dreams about Shiro and Kuro, essentially raping them in his imagination. He wasn't brave enough to meet them in the flesh, even if those dreams were beyond his control and there was no way they could possibly know what he'd been dreaming. Still, he was afraid they'd take one look at his face and know exactly what went on in his dreams, and then denounce him for his filthy, selfish illusions.

He refrained from masturbating as much as he could. Not because he felt guilty about the act itself, but because, as he touched himself, he couldn't help but picture Shiro and Kuro. He'd try to think of something else, but the two of them always stole inside his imagination. The problem was, the more he refrained from masturbating, the more frequent his erotic dreams became, almost always featuring the two girls. So the result was the same. But at least these weren't images he'd intentionally conjured. He knew he was just making excuses, but for him this explanation, basically just a rephrasing of events, held no small importance.

The contents of the dreams were nearly always the same. The setting and some of the details might change, but always the two girls were nude, entwined around him, caressing his whole body with their fingers and lips, stroking his penis, and then having sex with him. And in the end the one he always ejaculated in was Shiro. He might be having steamy sex with Kuro, but in the final moments, he'd suddenly realize he'd changed partners, and he'd come inside Shiro's body. He'd started having these dreams in the summer of his sophomore year, after he'd been expelled from the group and lost any chance to see the two women again, after he'd made up his mind to never think of his four friends again. He had no memory, before then, of ever having a dream like this. Why he started having these dreams was a mystery, another unanswered question to stuff deep inside the 'Pending' drawer in his unconscious.

Filled with desultory feelings of frustration, Tsukuru returned to Tokyo. There was still no word from Haida. He didn't show up at either the pool or the library. Tsukuru called Haida's dorm, and was told each time that Haida wasn't there. He realized he didn't know the address or phone number of Haida's home in Akita. While all this went on, the spring holidays ended and a new school year began. Tsukuru was now a senior. On the trees, cherry blossoms bloomed, then scattered, but still no word came from his younger friend.

He visited the dormitory where Haida had lived. The dorm manager told him that, at the end of the previous school year, Haida had submitted a form requesting to move out, and had taken away all his belongings. When Tsukuru heard this, he was speechless. The dorm manager knew nothing about why Haida had left the dorm or where he might have gone. Or perhaps he knew, but was merely claiming he didn't.

Tsukuru went to the college registrar's office and learned that Haida had been granted a leave of absence. The reason why he'd applied for this was confidential, and they wouldn't tell him anything more. All he knew was that, right after final exams, Haida had stamped his seal on the leave of absence form and the form to vacate his dorm. At that point, he was still seeing Tsukuru often. They were swimming together at the pool, and on weekends Haida was visiting Tsukuru's apartment, where they'd talk until late and Haida would stay over. And yet he had kept his plan to leave school a total secret. 'I'm just going back to Akita for a couple of weeks,' he'd informed Tsukuru, as if it were nothing important. And then he had vanished from sight.

I may never see him again, Tsukuru thought. For some reason Haida was determined to leave without a word of explanation. This didn't just happen by chance. There had to be a clear reason why he chose to act that way. No matter what the reason was, though, Tsukuru felt that Haida would never come back. And his hunch turned out to be right. At least while Tsukuru was in college, Haida never re-enrolled in school. And he never got in touch.

It's strange, Tsukuru thought at the time. Haida is repeating his father's fate. He leaves college when he's around twenty, and disappears, as if retracing his father's footsteps. Or was that whole story about his father a fabrication? Had he been trying to relate something about himself, making it sound as if it had happened to his father?

Somehow Haida's disappearance this time didn't confuse Tsukuru as deeply as he'd been confused before. He didn't feel bitter about Haida abandoning him. Rather, after losing his friend, he felt a strangely neutral quiet descending over his life. At times the odd thought struck him that Haida had partially absorbed Tsukuru's sin, his impurity, and as a result he had had to go far away.

Of course, Tsukuru felt lonely without his friend. He regretted that things had worked out this way. Haida was a good friend,

106

one of the few he'd ever had. But maybe it was unavoidable. All he'd left behind were his little coffee mill, a half-filled bag of coffee beans, the three-LP set of Lazar Berman playing Liszt's 'Le mal du pays,' and the memory of his unusually limpid eyes, and that gaze.

That May, a month after Tsukuru learned that Haida had left campus, he had his first real sexual relationship with a woman. He was twenty-one then, twenty-one and six months. Since the beginning of the school year he'd begun an internship doing drafting at an architectural firm, and the person he slept with was an unmarried woman, four years older than he, whom he met at the office. She did clerical work there. She was on the small side, with long hair, large ears, gorgeous legs, and a taut body. More cute than beautiful. When she joked around, her smile revealed beautiful white teeth. She was kind to him from the first day he started work, and he could sense she liked him. Raised with two older sisters, Tsukuru always felt comfortable around older women. The woman was the same age as his second sister.

Tsukuru found a chance to invite her to dinner, then back to his apartment, and there he took the plunge and lured her into bed. She accepted his overtures with barely a moment's hesitation. Though it was Tsukuru's first time with a woman, things went smoothly – no confusion, no nervousness – from start to finish. Because of this, the woman seemed convinced that he was more sexually experienced than most young men his age, even though the only sex he'd had with women had been confined to dreams.

Tsukuru really liked her. She was bright and attractive, and while she didn't provide intellectual stimulation like Haida, she had a cheerful, open personality, plenty of curiosity, and was an enjoyable conversationalist. She enjoyed making love, too, and being with her taught him much about women's bodies.

She wasn't good at cooking, but enjoyed cleaning, and before long she had his apartment sparkling clean. She replaced his curtains, sheets, pillowcases, towels, and bath mats with brand-new ones. She brought color and vitality into Tsukuru's post-Haida life. But he didn't choose to sleep with her out of passion, or because he was fond of her, or even to lessen his loneliness. Though he probably would never have admitted it, he was hoping to prove to himself that he wasn't gay, that he was capable of having sex with a real woman, not just in his dreams. This was his main objective.

And he achieved his goal.

She stayed overnight at his place on weekends, just as Haida had done not so long before. They would make love leisurely, sometimes having sex almost until dawn. As he made love to her, he tried hard to think of nothing beyond her and her body. He focused, switched off his imagination, and chased away everything that wasn't there – Shiro and Kuro's naked bodies, and Haida's lips – as best he could. She was on the pill, so he could come freely inside her. She enjoyed sex with him and seemed to be satisfied. When she orgasmed she always cried out in a strange voice. *It's okay*, Tsukuru told himself. *I'm normal, after all.* Thanks to this relationship, his erotic dreams disappeared.

They saw each other for eight months, then mutually agreed to break up, just before he graduated from college. A railroad company had offered him a job, and his part-time work at the architectural firm was over. While she was seeing Tsukuru she had another boyfriend, someone back in her hometown in

Niigata, whom she'd known since childhood (information she had disclosed from the first day they slept together). She was going to marry him in April. She planned to quit her job at the architectural firm and move to Sanjo City, where her fiancé worked. 'So I won't be able to see you anymore,' she told Tsukuru one day as they lay in bed.

'He's a very good person,' she said, resting her hand on Tsukuru's. 'We're well suited to each other.'

'I hate the thought of not seeing you again,' Tsukuru said, 'but I suppose I should congratulate you.'

'Thank you,' she said. Then, as if writing a tiny footnote at the corner of a page, she added, 'I might have a chance to see you again, someday.'

'That would be great,' Tsukuru said, though he found it hard to decipher that footnote. When she's with her fiancé, he suddenly wondered, does she cry out in the same way? The two of them made love again.

And he really did feel bad about not being able to see her once a week. He knew that if he wanted to avoid having graphic erotic dreams, and live more in the present, he needed a regular sexual partner. But still, her marriage was, if anything, a good development for him, as he'd never felt anything for her beyond a calm fondness and a healthy physical desire. And at that point Tsukuru was about to embark on a new stage in his life.

9.

When the call came in on his cell phone from Sara Kimoto, Tsukuru was killing time, sorting the documents that had piled up on his desk, discarding the ones he didn't need, reorganizing the clutter that had accumulated in his desk drawer. It was a Thursday, five days since he'd last seen her.

'Can you talk?'

'Sure,' Tsukuru said. 'I'm just taking it easy today for a change.'

'Good,' she said. 'Are you free later? Even for a little while? I have a dinner at seven, but I can see you before then. If you could come to Ginza, I'd really appreciate it.'

Tsukuru glanced at his watch. 'I can be there by five thirty. Just tell me where to meet you.'

She told him the name of a coffee shop near the Ginza-Yonchome intersection. Tsukuru knew the place.

He wrapped up work before five, left the office, and rode the Marunouchi line from Shinjuku to Ginza. Luckily he happened to be wearing the tie Sara had given him last time.

Sara was in the coffee shop when he arrived. She had already ordered coffee and was waiting for him. She beamed when she saw the tie. When she smiled, two charming little lines formed beside her lips. The waitress came over, and Tsukuru ordered coffee. The shop was crowded with people meeting up after work.

'Sorry to drag you out all this way,' Sara said.

'No, it's good for me to get to Ginza every once in a while,' Tsukuru said. 'I only wish we could go somewhere and have dinner together.'

Sara pursed her lips and sighed. 'I wish we could, but I have to attend a business dinner tonight. There's this VIP from France who's here and I have to take him to an expensive *kaiseki* restaurant. I hate these kinds of dinners. I get all tense and can't even taste what I'm eating.'

She'd taken even more care with her appearance than usual, Tsukuru noticed. She wore a nicely tailored coffee-brown suit and a brooch on her collar with a tiny diamond sparkling in the center. Her skirt was short, and below this were stockings with a detailed pattern the same color as her suit.

Sara snapped open the maroon enamel handbag on her lap and extracted a large white envelope. Inside were several printouts, folded. She snapped her handbag smartly shut. A pleasant sound, the kind you might expect would turn the heads of the people around her.

'I looked into your four friends, where they are, and what they're doing now. Like I promised.'

Tsukuru was taken aback. 'But that was less than a week ago.'

'I'm very quick when it comes to work. As long as I know the gist of something, I don't take long to get it done.'

'There's no way I could have done that.'

'Everyone has their specialty. I could never build a railroad station.'

'Or do drafting, either.'

She smiled. 'Not if I lived for two hundred years.'

'So, you know where the four of them are now?' Tsukuru asked.

'In a sense,' she said.

'*In a sense*,' Tsukuru repeated. The phrase had a strange ring to it. 'What do you mean?'

She took a sip of coffee and returned the cup to the saucer. She paused, and checked her enameled nails. They looked beautiful, painted in the same maroon color as her handbag (perhaps a little lighter). He was willing to bet a month's salary this wasn't a coincidence.

'Let me tell things in order,' Sara said. 'Otherwise it won't come out right.'

Tsukuru nodded. 'Of course. Whatever way works best for you.'

Sara quickly explained how she'd carried out the investigation. She started with various online search methods and social networks, including Facebook, Google, and Twitter, and had tracked down information about the four people's lives. Gathering information about Ao and Aka hadn't been difficult. Actually, they openly shared information about themselves online – most of it related to their businesses.

'It's sort of weird if you think about it,' Sara said. 'We live in a pretty apathetic age, yet we're surrounded by an enormous amount of information about other people. If you feel like it, you can easily gather that information about them. Having said that, we still hardly know anything about people.'

'Philosophical observations really suit the way you're dressed today,' Tsukuru said.

'Thank you,' Sara said, and smiled.

When it came to Kuro, the investigation hadn't been as easy. She had no business reasons for disclosing personal information to the world. Still, searching the website for the industrial arts department of the Aichi Prefectural Arts College, Sara had finally been able to trace her whereabouts.

The Aichi Prefectural Arts College? But Kuro was supposed to go into the English literature department of a private women's college in Nagoya. Tsukuru didn't mention this, though. He kept the question to himself.

'I couldn't find out much about her,' Sara said, 'so I called her parents' home. I made up a story about being a former high school classmate. I said I was editing an alumni newsletter and needed her present address. Her mother was very nice and told me all kinds of things.'

'I'm sure you were very good at drawing her out,' Tsukuru said.

'Maybe so,' Sara said modestly.

The waitress came over and was about to top off her coffee, but Sara held up a hand to refuse. After the waitress left, she spoke again.

'Gathering information about Shiro was both difficult and easy. I couldn't find any personal information about her at all, but a newspaper article told me all I needed to know.'

'A newspaper article?' Tsukuru asked.

Sara bit her lip. 'This is a very delicate area. So, like I said before, let me tell it in the right order.'

'Sorry,' Tsukuru said.

'The first thing I'd like to know is this: If you know where these four friends are now, do you want to see them again? Even if you find out that some of what I'm going to tell you is unpleasant? Facts you might wish you hadn't found out about?'

Tsukuru nodded. 'I can't guess what those might be, but I do plan to see the four of them. I've made up my mind.'

Sara gazed at his face for some time before speaking.

'Kuro – Eri Kurono – is living in Finland now. She rarely returns to Japan.'

'Finland?'

'She lives in Helsinki with her Finnish husband and two little daughters. So if you want to see her, you'll have to travel there.'

Tsukuru pictured a rough map of Europe in his mind. 'I've never really traveled before, and I have some vacation time saved up. And it might be nice to check out the railroads in northern Europe.'

Sara smiled. 'I wrote down the address and phone number of her apartment in Helsinki. Why she married a Finnish man, and how she came to live in Helsinki, you can look into yourself. Or you can ask her.'

'Thank you. Her address and phone number are more than enough.'

'If you feel like traveling to Finland, I can help with the arrangements.'

'Because you're a pro.'

'Not to mention capable and skilled.'

'Of course.'

Sara unfolded the next printout. 'Ao – Yoshio Oumi – is a salesman at a Lexus dealership in Nagoya City. He's done very well, apparently, and has won their last few top sales awards. He's still young, but he's already head of their sales department.'

'Lexus,' Tsukuru said, murmuring the name to himself.

Tsukuru tried to imagine Ao in a business suit in a brightly lit showroom, explaining to a customer the feel of the leather and the quality of the surface coating of a high-end sedan. But he just couldn't picture it. What he saw instead was Ao in a rugby jersey, sweaty, gulping cold barley tea directly from a teapot, scarfing down enough food for two people.

'Are you surprised?'

'It just feels a little strange,' Tsukuru said. 'But now that I think about it, Ao might be a really good salesman. He's a stand-up guy, and though he isn't the most eloquent person, people trust him. He isn't the type to resort to cheap tricks, and if he worked at it for a while, I can imagine him doing very well.'

'I understand Lexus is an outstanding type of car, very reliable.'

'If he's that great a salesman, he might convince me to buy a Lexus too, as soon as I meet with him.'

Sara laughed. 'Could be.'

Tsukuru remembered his father, and how he never rode in anything but a full-size Mercedes-Benz. Every three years, like clockwork, he would exchange it for a newer Mercedes of the same class. Or rather, without him doing anything, the dealer would show up every three years to replace his car with a brand-new, fully loaded model. His cars were always polished and shiny, without a single scratch or blemish. His father never drove the cars himself, but always had a driver. The windows were tinted dark gray, so the interior wasn't visible. The wheel covers were as shiny as newly minted silver coins, the doors made a solid, bank vault-like clunk as they closed, and the interior was like a locked room. Sinking into the backseat, you felt far away from the noise and confusion of the outside world. Tsukuru had never liked riding in his father's car. It was just too quiet. He much preferred a crowded station and trains, teeming with passengers.

'Ao has worked for Toyota dealers ever since he graduated from college, and because of his outstanding sales record in 2005, when the company moved to launch Lexus dealerships in Japan he was handpicked to move over to that division. Farewell Corolla, hello Lexus.' Sara again checked out the manicure on her left hand. 'So it won't be very hard for you to see Ao again. Just visit the Lexus showroom and he'll be there.'

'I see,' Tsukuru said.

Sara turned to the next page.

'Compared to Ao, Aka – Kei Akamatsu – has had a pretty stormy life. He graduated at the top of his class in economics from Nagoya University and worked for a major bank. One of the so-called megabanks. But for some reason, he quit after three years and went to work at a fairly well-known finance company, a firm financed out of Nagoya. One of those consumer-finance companies with a bit of an unsavory reputation. A pretty unexpected change in direction for him, but he didn't stay there long, either – it was only two and a half years before he quit. This time he got funding from somewhere and started his own company, one that provides a combination of personal development seminars and a company training center. He calls it a "creative business seminar." The business has been amazingly successful – so much so that now he has a large staff, and an office in a high-rise in downtown Nagoya. If you want to learn more about it, it's easy to find online. The company's name is BEYOND. Sounds a little New Agey, don't you think?'

'"Creative business seminar."'

'The name's new, but it's really not much different from a personal development seminar,' Sara said. 'Basically a quick, impromptu brainwashing course to educate your typical corporate warriors. They use a training manual instead of sacred scriptures, with promotion and a high salary as their equivalent of enlightenment and paradise. A new religion for a pragmatic age. No transcendent elements like in a religion, though, and everything is theorized and digitalized. Very transparent and easy to grasp. And quite a few people get positive encouragement from this. But the fact remains that it's nothing more than an infusion of the hypnotic into a system of thought that suits their goal, a conglomeration of only those theories and statistics that line up with their ultimate objectives. The company has an excellent reputation, though, and quite a lot of local businesses have contracts with them. Their website shows that they run a variety of new programs guaranteed to get people's attention, from boot-camp-like group training for new employees and a reeducation summer session for mid-level employees that's held at an upscale resort hotel, to high-class power lunches for top-level executives. The way these seminars are packaged, at least, makes them look really attractive. They focus on teaching business etiquette and correct communication skills for young employees. Personally it's the last thing I'd like to do, but I can understand how companies would find it appealing. Does this give you a general idea now of what sort of business we're talking about?'

'I think so,' Tsukuru said. 'But to launch a business like that you need a fair amount of capital. Where could Aka have possibly gotten it? His father's a university professor and kind of a straight arrow. As far as I know he isn't that well off, and I can't imagine he'd be willing to invest in something that risky.'

'I don't know. It's a mystery,' Sara said. 'That being said, when you knew him in high school, was this Akamatsu the sort of person you could imagine becoming a kind of guru?'

Tsukuru shook his head. 'No, he was more the calm, objective, academic type. He was quick, superintelligent, and had a way with words. Most of the time, though, he tried to not show any of that. Maybe I shouldn't say this, but he was more comfortable in the background, scheming on his own. I can't picture him standing up in front of people and trying to inspire and encourage them.'

'People change,' Sara said.

'True enough,' Tsukuru said. 'People do change. And no matter how close we once were, and how much we opened up to each other, maybe neither of us knew anything substantial about the other.'

Sara gazed at Tsukuru for a time before she spoke. 'Anyway, both of them are working in Nagoya City. They've basically never taken a step outside the city since the day they were born. Their schools were in Nagoya, their jobs are in Nagoya. Reminds me of Conan Doyle's *The Lost World*. Is Nagoya really that nice a place?'

Tsukuru couldn't answer, but he had a strange feeling. If circumstances had been different he might have spent his life entirely within the confines of Nagoya too, and never questioned it.

Sara was silent. She folded up the printouts, put them back in the envelope, placed it on the end of the table, and took a drink of water. When she spoke again, her tone was more formal.

'Now, about the last person, Shiro – Yuzuki Shirane – unfortunately, she does not have a present address.'

'Does not have a present address,' Tsukuru murmured.

That's an odd way of putting it, Tsukuru thought. If she'd said she didn't *know* her present address, that he could fathom. But saying she doesn't *have* a present address sounded strange. He considered the implications. Had Shiro gone missing? She wasn't homeless, was she?

'Sadly, she's no longer in this world,' Sara said.

'No longer in this world?'

For some reason an image flashed before his eyes of Shiro in a space shuttle, wandering in outer space.

'She passed away six years ago,' Sara said. 'That's why she has no present address. She does have a gravestone, in a suburb of Nagoya. It's very difficult for me to have to tell you this.'

Tsukuru didn't know what to say. The strength drained out of him, like water leaking from a small hole in a bag. The hum around him faded, Sara's voice the only thing that – barely – reached him. It was a far-off, meaningless echo, as if he were hearing it from the bottom of a pool. He roused himself, sat up straight, and raised his head above the water. He was finally able to hear again, and the words started to regain meaning. Sara was speaking to him.

'. . . I didn't write down the details of how she passed away. I think it's better if you find that out on your own. Even if it takes time.'

Tsukuru nodded automatically.

Six years ago? Six years ago she was thirty. Still only thirty. Tsukuru tried to picture her at that age, but couldn't. What he imagined was Shiro at sixteen or seventeen. A terrible sadness washed over him. What the hell was this? He couldn't even grow old with her?

Sara leaned across the table and gently laid her hand, small and warm, on his. Tsukuru was happy at this intimate touch, and grateful, yet it felt like something happening simultaneously, far away, to someone else.

'I'm very sorry it turned out this way,' Sara said. 'But you had to hear this someday.'

'I know,' Tsukuru said. Of course he knew this. But it would take a while for his mind to catch up to reality. It was nobody's fault.

'I have to get going,' Sara said, glancing at her watch. She handed him the envelope. 'I printed out all the information about your four friends. Only the bare minimum is written down here. It's more important that you meet them in person. You'll learn more that way.'

'I really appreciate it,' Tsukuru said. It took a while for him to locate the appropriate words, and to voice them. 'I should be able to let you know pretty soon how things turn out.'

'I'll wait to hear from you. In the meanwhile, if there's anything I can do, be sure to let me know.'

Tsukuru thanked her again.

They left the café and said goodbye. Tsukuru stood on the street, watching as Sara, in her milky coffee-brown summer suit, waved and disappeared into the crowd. He wished he could be with her longer, spend more time with her, have a good, leisurely talk. But she had her own life, most of which occurred offstage, in a place he didn't yet know about, doing things that had nothing to do with him.

Sara's envelope was tucked in the inside pocket of his suit jacket. It contained a neatly folded document that listed a concise summary of his four friends' lives. One of them no longer existed *here*. She was no more than a handful of white ash. Her thoughts, her opinions, her feelings, her hopes and dreams – all of them had vanished without a trace. All that remained were memories *of* her. Her long, straight black hair, her shapely fingers on the keyboard, her smooth, white, graceful (yet strangely eloquent) calves, her playing of Franz Liszt's 'Le mal du pays.' Her wet pubic hair, her hard nipples. *No* – that wasn't even a memory. That was a – Tsukuru decided not to go there.

Where to now? Tsukuru wondered as he leaned back against a streetlight. His watch showed it was just before seven. Some light remained in the sky, but the shop windows along the street were sparkling more by the minute, enticing those who wandered by. It was still early, and he had nothing in particular he needed to do. He didn't want to go home just yet. He didn't want to be alone in a quiet place. Tsukuru could go anywhere he liked. *Almost* anywhere. But he couldn't think of anyplace to go.

At a time like this it would be nice if I could drink more, he thought. At this point most men would find a bar and get drunk. But his body couldn't handle more than a fixed amount of alcohol. Liquor didn't give him deadened senses, or a pleasant forgetfulness, just a splitting headache the next morning.

So, where should I go?

There really was only one choice.

He walked along the main street to Tokyo Station, passed through the Yaesu entrance, and sat down on a bench on the Yamanote line platform. He spent over an hour watching as, almost every minute, another line of green train cars pulled up to the platform, disembarking hordes of people and hurriedly swallowing up countless more. His mind was a blank as he watched, absorbed in the scene. The view didn't soothe the pain in his heart, but the endless repetition enthralled him as always and, at the very least, numbed his sense of time.

Unceasing crowds of people arrived out of nowhere, automatically formed lines, boarded the trains in order, and were carried off somewhere. Tsukuru was moved by how many people *actually* existed in the world. And he was likewise moved by the sheer number of green train cars. It was surely a miracle, he thought – how so many people, in so many railroad cars, are systematically transported, as if it were nothing. How all those people have places to go, places to return to.

As the rush-hour surge finally receded, Tsukuru Tazaki slowly got to his feet, boarded one of the cars, and went home. The pain was still there, but now he knew there was something he had to do.

10.

At the end of May Tsukuru took a long weekend and returned to his home in Nagoya for three days. His family was holding a Buddhist memorial service for his father, so it was a particularly good time for him to go back.

Since his father's death, his oldest sister and her husband had been living with Tsukuru's mother in her spacious house, but Tsukuru's old room was as vacant as he had left it, so he stayed there. His bed, desk, and bookshelf were unchanged from his high school days, the bookshelf lined with old books, the drawers full of pens and notebooks he'd used as a boy.

The memorial service took place on his first day back. It was held at a temple and followed by a meal with relatives, which gave him sufficient time to catch up with his family. The next day he was totally free. Tsukuru decided to go see Ao first. It was a Sunday, when most businesses were usually closed, but not a new-car dealership. Tsukuru had decided that – no matter which of his friends he saw – he would casually show up without an appointment. He wanted to get an honest response when they saw him again, without giving them a chance to mentally prepare themselves for his visit. If he wasn't able to meet with them when he showed up, or if they refused to see him, he'd just have to live with it. If it came to that, he'd figure out another approach.

The Lexus showroom was in a quiet area near Nagoya Castle. Lexuses in a variety of colors were grandly lined up behind the wide glass show windows, every kind of car from sports cars to SUVs. Once inside the showroom, the distinctive new-car smell wafted toward him, a blend of new tires, plastic, and leather.

Tsukuru walked over to speak with a young woman seated behind the reception desk. She wore her hair up in a neat bun, revealing a slim white neck. A vase of large pink and white dahlias graced her desk.

'I'd like to see Mr. Oumi, please,' he told her.

She flashed him a calm, self-possessed smile that perfectly matched the bright, immaculate showroom. Her lipstick was a natural shade, her teeth beautifully even. 'Mr. Oumi? Of course, sir. And you would be—?'

'Tazaki,' he said.

'Mr. Tasaki. And would you have an appointment for today?'

He didn't correct her mispronunciation of his name, a common mistake. That would actually help.

'I'm afraid I don't.'

'I see. If you would pardon me for a moment.' The woman pushed an extension button on her phone and waited for about five seconds, then spoke. 'Mr. Oumi? A client named Mr. Tasaki is here to see you. Yes, that's correct. Mr. Tasaki.'

He couldn't hear what the other party was saying, just her short, clipped replies. Finally she said, 'Yes, sir, I will let him know.'

She hung up the phone and looked at Tsukuru. 'Mr. Tasaki, I'm afraid Mr. Oumi is busy at the moment and cannot get away.

124

I'm very sorry, but could I ask you to wait? He said it shouldn't take ten minutes.'

Her way of speaking was smooth and well trained, her use of Japanese honorifics flawless. She sounded truly apologetic at having to make him wait. Obviously she had been very well educated. Or maybe she was just naturally this kind of person?

'That's fine. I'm in no hurry,' Tsukuru said.

She led him to a plush black leather sofa. Next to it was a huge decorative potted plant, and in the background an Antônio Carlos Jobim tune played. Glossy Lexus catalogs lay on top of the narrow glass coffee table.

'Would you care for coffee or tea? Or perhaps green tea?'

'A coffee would be nice,' Tsukuru said.

As he leafed through the catalog for the latest Lexus sedans, she brought over the coffee in a cream-colored cup imprinted with the Lexus logo. He thanked her. The coffee was delicious. It had a fresh aroma, and was the perfect temperature.

Tsukuru was glad he had decided to wear a suit and nice leather shoes. He had no idea what people coming to buy a Lexus normally wore, but they might not have taken him seriously if he'd been decked out in a polo shirt, jeans, and sneakers. Just before he left the house, he had suddenly changed his mind and put on a suit and tie.

He was kept waiting for fifteen minutes, during which time he learned the entire lineup of Lexus models. He discovered that Lexus didn't give their different models names, like Corolla or Crown, but instead used numbers to distinguish models. Just like Mercedes-Benz and BMW. And Brahms symphonies.

A tall man finally appeared. He crossed the showroom in Tsukuru's direction. He was broad-shouldered, and carried himself in a decisive manner, letting those around him know he was not about to waste any time getting from point A to point B. It was definitely Ao. Even seen from a distance, he looked nearly the same as he had in high school. He'd grown a little bigger, that was all, like a house with an addition when the family grows. Tsukuru placed the catalogs back on the tabletop and rose from the sofa.

'I'm sorry to have kept you waiting. My name's Oumi.'

Ao stood in front of Tsukuru, giving a slight bow. The suit that encased his large frame was perfectly pressed, without a single wrinkle. A refined suit, a mix of blue and gray in a light fabric. Considering his size, it must have been made to order. A light gray shirt and dark gray necktie completed the outfit. Tsukuru recalled how Ao had looked in high school and found it surprising to now see him so impeccably dressed. Ao's hair, though, was unchanged, a rugby player's buzz cut. And he was, as before, quite tan.

Ao's expression changed slightly when he looked at Tsukuru. A slight doubt glinted in his eyes, as if he'd seen something in Tsukuru's face he remembered, but couldn't quite recall what it was. He smiled, swallowing back what he was about to say, waiting for Tsukuru to speak.

'It's been a while,' Tsukuru said.

As he heard Tsukuru's voice, the layer of doubt that had veiled Ao's face suddenly lifted. Tsukuru's voice hadn't changed at all.

'Tsukuru?' he said, narrowing his eyes.

Tsukuru nodded. 'I'm sorry to barge in on you at work like this, but I figured that was the best way.'

Ao took a deep breath, his shoulders lifting, and then slowly breathed out. He looked at Tsukuru's whole body, as if inspecting him, his gaze running from top to bottom, then back to the top again.

'I can't believe how much you've changed,' Ao said, sounding impressed. 'If I'd passed you on the street I wouldn't have recognized you.'

'You haven't changed at all.'

Ao's large mouth twisted to one side. 'No way. I've put on weight. Got a potbelly now. And I can't run fast anymore. Golf once a month with clients is about all I can manage.'

They were silent for a moment.

'You didn't come here to buy a car, am I right?' Ao asked, as if confirming it.

'You're right, I didn't come to buy a car. If you're free, I'd like to talk, just the two of us. Even for a short time.'

Ao gave a slight, unsure frown. His face always had given away his feelings, ever since Tsukuru had first known him.

'I have a pretty tight schedule today. I have to go visit some customers, and then I have a meeting in the afternoon.'

'Name a time that's convenient for you. I'm fine with whatever works for you. It's why I came back to Nagoya.'

Ao mentally reviewed his schedule, and glanced at the wall clock. It was eleven thirty. He rubbed the tip of his nose vigorously and then spoke, as if he'd made up his mind. 'Okay. I'll take a lunch break at twelve. I could meet you for a half hour. If you go out here, and turn left, you'll see a Starbucks down the street. I'll meet you there.'

Ao showed up at the Starbucks at five to twelve.

'It's too noisy here, so let's grab some drinks and go somewhere else,' Ao said. He ordered a cappuccino and a scone for himself. Tsukuru bought a bottle of mineral water. They walked to a nearby park and sat down on an unoccupied bench.

The sky was covered with a thin layer of clouds, not a patch of blue visible anywhere, though it did not look like rain. There was no wind, either. The branches of a nearby willow tree were laden with lush foliage and drooping heavily, almost to the ground, though they were still, as if lost in deep thought. Occasionally a small bird landed unsteadily on a branch, but soon gave up and fluttered away. Like a distraught mind, the branch quivered slightly, then returned to stillness.

'I might get a call on my cell while we're talking,' Ao said. 'I hope you'll forgive me. I have a couple of business-related things I'm working on.'

'No problem. I can imagine how busy you must be.'

'Cell phones are so convenient that they're an inconvenience,' Ao said. 'So tell me, are you married?'

'No, still single.'

'I got married six years ago and have a child. A three-year-old boy. Another one's on the way, and my wife's getting bigger by the day. The due date's in September. A girl this time.'

Tsukuru nodded. 'Life's moving along smoothly, then.'

'I don't know about smoothly, but it's moving along, at least. There's no going back now might be another way of putting it. How about you?'

'Not so bad,' Tsukuru said, taking a business card out of his wallet and passing it to Ao, who took it and read aloud.

'[——] Railroad Company. Facilities Department, Construction Division.'

'Mostly we build and maintain railroad stations,' Tsukuru said.

'You always liked stations, didn't you,' Ao said, sounding

impressed. He took a sip of cappuccino. 'So you got a job doing what you like.'

'But I work for a company, so I can't just do what I like. There are all kinds of boring things I have to do.'

'It's the same everywhere,' Ao said. 'As long as you work for somebody you have to put up with a lot of crap.' He shook his head a couple of times, as if remembering examples.

'So, are Lexuses selling well?' Tsukuru asked.

'Not bad. This is Nagoya, after all. Toyota's hometown. Toyotas practically sell themselves. But our competitors now aren't Nissan and Honda. We're targeting consumers who buy high-end imported cars, your Mercedes and your BMWs, trying to turn them into Lexus buyers. That's why Toyota's created a flagship brand. It might take time, but I'm sure it'll work out.'

'Losing is not an option.'

An odd look passed over Ao's face for a second and then he grinned broadly. 'Ah – my little rugby pep talk. You picked a strange thing to remember.'

'You were really good at boosting morale.'

'Yeah, but we lost most of the time. Business is actually going smoothly. The economy's still in bad shape, of course, but the rich manage to hold on to their money. Amazingly well.'

Tsukuru nodded, and Ao continued.

'I've driven a Lexus myself for quite a while. They're wonderful cars. Quiet, never need repairs. I took one out on a test course and got it up to 125 miles an hour. The steering wheel was stable, no vibration whatsoever. The brakes are solid, too. It's an amazing car. It's nice to be able to sell people something you believe in yourself. No matter how smooth-talking I might be, I could never sell something that I didn't actually like.'

Tsukuru agreed.

Ao looked him right in the eye. 'I bet I sound like a car salesman?'

'No, I don't think so,' Tsukuru said. He knew Ao was being honest about how he felt. Still, the fact remained that he had never talked like this back in high school.

'Do you drive?' Ao asked.

'I do, but I don't have a car. In Tokyo you can get by with trains, buses, and taxis. I get around by bike a lot. When I absolutely need a car, I rent one. It's different from Nagoya.'

'Yeah, that would be easier, and cost less,' Ao said. He let out a small sigh. 'People can get by without a car. So, how do you like living in Tokyo?'

'Well, my job's there, and I've lived there long enough to get used to it. I don't really have anywhere else to go. That's all. It's not like I'm that crazy about the place.'

They were silent for a while. A middle-aged woman with two border collies walked past, then a few joggers, heading toward the castle.

'You said there was something you wanted to talk about,' Ao said, as if addressing someone in the distance.

'During summer vacation in my sophomore year in college I came back to Nagoya and called you,' Tsukuru began. 'You told me then that you didn't want to see me anymore, not to ever call again, and that all four of you felt the same way. Do you remember that?'

'Of course I do.'

'I want to know why,' Tsukuru said.

'Just like that, after all this time?' Ao said, sounding a little surprised.

'Yes, after all this time. I wasn't able to ask you back then. It was too unexpected, too much of a shock. And I was afraid to hear the reason you guys so flat-out rejected me. I felt like if you told me, I'd never recover. So I tried to forget about all of it, without finding out what was going on. I thought time would heal the pain.'

Ao tore off a small piece of scone and popped it in his mouth. He chewed it slowly, washing it down with the cappuccino. Tsukuru went on.

'Sixteen years have gone by, but it feels like the wound is still there inside me. Like it's still bleeding. Something happened recently, something very significant to me, that made me realize this. That's why I came to Nagoya to see you. I apologize for showing up out of the blue like this.'

Ao stared for a time at the heavy, sagging branches of the willow. 'You have no idea why we did that?' he said, finally.

'I've thought about it for sixteen years, but I have no clue.'

Ao narrowed his eyes, seemingly perplexed, and rubbed the tip of his nose – his habit, apparently, when he was thinking hard. 'When I told you that back then you said, *I see*, and hung up. You didn't object or anything. Or try to dig deeper. So naturally I thought you knew why.'

'Words don't come out when you're hurt that deeply,' Tsukuru said.

Ao didn't respond. He tore off another piece of scone and tossed it toward some pigeons. The pigeons swiftly flocked around the food. He seemed to be used to doing this. Maybe he often came here on his break and shared his lunch with the birds.

'Okay, so tell me. What was the reason?' Tsukuru asked.

'You really don't have any idea?'

'I *really* don't.'

Just then a cheery melody rang out on Ao's cell phone. He slipped the phone from his suit pocket, checked the name on the screen, impassively pressed a key, and returned it to his pocket. Tsukuru had heard that melody somewhere before. An old pop song of some kind, probably popular before he was born, but he couldn't recall the title.

'If you have something you need to do,' Tsukuru said, 'please feel free to take care of it.'

Ao shook his head. 'No, it's okay. It's not that important. I can handle it later.'

Tsukuru took a drink of mineral water from the plastic bottle. 'Why did I have to be banished from the group?'

Ao considered this for some time before he spoke. 'If you're saying that you have no idea why, it means – what? – that you – didn't have any sexual relationship with Shiro?'

Tsukuru's lips curled up in surprise. 'A sexual relationship? No way.'

'Shiro said you raped her,' Ao said, as if reluctant to even say it. 'She said you forced her to have sex.'

Tsukuru started to respond, but the words wouldn't come. Despite the water, the back of his throat felt so dry that it ached.

'I couldn't believe you'd do something like that,' Ao continued. 'I think the other two felt the same way, both Kuro and Aka. You weren't the type to force someone to do something they didn't want to do. You weren't violent, we knew that. But Shiro was totally serious about it, obsessed even. You had a public face and a hidden, private face, she said. You had a dark, hidden side, something unhinged and detached from the side of you that

132

everyone knew. When she said that, there was nothing we could say.'

Tsukuru bit his lip for a time. 'Did Shiro explain how I supposedly raped her?'

'She did. Very realistically, and in great detail. I didn't want to hear any of it. Frankly, it was painful to hear. Painful, and sad. It hurt me, I guess I should say. Anyway, she got very emotional. Her body started trembling, and she was so enraged that she looked like a different person. According to Shiro, she traveled to Tokyo to see a concert by a famous foreign pianist and you let her stay in your apartment in Jiyugaoka. She told her parents she was staying in a hotel, but by staying with you, she saved money. Normally she might have hesitated to stay alone in a man's place, but it was you, so she felt safe. But she said that in the middle of the night you forced yourself on her. She tried to resist, but her body was numb and wouldn't move. You both had a drink before bedtime, and you might have slipped something into her glass. That's what she told us.'

Tsukuru shook his head. 'Shiro never visited my place in Tokyo once, let alone stay over.'

Ao shrugged his shoulders a touch. He made a face like he'd bitten into something bitter, and glanced off to one side. 'The only thing I could do was believe what she said. She told us she'd been a virgin. That you'd deflowered her by force, and it was painful and she'd bled. Shiro was always so shy and bashful, and I couldn't imagine a reason why she'd make up such a graphic story.'

Tsukuru turned to look at Ao's profile. 'Granted, but why didn't you ask me? Shouldn't you have given me a chance to explain? Instead of trying me in absentia like that?'

Ao sighed. 'You're absolutely right. In retrospect, yes, that's what we should have done. We should have listened to your side of the story. But at the time, we couldn't. It was impossible. Shiro was agitated and confused like you wouldn't believe. We had no idea what might happen. So our first priority was to calm her down. It wasn't like we believed every single thing she said. Some parts didn't add up. But we didn't think it was all fiction, either. It was so detailed, what she told us, that we figured there had to be some truth to it.'

'So you went ahead and cut me off.'

'You've got to understand, Tsukuru, that we were in shock ourselves, totally disoriented. We were hurt, too. We had no idea who to believe. In the midst of all this, Kuro stood by Shiro. She wanted us to cut you off, just like Shiro had asked. I'm not trying to excuse our actions, but Aka and I were sort of swept along, and we did what Kuro wanted.'

Tsukuru sighed. 'Whether or not you believe me, I never raped Shiro, and never had a sexual relationship with her. I don't remember doing anything even close to that.'

Ao nodded but didn't say anything. Whatever he believed or didn't believe, too much time had passed since then. That's what Tsukuru figured. For the other three as well. And for Tsukuru himself.

Ao's cell phone rang again. He checked the name and turned to Tsukuru.

'Sorry, but do you mind if I take this?'

'Go right ahead,' Tsukuru said.

Ao stood up from the bench, walked a little ways away, and began talking into his cell phone. His body language and expression made clear that it was a customer. Tsukuru suddenly remembered the ringtone melody. Elvis Presley's 'Viva Las Vegas!' No matter what sort of spin you put on it, it was not exactly the right ringtone for a shrewd Lexus salesman. Ever so slowly, Tsukuru felt reality drain from things around him.

Ao returned and sat back down on the bench.

'Sorry about that,' he said. 'I'm done.'

Tsukuru looked at his watch. It was close to the end of the thirty minutes Ao said he could spare.

'But why would Shiro claim such a ridiculous thing?' Tsukuru asked. 'And why did it have to be me she accused?'

'I couldn't say,' Ao said. He shook his head weakly a couple of times. 'I'm sorry, but I can't help you. Back then, and even now, I'm totally in the dark about the whole thing.'

Doubts about what was true, and what he should believe, had taken hold of Ao, and he was not the type of person who could handle being confused. He always worked best on a set field, with set rules and a set team.

'Kuro must know more,' Ao said. 'I got that impression. Like there were details we weren't told about. You know what I mean? Women open up more to each other.'

'Kuro's living in Finland now,' Tsukuru said.

'I know. She sends me a postcard every once in a while,' Ao said.

They fell silent again. A group of three high school girls in school uniforms were cutting across the park. The hems of their short skirts swished perkily, and they laughed loudly as they passed in front of the bench. The girls still looked like children. White socks and black loafers, and innocent expressions. It gave Tsukuru a strange feeling to think that not so long ago he and Ao and his friends were that age.

'You really look different now, you know that?' Ao said.

'Well, of course I've changed. You haven't seen me for sixteen years.'

'No, not just because it's been so long. At first I didn't recognize you. When I took a good look, of course I knew who you were. You look sort of – I don't know – gaunt and fearless-looking. You have these sunken cheeks, piercing eyes. Back then you had a rounder, softer kind of face.'

Tsukuru couldn't tell him how a half year spent obsessing over death, over destroying himself, had changed him, how those days had permanently transformed the person he was. He had the feeling he couldn't get across even half the despair he'd felt at the time. It was probably better not to bring it up at all. Tsukuru was silent, waiting for Ao to continue.

'In our group you were always the handsome one, the boy who made a good impression. Clean, neat, well dressed, and polite. You always made sure to greet people nicely, and never said anything stupid. You didn't smoke, hardly touched alcohol, were always on time. Did you know that all our mothers were big fans of yours?'

'Your mothers?' Tsukuru said in surprise. He hardly remembered a thing about their mothers. 'And I've never been handsome. Not then or now. I've got this kind of blah look.'

Ao shrugged his wide shoulders a touch. 'Well, at least in our group you were the best-looking. My face has personality, I suppose – the personality of a gorilla – and Aka is the stereotypical nerd with glasses. What I'm trying to say is, we all took on our different roles pretty well. While the group lasted, I mean.'

'We consciously played those roles?'

'No, I don't think we were that aware of it,' Ao replied. 'But we did sense which position each of us played. I was the happy-go-lucky jock, Aka the brilliant intellectual, Shiro the sweet young

136

girl, Kuro the quick-witted comedian. And you were the well-mannered, handsome boy.'

Tsukuru considered this. 'I've always seen myself as an empty person, lacking color and identity. Maybe that was my role in the group. To be empty.'

Ao shot him a baffled look. 'I don't get it. What role would being empty play?'

'An empty vessel. A colorless background. With no special defects, nothing outstanding. Maybe that sort of person was necessary to the group.'

Ao shook his head. 'You're weren't empty. Nobody ever thought that. You – how should I put it? – helped the rest of us relax.'

'Helped you relax?' Tsukuru repeated, surprised. 'Like elevator music, you mean?'

'No, not like that. It's hard to explain, but having you there, we could be ourselves. You didn't say much, but you had your feet solidly planted on the ground, and that gave the group a sense of security. Like an anchor. We saw that more clearly when you weren't with us anymore. How much we really needed you. I don't know if that's the reason, but after you left, we all sort of went our separate ways.'

Tsukuru remained silent, unable to find the right reply.

'You know, in a sense we were a perfect combination, the five of us. Like five fingers.' Ao raised his right hand and spread his thick fingers. 'I still think that. The five of us all naturally made up for what was lacking in the others, and totally shared our better qualities. I doubt that sort of thing will ever happen again in our lives. It was a one-time occurrence. I have my own family now, and of course I love them. But truthfully, I don't have the same spontaneous, pure feeling for them that I had for all of you back then.'

Tsukuru was silent. Ao crushed the empty paper bag into a ball and rolled it around in his large hand.

'Tsukuru, I believe you,' Ao said. 'That you didn't do anything to Shiro. If you think about it, it makes perfect sense. You'd never have done something like that.'

As Tsukuru was wondering how to respond, 'Viva Las Vegas!' blared out on Ao's cell phone again. He checked the caller's name and stuffed the phone back in his pocket.

'I'm sorry, but I really need to get back to the office, back to hustling cars. Would you mind walking with me to the dealership?'

They walked down the street, side by side, not speaking for a while.

Tsukuru was the first to break the silence. 'Tell me, why "Viva Las Vegas!" as your ringtone?'

Ao chuckled. 'Have you seen that movie?'

'A long time ago, on late-night TV. I didn't watch the whole thing.'

'Kind of a silly movie, wasn't it?'

Tsukuru gave a neutral smile.

'Three years ago I was invited, as the top salesman in Japan, to attend a conference in Las Vegas for U.S. Lexus dealers. More of a reward for my performance than a real conference. After meetings in the morning, it was gambling and drinking the rest of the day. "Viva Las Vegas!" was like the city's theme song – you heard it everywhere you went. When I hit it big at roulette, too, it was playing in the background. Since then that song's been my lucky charm.'

'Makes sense.'

'And the song's been surprisingly helpful in my business.

138

Older customers are happy when we're talking and they hear that ringtone. You're still so young, they ask, so why do you like that old song? Kind of an icebreaker, I guess. "Viva Las Vegas!" isn't one of Elvis's legendary songs, of course. There are songs that are a lot more famous. But there's something about it – something unexpected that gets people to open up. They can't help but smile. I don't know why, but there it is. Have you ever been to Las Vegas?'

'No, never been,' Tsukuru said. 'I've never been abroad, even once. But I'm thinking of going to Finland sometime soon.'

Ao looked taken aback. As he walked along, he kept his eyes fixed on Tsukuru.

'Yeah, that might be nice. If I could, I'd like to go, too. I haven't spoken with Kuro since her wedding. Maybe I shouldn't be saying this, but I used to like her.' Ao turned to face forward and took a few steps. 'But I've got one and a half kids now, and a busy job. A mortgage and a dog I have to walk every day. I can't see myself getting away to Finland. But if you see Kuro, tell her hello from me.'

'I will,' Tsukuru said. 'Before I do that, though, I'm thinking of going to see Aka.'

'Ah,' Ao said. An ambiguous look came over his face. His facial muscles twitched in an odd way. 'I haven't seen him lately.'

'How come?'

'Do you know what kind of work he's doing now?'

'Sort of,' Tsukuru replied.

'I guess I shouldn't be going into it here. I don't want to bias you before you see him. All I can say is that I'm not too fond of what he's doing. Which is partly why I don't see him very often. Unfortunately.'

Tsukuru was silent, keeping pace with Ao's long strides.

'It's not like I have doubts about him as a person. I have doubts about what he does. There's a difference.' Ao sounded like he was convincing himself. 'Maybe doubts is the wrong word. I just don't feel – comfortable with his way of thinking. Anyway, he's become pretty famous in this town. He's been on TV, in newspapers and magazines, as a real wheeler-dealer entrepreneur. He was featured in a women's magazine as one of the 'Most Successful Bachelors in Their Thirties.'

'"Most Successful Bachelors"?' Tsukuru said.

'I never saw that coming,' Ao said. 'I would never have imagined him appearing in a women's magazine.'

'Tell me – how did Shiro die?' Tsukuru said, changing the subject.

Ao came to an abrupt halt in the middle of the street. He stood stock-still, like a statue. The people walking behind him nearly crashed into him. He stared straight at Tsukuru.

'Hold on a second. You honestly don't know how she died?'

'How should I? Until last week I didn't even know she was dead. Nobody told me.'

'Don't you ever read the newspaper?'

'Sure, but I didn't see anything about it. I don't know what happened, but I'm guessing the Tokyo papers didn't give it much coverage.'

'Your family didn't know anything?'

Tsukuru shook his head.

Ao, seemingly unnerved, faced forward again and resumed his quick pace. Tsukuru kept up with him. A moment later Ao spoke.

'After Shiro graduated from music college she taught piano for a while from her house. She moved out, finally, to Hamamatsu, and was living alone. About two years later she was found, stran-gled to death, in her apartment. Her mother had been worried because she hadn't been able to reach Shiro. Her mother was the one who found her. She still hasn't recovered from the shock. And they still haven't arrested anyone.'

Tsukuru gasped. Strangled?

Ao went on. 'Shiro's body was discovered six years ago, on May 12th. By then we rarely got in touch with each other, so I don't know what sort of life she led in Hamamatsu. I don't even know why she moved there. When her mother found her, Shiro had already been dead for three days. She'd been lying on the kitchen floor for three days.

'I went to the funeral in Nagoya,' Ao continued, 'and I couldn't stop crying. I felt like a part of me had died, like I'd turned to stone. But like I said, by this time our group had pretty much split up. We were all adults, with different lives, so there really wasn't much we could do about it. We weren't naive high school students anymore. Still, it was sad to see what used to be so fundamental to our lives fade away, and disappear. We'd gone through such an exciting time together, and grown up together.'

When he inhaled, Tsukuru felt like his lungs were on fire. His tongue felt swollen, as if it were blocking his mouth.

'Viva Las Vegas!' rang out again on the cell phone, but Ao ignored it and kept walking. That out-of-place, cheery melody kept playing from his pocket, then stopped.

When they reached the entrance to the Lexus showroom, Ao held out a large hand to shake with Tsukuru. Ao had a strong grip. 'I'm glad I could see you,' he said, looking Tsukuru in the eye. Looking people right in the eye when he talked, giving them a good, firm handshake. This hadn't changed.

'I'm sorry to have bothered you when you're so busy,' Tsukuru finally managed to say.

'No problem. I'd like to see you again, when I have more time. I feel like there's so much more we should talk about. Make sure you get in touch the next time you're in Nagoya.'

'I will. I'm sure we'll see each other again before too long,' Tsukuru said. 'Oh, one more thing. Do you remember a piano piece that Shiro used to play a lot? A quiet, five- or six-minute piece by Franz Liszt called "Le mal du pays"?'

Ao thought for a minute and shook his head. 'If I heard the melody, maybe I'd remember. I can't tell from the title. I don't know much about classical music. Why do you ask?'

'I just happened to recall it,' Tsukuru said. 'One last question: What in the world does the word "Lexus" mean?'

Ao laughed. 'People ask that a lot. Actually, it doesn't mean anything. It's a made-up word. An ad agency in New York came up with it at Toyota's request. It sounds high class, expressive, and has a nice ring to it. What a strange world we live in. Some people plug away at building railroad stations, while others make tons of money cooking up sophisticated-sounding words.'

'"Industrial refinement" is the term for it. A trend of the times,' Tsukuru said.

Ao grinned broadly. 'Let's make sure neither of us gets left behind.'

They said goodbye. Ao went into the showroom, tugging his cell phone out as he strode inside.

This might be the last time I ever see him, Tsukuru thought as he waited for the signal to change at the crosswalk. A thirty-minute meeting after sixteen years was, arguably, too short a time for such old friends to fully catch up. Surely there was much more that they hadn't had time to talk about. Still, Tsukuru felt as if they had covered everything important that needed to be said.

Tsukuru grabbed a taxi, went to the local library, and requested the bound editions of newspapers from six years ago.

11.

The next morning, a Monday, at ten thirty, Tsukuru visited Aka's office. The company was located about five kilometers from the Lexus showroom in a modern, glass-enclosed commercial building, where it occupied half of the eighth floor. The other half was taken up by the offices of a well-known German pharmaceutical company. Tsukuru wore the same suit as on the previous day, and the blue tie Sara had given him.

At the entrance was a huge, smartly designed logo that announced BEYOND. The office was clean, open, and bright. On the wall behind the reception desk hung a large abstract painting, a splash of primary colors. What it was supposed to be was unclear, though it was not terribly puzzling. Aside from that one painting, the office was devoid of decorations. No flowers, no vases. From the entrance alone it was hard to know what sort of business the company was in.

At the reception desk he was greeted by a young woman in her early twenties, with hair perfectly curled at the ends. She had on a light blue short-sleeved dress and a pearl brooch. The sort of healthy girl lovingly raised in a well-off, optimistic sort of family. She took Tsukuru's business card, her whole face lighting up in a smile, then pushed an extension number on her phone as if pressing the soft nose of an oversized dog.

A short while later the inner door opened and a sturdy-looking woman in her mid-forties emerged, dressed in a dark suit with wide shoulders and thick-heeled black pumps. Her features were oddly flawless. Her hair was cut short, her jaw firm, and she looked extremely competent. There are certain middle-aged women who look like they are outstanding at whatever they do, and this woman was one of them. If she were an actress she would play a veteran chief nurse, or the madam of an exclusive escort service.

She looked at the business card Tsukuru proffered, a hint of doubt crossing her face. What possible business could the deputy section chief of the construction section of the facilities department of a Tokyo-based railroad company have with the CEO of a creative business seminar company in Nagoya? Not to mention showing up without an appointment. But she did not question him about his reasons for visiting.

'I'm sorry, but I wonder if I could have you wait here for a little while?' she said, mustering the barest minimalist smile. She motioned Tsukuru to take a seat and then vanished through the same door. The chair was a simple Scandinavian design of chrome and white leather. Beautiful, clean, and silent, with not an ounce of warmth, like a fine rain falling under the midnight sun. Tsukuru sat down and waited. The young woman at the reception desk was busy with some sort of task on her laptop. She glanced in his direction from time to time, shooting him an encouraging smile.

Like the woman at the Lexus dealership, she was a type Tsukuru often saw in Nagoya. Beautiful features, always immaculately dressed, the kind of woman that makes a great impression. Their hair is always nicely curled. They major in French literature at expensive private women's colleges, and after graduation find jobs as receptionists or secretaries. They work for a few years, visit Paris for shopping once a year with their girlfriends. They finally catch the eye of a promising young man in the company, or else are formally introduced to one, and quit work to get married. They then devote themselves to getting their children into famous private schools. As he sat there, Tsukuru pondered the kind of lives they led.

In five minutes the middle-aged secretary returned and led him to Aka's office. Her smile had ratcheted up a notch. Tsukuru could detect a certain respect for someone like him who showed up without an appointment and actually got to see her boss. It had to be a rare occurrence.

She led him down the hallway with long strides, heels clicking hard and precise like the sounds a faithful blacksmith makes early in the morning. Along the corridor were several doors with thick, opaque glass, but Tsukuru could hear no voices or sounds from the rooms beyond. Compared to his workplace – with its incessantly ringing phones, doors constantly banging open and shut, people yelling – this was a whole other world.

Aka's office was surprisingly small and cozy, considering the scale of the company. Inside was a desk, also a Scandinavian design, a small sofa set, and a wooden cabinet. On top of the desk were a sort of objet d'art stainless steel desk light and a Mac laptop. B&O audio components were set above the cabinet, and another large abstract painting that made copious use of primary colors hung on the wall. It looked like it was by the same artist. The window in the office was big and faced the

146

main street, but none of the sound from outside filtered in. Early-summer sunlight fell on the plain carpet on the floor. Gentle, subdued sunlight.

The room was simple, with a uniform design and nothing extraneous. Each piece of furniture and equipment was clearly high-end, but unlike the Lexus showroom, which went out of its way to advertise luxury, everything here was designed to be low-key and unobtrusive. Expensive anonymity was the basic concept.

Aka stood up from behind his desk. He had changed a lot from when he was twenty. He was still short, not quite five foot three, but his hair had receded considerably. He'd always had thinnish hair, but now it had become even sparser, his forehead more prominent, as was the shape of his head. As if to compensate for the hair loss, he now had a full beard. Compared to his thin hair, his beard was dark black, the contrast quite striking. His metal-framed glasses, narrow and wide, looked good on his long, oval face. His body was as thin as before, without an ounce of extra weight. He had on a white shirt with narrow pinstripes, and a brown knit tie. His sleeves were rolled up to the elbows. He wore cream-colored chinos, and soft brown leather loafers with no socks. The whole outfit hinted at a casual, free lifestyle.

'I'm sorry to barge in on you like this in the morning,' Tsukuru said. 'I was afraid if I didn't, you might not see me.'

'No way,' Aka said. He held out his hand and shook Tsukuru's. Unlike Ao's, his hand was small and soft, his grip gentle. It was not a perfunctory handshake, though, but full of warmth. 'How could I ever say no? I'm happy to see you anytime.'

'But you're pretty busy, I imagine?'

'Work keeps me busy, for sure. But this is my company, and

I make the ultimate decisions. My schedule can be pretty flex-
ible, if I want it to be. I can take more time with some things,
or shorten others. In the end, obviously, the accounts have to
balance, and I can't change the ultimate amount of time we get,
of course – only God can do that – but I can make some partial
adjustments.'

'If it's okay with you, I'd like to talk about some personal
things,' Tsukuru said. 'But if you're busy right now, I can come
back whenever's convenient.'

'Don't worry about the time. You've come all this way. We can
take our time and talk here, right now.'

Tsukuru sat down on the two-person black leather sofa, and
Aka sat on the facing chair. Between them was a small oval table
with a heavy-looking glass ashtray. Aka picked up Tsukuru's
business card again and studied it, his eyes narrowed.

'I see. So Tsukuru Tazaki's dream of building railroad stations
came true.'

'I'd like to say that's true, but unfortunately I don't get many
opportunities to actually construct a new station,' Tsukuru said.
'They rarely build new train lines in Tokyo, so most of the time
we rebuild and refurbish existing stations. Making them barrier-
free, creating more multifunction restrooms, constructing safety
fences, building more shops within the stations, coordinating
things so other rail lines can share the tracks . . . The social
function of stations is changing, so they keep us pretty busy.'

'But still, your job has something to do with railway stations.'

'True.'

'Are you married?'

'No, I'm still single.'

Aka crossed his legs and brushed away a thread on the cuff

of his chinos. 'I was married once, when I was twenty-seven. But I got divorced after a year and a half. I've been alone ever since. It's easier being single. You don't waste a lot of time. Are you the same way?'

'No, not really. I'd like to get married. I actually have too much spare time on my hands. I've just never met the right person.'

Tsukuru thought of Sara. If it were her, maybe he would feel like marrying. But they both needed to know more about each other first. Both of them needed a little more time.

'Your business seems to be doing well,' Tsukuru said, glancing around the tidy office.

Back when they were teenagers, Ao, Aka, and Tsukuru had used the rough, masculine pronouns *ore* and *omae* – 'I' and 'you' – when they talked to each other, but Tsukuru realized now, seeing them sixteen years later, that this form of address no longer felt right. Ao and Aka still called him *omae*, and referred to themselves as *ore*, but this casual way of speaking no longer came so easily to Tsukuru.

'Yes, business is going well at the moment,' Aka said. He cleared his throat. 'You know what we do here?'

'Pretty much. If what's online is accurate.'

Aka laughed. 'It's not lies. That's what we do. The most important part, of course, is all in here.' Aka tapped his temple. 'Like with a chef. The most critical ingredient isn't in the recipe.'

'The way I understand it, what you mainly do is educate and train human resources for companies.'

'Exactly. We educate new employees and reeducate mid-level employees. We offer that service to other companies. We create programs tailored to the clients' wishes, and carry them out efficiently and professionally. It saves companies time and effort.'

'Outsourcing employee education.'

'Correct. The business all started with an idea I had. You know, like in a comic book, where a light bulb goes off over the character's head? Startup funding came from the president of a consumer finance company who believed in me and fronted me the money. It just happened that's where the original funds came from.'

'So how did you come up with the idea?'

Aka laughed. 'It's not all that exciting a story. After I graduated from college I worked in a large bank, but the job was boring. The people above me were incompetent. They only thought about what was right in front of them, never thought long term, and only cared about covering their asses. I figured if a top bank was like this, then Japan's future looked pretty bleak. I put up with it for three years, but nothing improved. If anything, it got worse. So I switched jobs and went to work for a consumer finance company. The president of the company liked me a lot and had asked me to work for him. In a job like that you have much more freedom to maneuver, and the work itself was interesting. But there, too, my opinions didn't exactly conform with the higher-ups, and I quit after a little over two years. I apologized to the president, but there it was.'

Aka took out a packet of Marlboro Reds. 'Do you mind if I smoke?'

'Not at all,' Tsukuru said. Aka put a cigarette in his mouth and lit it with a small gold lighter. His eyes narrowed and he slowly inhaled, then exhaled. 'I tried quitting, but just couldn't. If I can't smoke, I can't work. Have you ever tried giving up smoking?'

Tsukuru had never smoked a cigarette in his life.

Aka continued. 'I'm more of a lone-wolf type. I might not look like it, and I didn't understand that part of my personality until I'd graduated from college and started work. But it's true. Whenever some moron ordered me to do something stupid, I'd blow my top. It was like you could actually hear my brain explode. No way a person like that can work for a company. So I made up my mind. I had to go out on my own.'

Aka paused and gazed at the purplish smoke rising up from his hand, as if tracing a far-off memory.

'One other thing I learned from working in a company was that the majority of people in the world have no problem following orders. They're actually happy to be told what to do. They might complain, but that's not how they really feel. They just grumble out of habit. If you told them to think for themselves, and make their own decisions and take responsibility for them, they'd be clueless. So I decided I could turn that into a business. It's simple. I hope this makes sense?'

Tsukuru said nothing. It was a rhetorical question.

'I compiled a list of things I dislike, things I don't like to do, and things I don't want others to do. And based on that list, I came up with a program to train people who follow orders from above, so that they could work more systematically. I guess you could call it an original idea, but in part I ripped off elements from elsewhere. The experience I had myself, the training I received as a newly hired bank clerk, was extremely valuable. I added methods taken from religious cults and personal development seminars, to spice things up. I researched companies in the U.S. that had been successful in the same sort of business. I read a lot of books on psychology as well. I included elements from manuals for new recruits in the

Nazi SS and the Marines. In the half year after I quit my job, I literally immersed myself in developing this program. I've always been good at focusing on one particular task.'

'It helps that you're so bright.'

Aka grinned. 'Thanks. I couldn't very well come right out and say that about myself.'

He took a puff on his cigarette and flicked the ash into the ashtray. He raised his head and looked at Tsukuru.

'Religious cults and personal development seminars mainly try to get money from people. To do that, they perform a rather crude form of brainwashing. We're different. If we did something that questionable, top corporations wouldn't agree to work with us. Using drastic measures, forcing people to do things – we're not into any of that. You might get impressive results for a while, but they won't last. Driving the idea of discipline into people's heads is important, but the program you use to do it has to be totally scientific, practical, and sophisticated. It has to be something society can accept. And the results need to be long lasting. We're not aiming at producing zombies. We want to create a workforce that does what their company wants them to do, yet still believes they're independent thinkers.'

'That's a pretty cynical worldview,' Tsukuru said.

'I suppose you could see it that way.'

'I can't imagine that everyone who attends your seminars allows themselves to be disciplined like that.'

'No, of course not. There are quite a few people who reject the program. You can divide them into two groups. The first is antisocial. In English you'd call them "outcasts." They just can't accept any form of constructive criticism, no matter what it is. They reject any kind of group discipline. It's a waste of time to deal with people like that, so we ask them to withdraw. The other group is comprised of people who *actually* think on their own. Those it's best to leave alone. Don't fool with them. Every system needs *elite* people like them. If things go well, they'll eventually be in leadership positions. In the middlc, between those two groups, are those who take orders from above and just do what they're told. That's the vast majority of people. By my rough estimate, 85 percent of the total. I developed this business to target the 85 percent.'

'And your business is doing as well as you hoped it would?'

Aka nodded. 'Things are working out now pretty much as I calculated. It was a small company at first, with just a couple of employees, but now it's grown larger, as you can see. Our brand's become pretty well known.'

'You've assessed the tasks that you don't like to do, or the things that you don't like to have done to you, analyzed them, and used this to launch your business. That was the starting point?'

Aka nodded. 'Exactly. It's not hard to think about what you don't want to do or have done to you. Just like it's not hard to think about what you would like to do. It's a difference between the positive and the negative. A question of emphasis.'

I'm not too fond of what he's doing. Tsukuru recalled Ao's words.

'Aren't you doing this, in part, to get personal revenge on society? As one of the elites, someone who thinks like an outcast.'

'You could be right,' Aka said. He laughed happily and snapped his fingers. 'Great serve. Advantage Tsukuru Tazaki.'

'Are you the organizer of these programs? Do you do the presentations yourself?'

'In the beginning I did. I was the only person I could count on at that point. Can you picture me doing that?'

153

'No, not really,' Tsukuru replied honestly.

Aka laughed. 'For some reason, though, I turned out to be really good at it. I shouldn't brag, but I was well suited for it. Of course, it's all an act, but I was good at seeming real and convincing. I don't do it anymore, though. I'm not a guru, but more of a manager. And I keep plenty busy. What I do now is train our instructors, and leave the practical side of things to them. These days I've been giving a lot of outside lectures. Corporations invite me to their meetings, and I give talks at university employment seminars. A publisher asked me to write a book, too, which I'm working on.'

Aka crushed out his cigarette in the ashtray.

'Once you get the knack, this kind of business isn't so hard. Just print up a glossy pamphlet, string together some high-blown self-advertising language, and get some smart office space in a high-end part of town. Purchase attractive furnishings, hire capable, sophisticated staff members, and pay them very well. Image is everything. You don't spare any expense to create the right image. And word of mouth is critical. Once you get a good reputation, momentum will carry you. But I'm not planning to expand beyond what we do now. We'll continue to focus solely on companies in the greater Nagoya area. Unless I can keep an eye on things myself, I can't ensure the level of quality.'

Aka gazed searchingly into Tsukuru's eyes.

'Come on, you're not all that interested in what I do, are you?'

'It just feels strange. I never would have thought, back when you were a teenager, that you would open this kind of business someday.'

'Me neither,' Aka said, and laughed. 'I was sure I would stay in a university and become a professor. But once I got to college

I realized I wasn't cut out for academic life. It's a stagnant, crushingly dull world, and I didn't want to spend the rest of my life there. Then, when I graduated, I found out that working for a company wasn't for me, either. It was all trial and error, and eventually, I was able to find my own niche. But what about you? Are you satisfied with your job?'

'Not really. But I'm not particularly dissatisfied with it, either,' Tsukuru said.

'Because you can do work related to railroad stations?'

'That's right. As you put it, I'm able to stay on the positive side.'

'Have you ever had doubts about your job?'

'Every day I just build things you can see. I have no time for doubts.'

Aka smiled. 'That's wonderful. And so very like you.'

Silence descended on them. Aka toyed with the gold lighter in his hand but didn't light another cigarette. He probably had a set number of cigarettes he smoked every day.

'You came here because there was something you wanted to talk about, right?' Aka said.

'I'd like to ask about the past,' Tsukuru said.

'Sure. Let's talk about the past.'

'It's about Shiro.'

Aka's eyes narrowed behind his glasses, and he stroked his beard. 'I was kind of expecting that. After my secretary handed me your business card.'

Tsukuru didn't reply.

'I feel sorry for Shiro,' Aka said quietly. 'Her life wasn't very happy. She was so beautiful, so musically talented, yet she died so horribly.'

Tsukuru felt uncomfortable at the way Aka summed up her life in just a couple of lines. But a time difference was at work here, he understood. Tsukuru had only recently learned of Shiro's death, while Aka had lived with the knowledge for six years.

'Maybe there's not much point in doing this now, but I wanted to clear up a misunderstanding,' Tsukuru said. 'I don't know what Shiro told you, but I never raped her. I never had a relationship like that with her of any kind.'

'The truth sometimes reminds me of a city buried in sand,' Aka said. 'As time passes, the sand piles up even thicker, and occasionally it's blown away and what's below is revealed. In this case it's definitely the latter. Whether the misunderstanding is cleared up or it isn't, you aren't the type of person to do something like that. I know that very well.'

'You know that?' Tsukuru repeated the words.

'*Now* I do, is what I mean.'

'Because the sand has blown away?'

Aka nodded. 'That's about the size of it.'

'It's like we're discussing history.'

'In a way, we are.'

Tsukuru gazed at the face of his old friend seated across from him, but couldn't read anything resembling an emotion in Aka's expression.

You can hide memories, but you can't erase history. Tsukuru recalled Sara's words, and said them aloud.

Aka nodded several times. 'Exactly. You can hide memories, but you can't erase history. That's precisely what I want to say.'

'Anyway, back then, the four of you cut me off. Totally, and mercilessly,' Tsukuru said.

156

'It's true, we did. That's a historical fact. I'm not trying to justify it, but at the time we had no other choice. Shiro's story was so real. She wasn't acting. She was *really* hurt. An actual wound, with real pain, and real blood. There was no room for us to doubt her at the time. But after we cut you off, and the more that time passed, the more confused we got about the whole thing.'

'How do you mean?'

Aka brought his hands together on his lap and thought for five seconds.

'In the beginning, it was small things. A few details that didn't fit. Parts of her story that didn't make sense. But it didn't bother us much. They didn't really matter at first. But these started to become more frequent, and we noticed them more and more. And then we thought, something's not right here.'

Tsukuru was silent, waiting for him to continue.

'Shiro might have had some mental issues.' Aka fiddled with the gold lighter, carefully choosing his words. 'Whether it was temporary, or more of a long-term condition, I don't know. But something was definitely *wrong* with her then. She had a lot of musical talent. The kind of beautiful music she played blew us away, but unfortunately she demanded more from herself. She had enough talent to make her way through the limited world where she lived, but not enough to go out into the wider world. And no matter how much she practiced, she couldn't reach the level she desired. You remember how serious and introverted she was. Once she entered the music conservatory, the pressure only mounted. And little by little, she started acting strangely.'

Tsukuru nodded but didn't say anything.

'It's not so unusual,' Aka said. 'It's a sad story, but in the art world it happens all the time. Talent is like a container. You can work as hard as you want, but the size will never change. It'll only hold so much water and no more.'

'I'm sure that kind of thing does happen a lot,' Tsukuru said. 'But saying that I drugged her in Tokyo and raped her – where did *that* come from? Granted, she might have had mental issues, but didn't that story just come out of nowhere?'

Aka nodded. 'Absolutely. It came out of nowhere. Which actually made us believe her at first. We couldn't conceive of Shiro making up something like that.'

Tsukuru pictured an ancient city, buried in sand. And himself, seated on top of a dune, gazing down at the desiccated ruins.

'But why was the other person in that story me, of all people? Why did it have to be me?'

'I couldn't tell you,' Aka said. 'Maybe Shiro secretly liked you. So she was disappointed and angry with you for going off to Tokyo by yourself. Or maybe she was jealous of you. Maybe she wanted to break free of this town. Anyway, there's no way now to understand what motivated her. Assuming there even was a motivation.'

Aka continued toying with the lighter.

'There's one thing I want you to know,' he said. 'You went to Tokyo, and the four of us stayed behind in Nagoya. I'm not trying to criticize you for that. But you had a new life in a new city. Back in Nagoya, the four of us had to draw closer together as a result. Do you know what I'm trying to say?'

'It was more realistic to cut off me, as the outsider, than to cut off Shiro. Right?'

Aka didn't reply, but let out a long, shallow sigh. 'Of the five of us maybe you were the toughest one, at least emotionally.

Unexpectedly so, considering how placid you seemed. The four of us who stayed behind weren't brave enough to venture out like you did. We were afraid of leaving the town we were brought up in, and saying goodbye to such close friends. We couldn't leave that warm comfort zone. It's like how hard it is to climb out of a warm bed on a cold winter morning. We came up with all kinds of plausible excuses at the time, but now I see how true this was.'

'But you don't regret staying here, do you?'

'No, I don't think so. There were lots of good, practical reasons for staying put, and I was able to use these to my advantage. Nagoya's a place where local connections really pay off. Take the president of the consumer finance company who invested in me. Years ago, he read about our volunteer efforts in high school in the paper, and that's why he trusted me. I didn't want to profit personally from our volunteer program, but it worked out that way. And many of our clients are people my father taught at the university. There's a tight social network like that in business circles in Nagoya, and a Nagoya University professor is like a respected brand name. But none of that would make any difference if I went to Tokyo. I'd be completely ignored. Don't you agree?'

Tsukuru was silent.

'Those practical reasons played a part, too, I think, in why the four of us never left town. We chose to keep soaking in the warm bath. But now it's only Ao and me who are still here. Shiro died, and Kuro got married and moved to Finland. And Ao and I are literally down the street from each other but never meet up. Why? Because even if we got together, we'd have nothing to talk about.'

'You could buy a Lexus. Then you'd have something to talk about.'

Aka winked. 'I'm driving a Porsche Carrera 4. Targa top. Six-gear manual transmission. The way it feels when you shift gears is amazing. The feeling when you downshift is especially great. Have you ever driven one?'

Tsukuru shook his head.

'I love it, and would never buy anything else,' Aka said.

'But you could buy a Lexus as a company car. Write it off.'

'I have clients whose companies are affiliated with Nissan and Mitsubishi, so that's not an option.'

A short silence followed.

'Did you go to Shiro's funeral?' Tsukuru asked.

'Yeah, I did. I'm telling you, I've never seen such a sad funeral, before or after. It's painful to think about, even now. Ao was there, too. Kuro couldn't come. She was already in Finland, about to have a baby.'

'Why didn't you let me know that Shiro had died?'

Aka didn't say anything for a while, gazing vacantly at him, his eyes unfocused. 'I really don't know,' he finally said. 'I was sure someone would tell you. Probably Ao would—'

'No, nobody ever told me. Until a week ago, I had no idea she'd died.'

Aka shook his head, and turned, as if averting his gaze, and gazed out the window. 'I guess we did something terrible. I'm not trying to excuse our actions, but you have to understand how confused we were. We didn't know what we were doing. We were positive you would hear about Shiro's murder. And when you didn't show up at the funeral, we figured you found it too hard to come.'

Tsukuru didn't say anything for a moment, and then spoke.

'I heard that at the time Shiro was murdered, she was living in Hamamatsu?'

'She was there for almost two years. She lived alone and taught piano to children. She worked for a Yamaha piano school. I don't know the details of why she moved all the way to Hamamatsu, though. She should have been able to find work in Nagoya.'

'What kind of life did she lead?'

Aka took a cigarette out of the box, put it between his lips, and, after a short pause, lit it.

'About half a year before she was murdered, I had to go to Hamamatsu on business. I called her and invited her to dinner. By this time the four of us had really gone our separate ways and hardly ever saw each other. We'd get in touch every once in a while, but that was it. My work in Hamamatsu was over sooner than I expected, and I had some free time, so I wanted to see Shiro for the first time in a while. She was more collected and calm than I'd imagined. She seemed to be enjoying having left Nagoya behind and living in a new place. We had dinner together and reminisced. We went to a famous unagi eel restaurant in Hamamatsu, had a few beers, and really relaxed. It surprised me that she was able to drink. Still, there was a bit of tension in the air. What I mean is, we had to avoid a particular topic . . .'

'That *particular* topic being me?'

Aka shot him a hard look and nodded. 'It still made her uneasy. She hadn't forgotten it. Apart from that, though, she seemed perfectly fine. She laughed a lot, and seemed to enjoy talking. And everything she said sounded normal. It struck me that moving to a new place had been great for her. But there *was* one thing. I don't enjoy bringing this up, but – she wasn't attractive like she used to be.'

'Wasn't attractive?' Tsukuru repeated the words, his voice sounding far away.

'No, that isn't quite the right expression,' Aka said, and thought it over. 'How should I put it? Her features were basically the same as before, of course, and by all standards, she was definitely still a beautiful woman. If you hadn't known her when she was a teenager, you'd think she was pretty. But I knew her from before, knew her very well. I could never forget how appealing she was. The Shiro in front of me now, though – she wasn't.'

Aka frowned slightly, as if recalling that scene.

'Seeing Shiro like that was very painful. It hurt to see that she no longer had that burning *something* she used to have. That what had been remarkable about her had vanished. That the special *something* would no longer be able to move me the way it used to.'

Smoke rose from Aka's cigarette above the ashtray. He continued.

'Shiro had just turned thirty then, and she was still young. When she met me she had on very plain clothes, with her hair pulled back in a bun, and hardly any makeup. But that's not really the point. Those are just details. My point is that she'd lost the glow she used to have, her vitality. She was always an introvert, but at her core there had been *something* vital and alive, something that even she wasn't totally aware of. That light, that radiance used to leak out by itself, emerging from between the cracks. Do you know what I mean? But the last time I saw her, it was all gone, like someone had slipped in behind her and pulled the plug. The kind of fresh, sparkling glow, what used to visibly set her apart, had disappeared, and it made me sad to look at her. It wasn't a question of age. She didn't get that way simply because she'd gotten older. When I heard that someone had strangled Shiro, I was devastated, and felt really sorry for her. Whatever the circumstances might have been, she didn't deserve to die like that. But at the same time I couldn't help but feel that the life had already been sucked out of her, even before she was physically murdered.'

Aka picked up the cigarette from the ashtray, took a deep drag, and closed his eyes.

'She left a huge hole in my heart,' Aka said. 'One that's still not filled.'

Silence descended on them, a hard, dense silence.

'Do you remember the piano piece Shiro used to play a lot?' Tsukuru asked. 'A short piece, Liszt's "Le mal du pays"?'

Aka considered this and shook his head. 'No, I don't recall that. The only one I remember is the famous piece from Schumann's *Scenes from Childhood*. "Träumerei." She used to play that sometimes. I'm not familiar with the Liszt piece, though. Why are you asking?'

'No special reason. I just happened to recall it,' Tsukuru said. He glanced at his watch. 'I've taken so much of your time. I should be going. I'm really happy we could talk like this.'

Aka stayed still in his chair, and gazed straight at Tsukuru. He was expressionless, like someone staring at a brand-new lithograph with nothing etched in it yet. 'Are you in a hurry?' he asked.

'Not at all.'

'Can we talk a little more?'

'Of course. I have plenty of time.'

Aka weighed what he was about to say before he spoke. 'You don't really like me very much anymore, do you?'

Tsukuru was speechless. Partly because the question had blindsided him, but also because it didn't seem right to reduce his feelings for the person seated before him into a simple binary equation of like or dislike.

Tsukuru carefully chose his words. 'I really can't say. My feelings are definitely different from back when we were teenagers. But that's—'

Aka held up a hand to cut him off.

'No need to mince words. And you don't need to force yourself to like me. No one likes me now. It's only to be expected. I don't even like myself much. I used to have a few really good friends. You were one of them. But at a certain stage in life I lost them. Like how Shiro at a certain point lost that special spark . . . But you can't go back. Can't return an item you've already opened. You just have to make do.'

He lowered his hand and placed it on his lap. He began tapping out an irregular rhythm on his kneecap, like he was sending a message in Morse code.

'My father worked so long as a college professor that he picked up the habits professors have. At home he always sounded like he was preaching at us, looking down on us from on high. I hated that, ever since I was a child. But at a certain point it hit me – I've started to talk just like him.'

He went on tapping his kneecap.

'I always felt I did a horrible thing to you. It's true. I – we – had no right to treat you that way. I felt that someday I needed to properly apologize to you. But somehow I never made it happen.'

'It doesn't matter,' Tsukuru said. 'That's another situation where you can't go back.'

Aka seemed lost in thought. 'Tsukuru,' he finally said, 'I have a favor to ask.'

164

'What kind?'

'I have something I want to tell you. A confession, you might call it, that I've never told anybody before. Maybe you don't want to hear it, but I want to open up about my own pain. I'd like you to know what I've been carrying around with me. Not that this will make amends for all the pain you endured. It's just a question of my own feelings and emotions. Will you hear me out? For old times' sake?'

Tsukuru nodded, uncertain where this was going.

Aka began. 'I told you how, until I actually went to college, I didn't know I wasn't cut out for academic life. And how I didn't know I wasn't cut out for company life, either, until I started working in a bank. You remember? It's kind of embarrassing. I probably had never taken a good, hard look at myself. But that's not all there was to it. Until I got married I didn't understand how I wasn't suited for marriage. What I'm saying is, the physical relationship between a man and a woman wasn't for me. Do you see what I'm getting at?'

Tsukuru was silent, and Aka went on.

'What I'm trying to say is, I don't really feel desire for women. Not that I don't have any desire at all, but I feel it more for men.'

A deep silence descended on the room. Tsukuru couldn't hear a single sound. It was a quiet room to begin with.

'That's not so unusual,' Tsukuru said to fill in the silence.

'You're right, it's not so unusual. But to confront that reality at a certain point in your life is a hard thing. Very hard. You can't just dismiss it with generalities. How should I put it? It's like you're standing on the deck of a ship at sea at night and suddenly you're thrown overboard, alone, into the ocean.'

Tsukuru thought of Haida. About how in the dream – and he

presumed it was a dream – he'd come in Haida's mouth. Tsukuru remembered the utter confusion he'd felt at the time. Being thrown overboard, alone, into the sea at night – the expression hit the mark exactly.

'I think you just need to be honest with yourself, as much as you can,' Tsukuru said, choosing his words. 'All you can do is be as honest and free as you can. I'm sorry, but that's about all I can say.'

'I know you're aware of this,' Aka said, 'but although Nagoya's one of the largest cities in Japan, in a way it's not all that big. The population's large, industries are doing well, and people are affluent, yet the choices you have are unexpectedly limited. It's not easy for people like us to live here and still be honest with ourselves and free . . . Kind of a major paradox, wouldn't you say? As we go through life we gradually discover who we are, but the more we discover, the more we lose ourselves.'

'I hope everything will work out for you. I really do,' Tsukuru said. He truly felt that way.

'You're not angry with me anymore?'

Tsukuru gave a short shake of his head. 'No, I'm not angry with you. I'm not angry with anybody.'

Tsukuru suddenly realized he was using the familiar *omae* to address Aka. It came out naturally at the end.

Aka walked with Tsukuru to the elevators.

'I may not have a chance to see you again,' Aka said as they walked down the hallway. 'So there's one more thing I wanted to tell you. You don't mind, do you?'

Tsukuru shook his head.

'It's the first thing I always say at our new employee training seminars. I gaze around the room, pick one person, and have

166

him stand up. And this is what I say: *I have some good news for you, and some bad news. The bad news first. We're going to have to rip off either your fingernails or your toenails with pliers. I'm sorry, but it's already decided. It can't be changed.* I pull out a huge, scary pair of pliers from my briefcase and show them to everybody. Slowly, making sure everybody gets a good look. And then I say: *Here's the good news. You have the freedom to choose which it's going to be – your fingernails, or your toenails. So, which will it be? You have ten seconds to make up your mind. If you're unable to decide, we'll rip off both your fingernails and your toenails.* I start the count. At about eight seconds most people say, "The toes." *Okay,* I say, *toenails it is. I'll use these pliers to rip them off. But before I do, I'd like you to tell me something. Why did you choose your toes and not your fingers?* The person usually says, "I don't know. I think they probably hurt the same. But since I had to choose one, I went with the toes." I turn to him and warmly applaud him. And I say, *Welcome to the real world.'*

Tsukuru gazed wordlessly at his old friend's delicate face.

'Each of us is given the freedom to choose,' Aka said, winking and smiling. 'That's the point of the story.'

The silver door of the elevator slid open soundlessly, and they said goodbye.

12.

Tsukuru got back to his apartment in Tokyo at 7 p.m. on the day he had met Aka. He unpacked, tossed his laundry in the washer, took a shower, then called Sara's cell phone. It went to voicemail and he left a message telling her he had just gotten back from Nagoya and to get in touch with him when she could.

He waited up until after eleven, but she didn't call. When she did call back, the next day, a Tuesday, Tsukuru was in the cafeteria at work eating lunch.

'Did everything go well in Nagoya?' Sara asked.

He stood up and went out into the corridor, which was quieter. He summarized his meetings with Ao and Aka, at the Lexus showroom and Aka's office on Sunday and Monday respectively, and what they'd talked about.

'I'm glad I could talk to them. I could understand a little better what happened,' Tsukuru said.

'That's good,' Sara said. 'So it wasn't a waste of time.'

'Could we meet somewhere? I'd like to tell you all about our conversations.'

'Just a minute. Let me check my schedule.'

There was a fifteen-second pause. While he waited, Tsukuru

gazed out the window at the streets of Shinjuku. Thick clouds covered the sky, and it looked like it was about to rain.

'I'm free in the evening the day after tomorrow. Does that work for you?' Sara asked.

'Sounds good. Let's have dinner,' Tsukuru said. He didn't need to check his schedule. It was blank almost every night.

They decided on a place and hung up. After he switched off the cell phone, Tsukuru felt a physical discomfort, as if something he'd eaten wasn't digesting well. He hadn't felt it before he'd spoken to Sara. That was for certain. But what it meant, or whether it meant anything at all, he couldn't tell.

He tried to replay the conversation with her, as accurately as he could remember it. What they'd said, her tone of voice, the way she'd paused. Nothing seemed any different from usual. He put the cell phone in his pocket and went back to the cafeteria to finish his lunch. But he no longer had any appetite.

—

That afternoon and the whole next day, Tsukuru, accompanied by a brand-new employee as his assistant, inspected several stations that required new elevators. With the new employee helping him to measure, Tsukuru checked the blueprints, one by one, that they kept at the office against the actual measurements at the sites. He found a number of unexpected errors and discrepancies between the blueprints and the actual sites. There could be several reasons for this, but what was more important at this point was to draw up accurate, reliable blueprints before construction began. If errors were discovered after they'd begun construction, it would be too late, like combat troops relying on a faulty map when landing on a foreign island.

After they'd finished their measurements, they went to talk with the stationmaster about potential problems the rebuilding might cause. Repositioning the elevators would change the configuration of the entire station, which in turn would affect passenger flow, and they had to make sure they could structurally incorporate these changes. Passenger safety was always the top priority, but they also had to be certain that the station staff could perform their duties with the new layout. Tsukuru's job was to synthesize all these elements, come up with a rebuilding plan, and include this in an actual blueprint. It was a painstaking process, but critical because people's safety was at stake. Tsukuru patiently managed it all. This was the kind of process that was exactly his forte – clarifying any problems, creating a checklist, and carefully making sure each and every point was handled correctly. At the same time, it provided a wonderful opportunity for the young, inexperienced new employee to learn the ropes on site. The employee, whose name was Sakamoto, had just graduated from the science and engineering department at Waseda University. He was a taciturn young man, with a long, unsmiling face, but he was a quick study and followed directions. He was skilled when it came to taking measurements, too. This guy might work out, Tsukuru thought.

They spent an hour at an express-train station with the stationmaster, going over the details of the rebuilding project. It was lunchtime, so they ordered in bentos and ate together in the stationmaster's office. Afterward they chatted over tea. The stationmaster, a friendly, heavyset middle-aged man, told them some fascinating stories about things he'd experienced in his career. Tsukuru loved going to sites and hearing these kinds of stories. The topic turned to lost property, more specifically to the huge amount of lost-and-found items left behind on trains and in stations, and the unusual, strange items among them – the ashes of cremated people, wigs, prosthetic legs, the manuscript of a novel (the stationmaster read a little bit of it and found it dull), a neatly wrapped, bloodstained shirt in a box, a live pit viper, forty color photos of women's vaginas, a large wooden gong, the kind Buddhist priests strike as they chant sutras . . .

'Sometimes you're not sure what to do with them,' the stationmaster said. 'A friend of mine who runs another station turned in a Boston bag once that had a dead fetus inside. Thankfully, I've never had that kind of experience myself. But once, when I was a stationmaster at another station, someone brought in two fingers preserved in formaldehyde.'

'That's pretty grotesque,' Tsukuru said.

'Yes, it sure was. Two small fingers floating in liquid, kept in what looked like a small mayonnaise jar, all inside a pretty cloth bag. Looked like a child's fingers severed at the base. Naturally we contacted the police since we thought it might be connected to a crime. The police came over immediately and took the jar away.'

The stationmaster drank a sip of tea.

'A week later the same police officer who'd taken the fingers stopped by. He questioned the station employee who'd found the jar in the restroom again. I was present for the questioning. According to the officer, the fingers in the jar weren't those of a child. The forensics lab determined that they belonged to an adult. The reason they were so small was that they were sixth, vestigial fingers. The officer said that sometimes people have extra fingers. Most of the time the parents want to get rid of the deformity, so they have the fingers amputated when the child's still a baby, but there are some people who, as adults, still have all six fingers. The ones that were found were an example – the fingers of an adult who had had them surgically removed, then preserved in formaldehyde. The lab estimated the fingers to be those of man, age mid-twenties to mid-thirties, though they couldn't tell how long it had been since the fingers had been amputated. I can't imagine how they'd come to be forgotten, or perhaps thrown away, in the station restroom. But it doesn't seem that they were connected to any crime. In the end the police kept them, and no one ever came forward to claim them. For all I know, they may still be in a police warehouse somewhere.'

'That's a weird story,' Tsukuru said. 'Why would he keep those sixth fingers until he became an adult and then suddenly decide to amputate them?'

'It's a mystery. It got me interested in the phenomenon, though, and I started looking into it. The technical term is hyperdactyly, and there have been lots of famous people who've had it. It's unclear whether it's true or not, but there was some evidence that Hideyoshi Toyotomi, the famous leader of the Sengoku period, had two thumbs. There are plenty of other examples. There was a famous pianist who had the condition, a novelist, an artist, a baseball player. In fiction, Hannibal Lecter of *The Silence of the Lambs* had six fingers. It's not all that unusual, and genetically it's a dominant trait. There are variations among different races, but in general, one out of every five hundred people is born with six fingers. As I said, though, the vast majority of their parents have the extra fingers amputated before their children's first birthdays, when kids begin to develop fine-motor skills. So we hardly ever run across someone with the condition. It was the same for me. Until that jar was found in the station, I'd never even heard of such a thing.'

'It is strange, though,' Tsukuru said. 'If having six fingers is a dominant trait, then why don't we see more people with them?'

The stationmaster inclined his head. 'Don't know. That kind of complicated stuff is beyond me.'

Sakamoto, who'd eaten lunch with them, opened his mouth for the first time. Hesitantly, as if rolling away a massive stone that blocked the mouth of a cave. 'I wonder if you wouldn't mind if I venture an opinion?'

'Of course,' Tsukuru said, taken by surprise. Sakamoto was not the type of young man who voiced his own opinion in front of others. 'Go right ahead.'

'People tend to misunderstand the meaning of the word "dominant,"' Sakamoto said. 'Even if a certain tendency is domin-ant, that doesn't mean it becomes widespread throughout the population. There are quite a few rare disorders where genetically there is a dominant gene, but these conditions don't, as a result, become common. Thankfully, in most cases these are checked at a fixed number, and remain rare disorders. Dominant genes are nothing more than one among many elements in tendency distribution. Other elements would include the survival of the fittest, natural selection, and so on. This is personal conjecture, but I think six fingers are too many for human beings. For what the hand has to do, five fingers are all that are necessary, and the most efficient number. So even if having six fingers is a dominant gene, in the real world it only manifests in a tiny minority. In other words, the law of selection trumps the domin-ant gene.'

After holding forth at such length, Sakamoto stepped back into silence.

'That makes sense,' Tsukuru said. 'I get the feeling it's connected with the process of how the world's counting systems have mainly standardized, moving from the duodecimal system to the decimal system.'

'Yes, that might have been a response to six and five fingers, digits, now that you mention it,' Sakamoto said.

'So how come you know so much about this?' Tsukuru asked Sakamoto.

'I took a class on genetics in college. I sort of had a personal interest in it.' Sakamoto's cheeks reddened as he said this.

The stationmaster gave a merry laugh. 'So your genetics class came in handy, even after you started work at a railway company. I guess getting an education isn't something to be sneezed at, is it.'

Tsukuru turned to the stationmaster. 'Seems like for a pianist, though, having six fingers could come in pretty handy.'

'Apparently it doesn't,' the stationmaster replied. 'One pianist who has six fingers said the extra ones get in the way. Like Mr. Sakamoto said just now, moving six fingers equally and freely might be a little too much for human beings. Maybe five is just the right number.'

'Is there some advantage to having six fingers?' Tsukuru asked.

'From what I learned,' the stationmaster replied, 'during the Middle Ages in Europe, they thought people born with six fingers were magicians or witches, and they were burned at the stake. And in one country during the era of the Crusaders, anybody who had six fingers was killed. Whether these stories are true or not, I don't know. In Borneo children born with six fingers are automatically treated as shamans. Maybe that isn't an advantage, however.'

'Shamans?' Tsukuru asked.

'Just in Borneo.'

Lunchtime was over, and so was their conversation. Tsukuru thanked the stationmaster for the lunch, and he and Sakamoto returned to their office.

As Tsukuru was writing some notes on the blueprints, he suddenly recalled the story Haida had told him, years ago, about his father. How the jazz pianist who was staying at the inn deep in the mountains of Oita had, just before he started playing, put a cloth bag on top of the piano. Could there have been, inside the bag, a sixth right and left finger, preserved in formaldehyde inside a jar? For some reason maybe he'd waited until he was an adult to get them amputated, and always carried the jar around with him. And just before he performed he'd put them on top of the piano. Like a talisman.

Of course, this was sheer conjecture. There was no basis for it. And that incident had taken place – if indeed it had actually occurred – over forty years ago. Still, the more Tsukuru thought about it, the more it seemed like this piece of the puzzle fit the lacuna in Haida's story. Tsukuru sat at his drafting table until evening, pencil in hand, mulling over the idea.

The following day Tsukuru met Sara in Hiroo. They went into a small bistro in a secluded part of the neighborhood – Sara was an expert on secluded, small bars and restaurants all over Tokyo – and before they ate, Tsukuru told her how he had seen his two former friends in Nagoya, and what they had talked about. It wasn't easy for him to summarize, so it took a while for him to tell her the whole story. Sara listened closely, occasionally stopping him to ask a question.

'So Shiro told the others that when she stayed at your apartment in Tokyo, you drugged her and raped her?'

'That's what she said.'

'She described it in great detail, very realistically, even though she was so introverted and always tried to avoid talking about sex.'

'That's what Ao said.'

'And she said you had two faces?' Sara asked.

'She said I had another *dark, hidden side*, something unhinged and detached from the side of me that everyone knew.'

Sara frowned and thought this over for a while.

'Doesn't this remind you of something? Didn't you ever have some special, intimate moment that passed between you and Shiro?'

Tsukuru shook his head. 'Never. Not once. I was always conscious of not letting something like that happen.'

'Always conscious?'

'I tried not to view her as someone of the opposite sex. And I avoided being alone with her as much as I could.'

Sara narrowed her eyes and inclined her head for a moment. 'Do you think the others in the group were just as careful? In other words, the boys not viewing the girls as members of the opposite sex, and vice versa?'

'I don't know what the others were thinking, deep down inside. But like I said, it was a kind of unspoken agreement between us that we wouldn't let male–female relationships be a part of the group. We were pretty insistent about that.'

'But isn't that unnatural? If boys and girls that age get close to each other, and are together all the time, it's only natural that they start to get interested in each other sexually.'

'I wanted to have a girlfriend and to go out on dates, just the two of us. And of course I was interested in sex. Just like anybody else. And no one was stopping me from having a girlfriend outside the group. But back then, that group was the most important part of my life. The thought hardly ever occurred to me to go out and be with anyone else.'

'Because you found a wonderful harmony there?'

Tsukuru nodded. 'When I was with them, I felt like an indispensible part of the whole. It was a special feeling that I could never get anywhere else.'

'Which is why all of you had to look past any sexual interest,' Sara said. 'In order to preserve the harmony the five of you had together. So as not to destroy the perfect circle.'

'Looking back on it now, I can see there was something unnatural about it. But at the time, nothing seemed more natural. We were still in our teens, experiencing everything for the first time. There was no way we could be that objective about our situation.'

'In other words, you were locked up inside the perfection of that circle. Can you see it that way?'

Tsukuru thought about this. 'Maybe that's true, but we were happy to be locked up inside it. And I don't regret it, even now.'

'Intriguing,' Sara said.

Sara was also quite interested to hear about Aka's visit with Shiro in Hamamatsu six months before she was murdered.

'It's a different situation, of course,' Sara said, 'but it reminds me of a classmate of mine from high school. She was beautiful, with a nice figure, from an affluent family, raised partly abroad and fluent in English and French, always at the top of her class. People noticed her, no matter what she did. She was revered by everybody, the heartthrob of all the younger students. We went to a private all-girls high school, so that sort of admiration by underclassmen could be pretty intense.'

Tsukuru nodded.

'She went on to Seishin University, the famous women's private college, and studied abroad in France for two years. A couple of years after she got back I had a chance to see her, and when I did, I was floored. I'm not sure how to put it, but she seemed faded. Like something that's been exposed to strong sunlight for a long time and the color fades. She looked much the same as before. Still beautiful, still with a nice figure . . . but she seemed paler, fainter than before. It made me feel like I should grab the TV remote to ramp up the color intensity. It was a weird experience. It was hard to imagine that someone could, in the space of just a few years, visibly diminish like that.'

Sara had finished her meal and was waiting for the dessert menu.

'She and I weren't all that close, but we had a few friends in common, so I'd run into her every now and again. And each time I saw her, she'd faded a little more. From a certain point on, it was clear to everyone that she wasn't pretty anymore, that she was no longer attractive. It was like she'd gotten less intelligent, too. The topics she talked about were boring, her opinions stale and trite. She married at twenty-seven, and her husband was some elite government official, an obviously shallow, boring man. But the woman couldn't seem to grasp the fact that she was no longer beautiful, no longer attractive, no longer the sort of person people notice. She still acted like she was the queen. It was pretty pathetic to watch.'

The dessert menu arrived, and Sara inspected it closely. Once

178

she'd made up her mind, she closed the menu and laid it on the table.

'Her friends gradually stopped seeing her. It was just too painful to witness. Maybe it wasn't exactly pain they felt when they saw her, but more a kind of fear, the kind of fear most women have. The fear that your peak attractiveness as a woman is behind you, and you either don't realize it or refuse to accept it, and go on acting the way you always have, and then people snub you and laugh at you behind your back. For her, that peak came earlier than for others. That's all it was. In her teens, all her natural gifts burst into bloom, like a garden in spring, and once those years had passed, they quickly withered.'

The white-haired waiter came over, and Sara ordered the lemon soufflé. Tsukuru was always impressed at how she never skipped dessert yet managed to keep her trim figure.

'I imagine Kuro could tell you more details about Shiro,' Sara said. 'Even if your group of five was a harmonious, perfect community, there are always things that only girls can discuss between themselves. Like Ao told you. And what they talk about doesn't go outside the world of girls. Sometimes it's just chatter, but there are certain secrets we tightly protect, especially so boys don't get wind of them.'

She gazed at the waiter, who was standing far off, almost as if she regretted ordering the lemon soufflé. But then she seemed to reconsider and turned her gaze back to Tsukuru.

'Did the three of you boys have confidential talks like that?' she asked.

'Not that I recall,' Tsukuru said.

'Then what did you talk about?' Sara asked.

What *did* we talk about back then? Tsukuru thought about

it, but couldn't remember. He was sure they'd talked a lot, enthusiastically, really opening up to each other, yet for the life of him, he couldn't recall a thing.

'You know, I can't remember,' Tsukuru said.

'That's weird,' Sara said. And she smiled.

'Next month I should be able to take a break from work,' Tsukuru said. 'Once I get to that point, I'm thinking of going to Finland. I've cleared it with my boss, and there's no problem with me taking time off.'

'When you've set the dates, I can arrange the travel schedule for you. Plane tickets, hotel reservations, and the like.'

'I appreciate it,' Tsukuru said.

She lifted her glass and took a sip of water. She traced the lip of the glass with her finger.

'What was your time in high school like?' Tsukuru asked.

'I didn't stand out very much. I was on the handball team. I wasn't pretty, and my grades were just so-so.'

'You're sure you're not being modest?'

She laughed and shook her head. 'Modesty is a wonderful virtue, but it doesn't suit me. It's true, I didn't stand out at all. I don't think I meshed well with the whole education system. I never was a teacher's pet, or had any underclassmen who thought I was cool. There was no sign of any boyfriends, and I had a bad case of acne. I owned every Wham! CD imaginable, and always wore the boring white underwear my mother bought for me. But I did have a few good friends. Two of them. We were never as close a group as you five, but we were good friends and could tell each other anything. They helped me get through those dull teenage years.'

'Do you still see them?'

She nodded. 'Yes, we're still good friends. They're both married, with children, so we can't meet that often, but we do get together for dinner every once in a while, and talk nonstop for three hours. We tell each other everything.'

The waiter brought over the lemon soufflé and espresso. Sara dug right in. Lemon soufflé seemed to have been the right choice after all. Tsukuru looked back and forth between Sara, as she ate, and the steam that rose from her espresso.

'Do you have any friends now?' Sara asked.

'No, nobody I would call a friend.'

Only the four people back in his Nagoya days were what he could have called friends. After that, although for just a short time, Haida was something close to it. But there was nobody else.

'Aren't you lonely without friends?'

'I don't know,' Tsukuru said. 'Even if I had some, I don't think I'd be able to open up and share secrets.'

Sara laughed. 'Women find that necessary. Though sharing secrets is only one function of a friend.'

'Of course.'

'Would you like a bite of this soufflé? It's delicious.'

'No, you go ahead and finish it.'

Sara carefully ate the last bite of the soufflé, then put her fork down, dabbed at her mouth with her napkin, and seemed lost in thought. Finally she raised her head and looked across the table, straight at Tsukuru.

'After this, can we go to your place?'

'Of course,' Tsukuru said. He motioned to the waiter to bring the check.

181

'The handball team?' Tsukuru asked.

'Don't ask,' Sara said.

Back at his apartment, they held each other. Tsukuru was over-joyed to make love to her again, that she'd given him the chance to do so. On the sofa they caressed each other, then got into bed. Under her mint-green dress she had on tiny black lace underwear.

'Did your mom buy these for you too?' Tsukuru asked.

'You dummy,' Sara laughed. 'I bought them myself. Like you need to ask.'

'I don't see any more acne, either.'

'What did you expect?'

She reached out and gently took his hard penis in her hand.

But a little later, as he was entering her, his penis went limp. It was the first time in his life that this had happened to him, and it left him baffled and mystified. Everything around him became strangely quiet. Total silence in his ears, only the sound of his heart beating.

'Don't let it bother you,' Sara said, stroking his back. 'Just keep holding me. That's enough. Don't worry about anything.'

'I don't get it,' Tsukuru said. 'All I've been thinking about these days is making love to you.'

'Maybe you were looking forward to it too much. Though I am happy you were thinking about me like that.'

They lay in bed, naked, leisurely stroking each other, but Tsukuru still wasn't able to get a decent erection. Finally, it was time for her to go home. They silently dressed, and Tsukuru walked her to the station. As they went, he apologized that things hadn't worked out.

'It doesn't matter at all, really. So there's nothing to worry about,' Sara told him, tenderly. And she took hold of his hand. Her hand was small, and warm.

Tsukuru felt he should say something, but nothing came out. He just continued to feel her hand in his.

'I think there's something still bothering you,' Sara said. 'Going back to Nagoya and seeing your old friends for the first time in years, talking with them, learning all kinds of things at once – it must have shaken you up. More than you realize.'

He did feel confused, that much was true. A door that had been shut for so long had swung open, and a reality he had turned his eyes away from until now – a reality he never could have anticipated – had come rushing back inside. And these facts were still jumbled in his mind, unable to settle.

'There's still something stuck inside you,' Sara said. 'Something you can't accept. And the natural flow of emotions you should have is obstructed. I just get that feeling about you.'

Tsukuru thought about what she had said. 'Not all the questions I had were cleared up by this trip to Nagoya. Is that what you mean?'

'Yes. It seems like it. I'm just saying,' Sara said. Her expression turned serious, and then she added, 'Now that certain things have become clear to you, it may have had the opposite effect – making the missing pieces even more significant.'

Tsukuru sighed. 'I wonder if I've pried opened a lid that I never should have touched.'

'*Temporarily* you might have,' she said. 'There may be some pushback for a while. But at least you've moved closer to solving it. That's what's important. Keep going a little further, and I'm sure you'll discover the right pieces that fill in the gaps.'

'But it might take a long time.'

Sara held on tightly to his hand, her grip surprisingly strong.

'There's no need to hurry. Just take your time. What I want to know most of all is whether or not you're hoping for a long-term relationship with me.'

'Of course I am. I want to be with you for a long time.'

'Really?'

'It's true,' Tsukuru said firmly.

'Then I have no problem. We still have time, and I'll wait. In the meantime, there are a couple of things I need to take care of.'

'Take care of?'

Sara didn't respond, instead flashing him a cryptic smile.

'As soon as you can, I want you to go to Finland to see Kuro,' she said. 'And tell her exactly what's in your heart. I'm sure she'll tell you something important. Something very important. I have a hunch.'

As he walked back alone from the station to his apartment, Tsukuru was seized by random thoughts. He had a strange sensation, as if time had, at a certain point, forked off into two branches. He thought of Shiro, of Haida, and of Sara. The past and present, memory and emotions, ran together as equals, side by side.

Maybe there really is something about me as a person, something deep down, he thought, *that is crooked and warped. Maybe Shiro was right, that I have something unhinged and detached inside of me.* Like the far side of the moon, forever cloaked in darkness. Maybe without realizing it, in a different place and different temporality, he *really had* raped Shiro and ripped her heart to shreds. Crudely, brutally. And maybe that dark, hidden side will one day outstrip the outer side and completely consume it. Tsukuru nearly crossed the street against the light and a taxi slammed on his brakes, the driver yelling an obscenity.

Back in his apartment he changed into pajamas and got into bed just before midnight. And right then, as if finally remembering to do so, he had an erection. A heroic, perfect, rock-hard erection. So massively hard he could barely believe it. He sighed deeply in the darkness at the irony of it. He got out of bed, switched on the light, took a bottle of Cutty Sark down from the shelf, and poured some into a small glass. He opened a book. After 1 a.m. it suddenly began to rain and gusts of wind began to blow. It was almost a storm, with plump raindrops pelting sideways against the window.

Supposedly I raped Shiro in this very bed, Tsukuru suddenly thought. Drugged her, numbed her, ripped off her clothes, and forced myself on her. She was a virgin. She felt terrible pain, and she bled. And with that, everything changed. Sixteen years ago.

As he listened to the rain drum against the window, with these thoughts swirling around in his head, his room began to feel like an alien space. As if the room itself had developed its own will. Just being in there steadily drained away any ability to distinguish the real from the unreal. On one plane of reality, he'd never even touched Shiro's hand. Yet on another, he'd brutally raped her. Which reality had he stepped into now? The more he thought about it, the less certain he became.

It was two thirty when he finally got to sleep.

13.

On weekends Tsukuru went to the pool at the gym, a ten-minute bike ride from his apartment. He always swam the crawl at a set pace, completing 1,500 meters in thirty-two or thirty-three minutes. He let faster swimmers pass him. Trying to compete against other people wasn't in his nature. As always, on this day he found another swimmer whose speed was close to his, and joined him in the same lane. The other man was young and lanky and wore a black competitive swimsuit, a black cap, and goggles.

Swimming eased Tsukuru's accumulated exhaustion, and relaxed his tense muscles. Being in the water calmed him more than any other place. Swimming a half hour twice a week allowed him to maintain a calm balance between mind and body. He also found the water a great place to think. A kind of Zen meditation, he discovered. Once he got into the rhythm of the swimming, thoughts came to him, unhampered, like a dog let loose in a field.

'Swimming feels wonderful – almost as good as flying through the air,' Tsukuru explained to Sara one time.

'Have you ever flown through the air?' she asked.

'Not yet,' Tsukuru said.

This morning, as he swam, thoughts of Sara came to him. He pictured her face, her body, and how he'd failed in bed. And he remembered several things she'd said. Something is stuck inside you, she'd told him, and the natural flow of emotions you should have is obstructed.

She might be right, Tsukuru thought.

At least from the outside, Tsukuru Tazaki's life was going well, with no particular problems to speak of. He'd graduated from a well-known engineering school, found a job in a railway company, working as a white-collar professional. His reputation in the company was sound, and his boss trusted him. Financially he had no worries. When his father died, Tsukuru had inherited a substantial sum of money and the one-bedroom condo in a convenient location near the center of Tokyo. He had no loans. He hardly drank and didn't smoke, and had no expensive hobbies. He spent very little money. It wasn't that he was especially trying to economize or live an austere life, but he just couldn't think of ways to spend money. He had no need for a car, and got by with a limited wardrobe. He bought books and CDs occasionally, but that didn't amount to much. He preferred cooking his own meals to eating out, and even washed his own sheets and ironed them.

He was generally a quiet person, not good at socializing. Not that he lived a solitary life. He got along with others pretty well. He didn't go out looking for women on his own, but hadn't lacked for girlfriends. He was single, not bad-looking, reserved, well groomed, and women tended to approach him. Or else, acquaintances introduced him to women (which is how he had gotten to know Sara).

To all appearances, at thirty-six he was enjoying a comfortable bachelor life. He was healthy, kept the pounds off, and had never been sick. Most people would see his life as going smoothly, with no major setbacks. His mother and older sisters certainly saw it that way. 'You enjoy being single too much, that's why you don't feel like getting married,' they told Tsukuru. And they finally gave up on trying to set him up with potential marriage partners. His coworkers seemed to come to the same conclusion.

Tsukuru had never lacked for anything in his life, or wanted something and suffered because he had been unable to obtain it. Because of this, he'd never experienced the joy of *really wanting something* and struggling to get it. His four high school friends had probably been the most valuable thing he'd ever had in his life. This relationship wasn't something he'd chosen himself, but more like something that had come to him naturally, like the grace of God. And long ago, again not through any choice of his own, he'd lost all of it. Or rather, had it stripped away.

Sara was now one of the very few things he desired. He wasn't 100 percent certain of this, but he was powerfully drawn to her. And each time he saw her, this desire only grew. He was ready to sacrifice in order to have her. It was unusual for him to feel such a strong, raw emotion. Even so – he didn't know why – when he had tried to make love to her, he hadn't been able to perform. Something had impeded his desire. *Take your time. I can wait*, Sara had said. But things weren't that simple. People are in constant motion, never stationary. No one knows what will happen next.

These were the thoughts that ran through his head as he swam the twenty-five-meter pool. Keeping a steady pace so as not to get out of breath, he'd turn his head slightly to one side and take a short breath, then slowly exhale under water. The longer he swam, the more automatic this cycle became. The number of strokes he needed for each lap was the same each time. He gave himself up to the rhythm, counting only the number of turns.

He suddenly noticed that he recognized the soles of the swimmer sharing the same lane. They were exactly the same as Haida's. He gulped, his rhythm thrown off, and inhaled water through his nose. His heart was pounding in his rib cage, and it took a while for his breathing to settle down.

These have to be Haida's soles, Tsukuru thought. The size and shape are exactly the same. That simple, confident kick was identical – even the bubbles the swimmer kicked up underwater, small, gentle, and as relaxed as his kick, were the same. Back when he and Haida had swum together in the college pool, he'd always kept his eyes riveted on Haida's soles, like a person driving at night never takes his eyes off the taillights of the car ahead. Those feet were etched in his memory.

Tsukuru stopped swimming, climbed out of the pool, and sat on the starting platform, waiting for the swimmer to turn and come back.

But it wasn't Haida. The cap and goggles hid his facial features, but now he realized this man was too tall, his shoulders too muscular. His neck was totally different, too. And he was too young, possibly still a college student. By now Haida would be in his mid-thirties.

Even though he knew it was someone else, Tsukuru's heart wouldn't settle down. He sat on a plastic chair by the side of the pool and watched the man continue to swim. His overall form, too, resembled Haida's, almost exactly the same. No splash, no unnecessary sound. His elbows rose beautifully and smoothly in the air, his arms quietly entering the water again, thumb first. Smooth,

189

nothing forced. Maintaining an introspective quiet seemed to be the main theme of his swimming style. Still, no matter how much his swimming style resembled Haida's, this was not Haida. The man finally stopped, got out of the pool, tugged off his black goggles and cap, and, rubbing his short hair vigorously with a towel, walked away. His face was angular, not anything like Haida's at all.

Tsukuru decided to call it a day, went to the locker room, and showered. He biked back to his apartment, and ate a simple breakfast. As he ate, a sudden thought struck him. *Haida is also one of the things that's blocking me inside.*

He was able to get the time off that he needed to travel to Finland without any trouble. His unused vacation time had piled up, like frozen snow underneath eaves. All his boss had said was 'Finland?' and shot him a dubious look. Tsukuru explained how a high school friend was living there, and he wanted to go visit. He figured he wouldn't have many chances to go to Finland in the future.

'What's there in Finland?' his boss asked.

'Sibelius, Aki Kaurismaki films, Marimekko, Nokia, Moomin.' Tsukuru listed all the names of famous Finnish things that he could think of.

His boss shook his head, obviously indifferent to all of them.

Tsukuru phoned Sara and decided on the departure date, setting the itinerary so he could take the nonstop Narita–Helsinki flight both ways. He'd leave Tokyo in two weeks, stay in Helsinki four nights, and then return to Tokyo.

'Are you going to get in touch with Kuro before you go?' Sara asked.

'No, I'll do what I did when I went to Nagoya, and not let her know I'm coming.'

'Finland's a lot further away than Nagoya. The round trip takes a long time. Maybe you'll get there and find out she left three days before for a summer holiday in Majorca.'

'If that's how it turns out, I can live with it. I'll just do some sightseeing in Finland and come home.'

'If that's what you want, fine,' Sara said, 'but since you're traveling all that way, how about seeing some other places while you're there? Tallinn and Saint Petersburg are just around the corner.'

'Finland's enough,' Tsukuru said. 'I'll fly from Tokyo to Helsinki, spend four nights there, and then come back.'

'I assume you have a passport?'

'When I joined the company, they told us to keep it renewed so we could go on an overseas business trip if one came up. But I've never had an opportunity to use it.'

'In Helsinki you can get around well using English, but if you travel to the countryside, I'm not so sure. Our company has a small office in Helsinki. Kind of a sub-branch. I'll contact them and let them know you're coming, so if you have any problems, you should stop by. A Finnish girl named Olga works there and I'm sure she can help you.'

'I appreciate it.'

'The day after tomorrow, I have to go to London on business. Once I make the airline and hotel reservations, I'll email you the particulars. Our Helsinki office address and phone number, too.'

'Sounds good.'

'Are you *really* going to go all the way to Helsinki to see her without getting in touch first? All the way across the Arctic Circle?'

'Is that too weird?'

She laughed. '*Bold* is the word I'd use for it.'

'I feel like things will work out better that way. Just intuition, of course.'

'Then I wish you good luck,' Sara said. 'Could I see you once before you go? I'll be back from London at the beginning of next week.'

'Of course I'd like to see you,' Tsukuru said, 'but I get the feeling it would be better if I go to Finland first.'

'Did something like intuition tell you that too?'

'I think so. Something like intuition.'

'Do you rely on intuition a lot?'

'Not really. I've hardly ever done anything based on it, up until now. Just like you don't build a railway station on a hunch. I mean, I don't even know if intuition's the right word. It's just something I felt, all of a sudden.'

'Anyway, you feel that's the best way to go this time, right? Whether that's intuition or not.'

'While I was swimming in the pool the other day, I was thinking about all kinds of things. About you, about Helsinki. I'm not sure how to put it, maybe like swimming upstream, back to my gut feelings.'

'While you were swimming?'

'I can think well when I'm swimming.'

Sara paused for a time, as if impressed. 'Like a salmon.'

'I don't know much about salmon.'

'Salmon travel a long way. Driven by something,' Sara said. 'Did you ever see *Star Wars*?'

'When I was a kid.'

'May the force be with you,' she said. 'So you don't lose out to the salmon.'

'Thanks. I'll get in touch when I'm back from Helsinki.'

'I'll be waiting.'

She hung up.

—

But it turned out that, a few days before he was due to board the flight for Helsinki, Tsukuru did see Sara again, by chance. Sara, though, had no idea.

That evening he went out to Aoyama to buy some presents for Kuro – some small accessories for her, and some Japanese picture books for her children. There was a good shop for these kinds of presents in a backstreet behind Aoyama Boulevard. After an hour or so of shopping, he felt like taking a break and went inside a café. He took a seat next to the large plate glass window, which faced Omotesando, ordered coffee and a tuna-salad sandwich, and sat back to watch the scene outside on the twilight-bathed street. Most of the people passing by were couples. They looked extremely happy, as if they were on their way to someplace special, where something delightful awaited them. As he watched, Tsukuru's mind grew still and tranquil. A quiet feeling, like a frozen tree on a windless winter night. But there was little pain mixed in. Over the years Tsukuru had grown used to this mental image, so much so that it no longer brought him any particular pain.

Still, he couldn't help thinking how nice it would be if Sara were with him. There was nothing he could do about that, though, as he was the one who'd turned her down. That was what he had wanted. He had frozen his own bare branches, on this invigorating summer evening.

Was that the right thing to have done?

Tsukuru wasn't at all sure. Could he really trust his *intuition*? Maybe this wasn't intuition, or anything like it, but just a baseless passing thought? *May the force be with you*, Sara had said.

For a while Tsukuru thought about salmon and their long journey through dark seas, following instinct or intuition.

Just then, Sara passed by, in front of him. She was wearing the same mint-green short-sleeved dress she'd had on the other day, and the light brown pumps, and was walking down the gentle slope from Aoyama Boulevard toward Jingumae. Tsukuru caught his breath, and grimaced in spite of himself. He couldn't believe what he was seeing was real. For a few seconds it felt as if she were an elaborate illusion generated by his solitary mind. But there was no doubt about it, this was the real, live Sara. Reflexively, he rose to his feet and nearly knocked over the table. Coffee spilled into the saucer. He soon sat back down.

Beside Sara stood a middle-aged man, a powerfully built man of medium height, wearing a dark jacket, a blue shirt, and a navy-blue tie with small dots. Neatly groomed hair, with a touch of gray. He looked to be in his early fifties. Nice features, despite the somewhat severe chin. His expression showed the sort of quiet, unassuming confidence that a certain kind of man that age exhibited. He and Sara were walking happily down the street, hand in hand. Tsukuru, openmouthed, like someone who'd lost the words he was just forming, watched them through the large window. They slowly passed in front of him, but Sara didn't glance in his direction. She was completely absorbed in talking with the man, and paid no attention to her surroundings. The man said something, and she opened her mouth and laughed. Her white teeth showed clearly.

Sara and the man were swallowed up into the evening crowd. Tsukuru kept looking in the direction they had disappeared in, clinging to a faint hope that Sara would return. That she might notice he was there and come back to explain. But she never came. Other people, with different faces and different looks, passed by, one after another.

He shifted in his chair and gulped down some ice water. All that remained now was a quiet sorrow. He felt a sudden, stabbing pain in the left side of his chest, as if he'd been pierced by a knife. It felt like hot blood was gushing out. Most likely it was blood. He hadn't felt such pain in a long time, not since the summer of his sophomore year in college, when his four friends had abandoned him. He closed his eyes and, as if floating in water, drifted in that world of pain. Still, being able to feel pain was good, he thought. It's when you can't even feel any pain anymore that you're in real trouble.

All sorts of sounds mixed together into a sharp, terrible static deep within his ears, the kind of noise that could only be perceived in the deepest possible silence. Not something you can hear from without, but a silence generated from your own internal organs. Everyone has their own special sound they live with, though they seldom have the chance to actually hear it.

When he opened his eyes again, it was as if the world had been transformed. The plastic table, the plain white coffee cup, the half-eaten sandwich, the old self-winding Heuer watch on his left wrist (the memento from his father), the evening paper he'd been reading, the trees lining the street outside, the show window of the store across the way, growing brighter as evening came on – everything around him looked distorted. The outlines were uncertain, the sense of depth lacking, the scale entirely wrong. He breathed in deeply, again and again, and finally began to calm down.

The pain he'd felt in his heart didn't stem from jealousy. Tsukuru knew what jealousy was like. He'd experienced it very vividly once, back in that dream, and the feeling remained with him even now. He knew how suffocating, how hopeless that sensation could be. But the pain he was feeling now was different. All he felt was sorrow, as if he'd been abandoned at the bottom of a deep, dark pit. That's all it was – sorrow. That, and simple physical pain. He actually found this comforting.

What hurt him most wasn't the fact that Sara was walking down the street holding hands with another man. Or the possibility that she might be going to sleep with the man. Of course it pained him to imagine her undressing and getting into bed with someone else. It took great effort to wipe that mental picture from his mind. But Sara was a thirty-eight-year-old, independent woman, single and free. She had her own life, just as Tsukuru had his. She had the right to be with whomever she liked, wherever she wanted, to do whatever she wanted.

What really shocked him, though, was how happy she looked. When she talked with that man, her whole face lit up. She had never showed such an unguarded expression when she was with Tsukuru, not once. With him, she always maintained a cool, controlled look. More than anything else, that's what tore, unbearably, at his heart.

Back in his apartment he got ready for the trip to Finland. Keeping busy would take his mind off things. Not that he had that much luggage to pack – just a few days' change of clothes, a pouch with toiletries, a couple of books to read on the plane, swimsuit and goggles (which he never went anywhere without), and a folding umbrella. Everything would fit neatly into one carry-on shoulder bag. He didn't even take a camera. What good were photos? What he was seeking was an actual person, and actual words.

Once he finished packing, he took out Liszt's *Years of Pilgrimage* for the first time in ages. The three-record set performed by Lazar Berman, the set Haida had left behind fifteen years before. He still kept an old-style record player for the sole purpose of playing this record. He placed the first LP on the turntable, B side up, and lowered the needle.

'First Year: Switzerland.' He sat down on the sofa, closed his eyes, and focused on the music. 'Le mal du pays' was the eighth piece in the suite, the first track on the B side. Usually he started with that piece and listened until the fourth composition in 'Second Year: Italy,' 'Petrarch's Sonnet 47.' At that point, the side ended, and the needle automatically lifted from the record.

'Le mal du pays.' The quiet, melancholy music gradually gave shape to the undefined sadness enveloping his heart, as if countless microscopic bits of pollen adhered to an invisible being concealed in the air, ultimately revealing, slowly and silently, its shape. This time the being took on the shape of Sara – Sara in her mint-green short-sleeved dress.

The ache in his heart returned. Not an intense pain, but the memory of intense pain.

What did you expect? Tsukuru asked himself. A basically empty vessel has become empty once again. Who can you complain to about that? People come to him, discover how empty he is, and leave. What's left is an empty, perhaps even emptier, Tsukuru Tazaki, all alone. Isn't that all there is to it?

Still, sometimes they leave behind a small memento, like Haida and the boxed set of *Years of Pilgrimage*. He probably didn't simply forget it, but intentionally left it behind in Tsukuru's apartment. And Tsukuru loved that music, for it connected him to Haida, and to Shiro. It was the vein that connected these three scattered people. A fragile, thin vein, but one that still had living, red blood coursing through it. The power of music made it possible. Whenever he listened to that music, particularly 'Le mal du pays,' vivid memories of the two of them swept over him. At times it even felt like they were right beside him, quietly breathing.

At a certain point the two of them had vanished from his life. Suddenly, without warning. No – it was less that they had left than that they had deliberately cut him off, abandoned him. Of course that had hurt Tsukuru deeply, and that wound remained to this day. But in the end, wasn't it the two of them – Shiro and Haida – who had, in a real sense of the term, been wounded or injured? Recently, that view had taken hold of his mind.

Maybe I *am* just an empty, futile person, he thought. But it was precisely because there was nothing inside of me that these people could find, if even for a short time, a place where they belonged. Like a nocturnal bird seeks a safe place to rest during the day in a vacant attic. The birds like that empty, dim, silent place. If that were true, then maybe he should be happy he was hollow.

The final strains of 'Petrarch's Sonnet 47' vanished in the air, the recording ended, and the needle automatically lifted, moved to the side, returned to the armrest. He lowered the needle back to the beginning of the B side of the LP. The needle quietly traced the grooves of the record and once more Lazar Berman was playing, beautifully, ever so delicately.

He listened to the whole side again, then changed into pajamas and got into bed. He switched off the light beside his bed, and once more felt grateful that what had taken hold of his heart was a deep sorrow, not the yoke of intense jealousy. That would have snatched away any hope for sleep.

Finally sleep came, wrapping him in its embrace. For several fleeting moments he felt that familiar softness throughout his body. This, too, was one of the few things Tsukuru felt thankful for that night.

In the midst of sleep he heard birds calling out in the night.

14.

As soon as he arrived at the Helsinki airport, Tsukuru exchanged his yen for euros, found a cell phone store, and bought the most basic, prepaid phone they had. This done, he walked out of the terminal, his carry-on bag hanging from his shoulder, and walked to the taxi stand. He got into a taxi, an older model Mercedes-Benz, and told the driver the name of his hotel in the city.

They left the airport and drove onto the highway. Though this was Tsukuru's first trip abroad, neither the deep green woods they passed nor the billboards in Finnish gave him the sense he had come – for the first time ever – to a foreign country. Obviously it took much longer to come here than to go to Nagoya, but he felt no different than when he'd gone back to his home-town. Only the currency in his wallet had changed. He wore his usual outfit – chinos, black polo shirt, sneakers, and a light brown cotton jacket. He'd brought the bare minimum when it came to extra clothes. He figured if he needed anything more, he could always buy it.

'Where are you from?' asked the taxi driver in English, shooting Tsukuru a glance in the rearview mirror. He was a middle-aged man with a full, thick beard.

'Japan,' Tsukuru replied.

'That's a long way to come with so little luggage.'

'I don't like heavy baggage.'

The driver laughed. 'Who does? But before you know it, you're surrounded by it. That's life. *C'est la vie.*' And again, he laughed happily.

Tsukuru laughed along with him.

'What kind of work do you do?' the driver asked.

'I build railroad stations.'

'You're an engineer?'

'Yes.'

'And you came to Finland to build a station?'

'No, I came here on vacation to visit a friend.'

'That's good,' the driver said. 'Vacations and friends are the two best things in life.'

Did all Finns like to make clever witticisms about life? Or was it just this one driver? Tsukuru hoped it was the latter.

Thirty minutes later, when the taxi pulled up in front of a hotel in downtown Helsinki, Tsukuru wasn't sure whether or not he should add a tip. He realized he hadn't checked this in the guidebook (or anything else about Finland, in fact). He added a little under 10 percent of what the meter said and gave it to the driver. The driver looked pleased and handed him a blank receipt, so it was probably the right decision. Even if it wasn't, the driver clearly wasn't upset.

The hotel Sara had chosen for him was an old-fashioned place in the center of the city. A handsome blond bellboy escorted him via an antique elevator to his room on the fourth floor. The furniture was old, the bed substantial, the walls covered with faded wallpaper with a pine needle pattern. There was an old claw-foot tub, and the windows opened vertically. The drapes were thick, with a thin lace curtain over the window. The whole place had a faintly nostalgic odor. Through the window, he could see green tram cars running down the middle of a broad boulevard. Overall, a comfortable, relaxing room. There was no coffee maker or LCD TV, but Tsukuru didn't mind. He wouldn't have used them anyway.

'Thank you. This room is fine,' Tsukuru told the bellboy, and handed him two one-euro coins as a tip. The bellboy grinned and softly slipped out of the room like a clever cat.

By the time he'd showered and changed, it was already evening. Outside, though, it was still bright as noon. A distinct half moon hung above, like a battered piece of pumice stone that had been tossed by someone and gotten stuck in the sky.

He went to the concierge desk in the lobby and got a free city map from the red-haired woman working there. He told her the address of Sara's travel agency, and the woman marked it in pen on the map. It was less than three blocks from the hotel. He followed the concierge's advice and bought a pass that was good for the city buses, subway, and streetcars. She told him how to ride these, and gave him a map of the lines. The woman looked to be in her late forties. She had light green eyes, and was very kind. Every time he talked with an older woman, Tsukuru got a natural, calm feeling. This seemed true no matter where in the world he found himself.

He went to a quiet corner of the lobby and used the cell phone he had bought at the airport to call Kuro's apartment in the city. The phone went to voicemail. A man's deep voice spoke in Finnish for about twenty seconds and then there was a beep where he could leave a message, but Tsukuru hung up without saying anything. He waited a while and dialed again, with the same result. The voice on the message was probably Kuro's husband. Tsukuru had no idea what he was saying, of course, but he got an impression of a straightforward, positive person. The voice of a healthy man who lived a comfortable, relaxed life.

Tsukuru hung up, put the phone back in his pocket, and took a deep breath. He didn't have a good feeling about this. Kuro might not be in the apartment now. She had a husband and two small children. It was July, and maybe, as Sara had thought, the whole family had decamped on a summer vacation to Majorca.

It was six thirty. The travel agency Sara had told him about was no doubt closed, but it couldn't hurt to try them. He took the cell phone out again and dialed the office number. Surprisingly, someone was still there.

A woman's voice answered in Finnish.

'Excuse me, is Olga there?' Tsukuru asked in English.

'I'm Olga,' the woman replied in unaccented English.

Tsukuru introduced himself and explained that Sara had suggested that he call.

'Yes, Mr. Tazaki. Sara told me about you,' Olga said.

Tsukuru explained the situation. How he'd come to see a friend, but when he called her, all he got was a recording in Finnish.

'Are you at your hotel now?'

'I am,' Tsukuru said.

'I'm about to close the office for the day. I can be over there in a half hour. Can we meet in the lobby?'

Olga was blond and wore tight jeans and a long-sleeved white T-shirt. She looked to be in her late twenties. She stood about five foot seven and had a full face with a rosy complexion. She looked liked a girl born to a well-off farming family, raised with a gaggle of garrulous geese. Her hair was pulled back, and a black enamel bag dangled from her shoulder. She had good posture, like a courier with an important package to deliver, and took long strides as she walked into the hotel.

They shook hands and sat down next to each other on a sofa in the middle of the lobby.

Sara had been to Helsinki a number of times, and each time she visited, she had worked with Olga. So Olga was not only a business partner but also, it seemed, a friend.

'I haven't seen Sara for a while. How is she?' Olga asked.

'She's fine,' Tsukuru replied. 'Work keeps her busy, and she's always flying off somewhere.'

'When she called me she said you were a close, personal friend.'

Tsukuru smiled. *A close, personal friend*, he repeated to himself.

'I'll be happy to help in any way I can. Don't hesitate to ask.' Olga beamed and looked him right in the eye.

'Thank you.' He felt like she was sizing him up, deciding if he was good enough to be Sara's boyfriend. He hoped that he passed the test.

'If you don't mind, let me listen to the message,' Olga said.

Tsukuru took out his cell phone and dialed the number for Kuro's apartment. Olga, meanwhile, took out a memo pad and a thin gold pen from her bag and placed them on her lap. As soon as he heard it ring he handed her the phone. Olga listened to the message, with a serious look on her face, and quickly noted down the requisite information. Then she hung up. She seemed like a smart, capable woman, and Tsukuru could imagine her and Sara getting along well.

'The voice is the woman's husband, I think,' Olga said. 'Last Friday they left their apartment and went to their summer cottage. They won't be back until the middle of August. He gave the phone number for the cottage.'

'Is it far away?'

She shook her head. 'He didn't say where it is. What we know from the message is just the phone number, and that it's in Finland. If you call the number, you should be able to find out where it is.'

'If you could do that for me, I'd really appreciate it. But I do have one request,' Tsukuru said. 'I don't want you to mention my name on the phone. If possible, I'd like to visit her without her knowing that I'm coming.'

Olga seemed curious.

Tsukuru explained. 'She's a really good friend of mine from high school, but I haven't seen her for a long time. I don't think she has any idea that I came to see her. I'm hoping to surprise her.'

'A surprise,' she said, opening her hands on her lap palms up. 'That sounds like a lot of fun.'

'I hope she'll agree.'

'Was she your girlfriend?' Olga asked.

Tsukuru shook his head. 'No, it wasn't that kind of relationship. We belonged to the same group of friends. That's all. But we were very close.'

She inclined her head a bit. 'Good friends in high school are hard to come by. I had one good friend in high school. We still see each other often.'

Tsukuru nodded.

'And your friend married a Finnish man and moved here. You haven't seen her for a long time. Is that correct?'

'I haven't seen her for sixteen years.'

Olga rubbed her temple with her index finger a couple of times. 'I understand. I'll try to get her address without mentioning your name. I'll think of a good way. Can you tell me her name?'

Tsukuru wrote down Kuro's name in her memo pad.

'What's the name of the town your high school was in?'

'Nagoya,' Tsukuru told her.

Olga took his cell phone again and dialed the number given on the answering machine. The phone rang a few times, and then someone answered. Olga spoke to the person in Finnish, using a friendly tone. She explained something, the other person asked her a question, and again she gave a concise explanation. She said the name Eri several times. After a few rounds of this, the other person seemed convinced. Olga picked up her ballpoint pen and noted something down. She politely thanked the person and hung up.

'It worked,' she said.

'I'm glad.'

'Their last name is Haatainen. The husband's first name is Edvard. He's spending the summer at their lakeside cottage outside a town called Hämeenlinna, northwest of Helsinki. Eri and the children are with him, of course.'

'How did you find that out without mentioning my name?'

Olga smiled impishly. 'I told a tiny lie. I pretended to be a FedEx delivery person. I said I had a package addressed to Eri from Nagoya, Japan, and asked him where I should forward it. Her husband answered the phone and didn't hesitate to give me the forwarding address. Here it is.'

She passed him a sheet from her memo pad. She stood up, went over to the concierge desk, and got a simple map of southern Finland. She spread the map open and marked the location of Hämeenlinna.

'Here's where Hämeenlinna is. I'll look up the address of their summer cottage on Google. The office is closed now, so I'll print it out tomorrow and give it to you then.'

'How long would it take to get there?'

'Well, it's about 100 kilometers, so from here by car you should allow about an hour and a half. The highway runs straight there. There are trains, too, but then you'd still need a car to get to their house.'

'I'll rent a car.'

'In Hämeenlinna there's a lovely castle by the lakeside, and the house where Sibelius was born. But I imagine you have more important matters. Tomorrow why don't you come by office whenever's convenient for you? We open at nine. There's a car rental place nearby, and I'll take care of renting a car for you.'

'You've been a big help,' Tsukuru said, thanking her.

'A good friend of Sara's is a friend of mine,' Olga said, and winked. 'I hope you can meet Eri. And that she'll be surprised.'

'I hope so. That's really why I came here.'

Olga hesitated for a moment, then said, 'I know this is none of my business, but is there something very important that made you come all the way here to see her?'

'Important to me, perhaps. But maybe not to her. I came here to find that out.'

'It sounds kind of complicated.'

'Maybe too complicated for me to explain in English.'

Olga laughed. 'Some things in life are too complicated to explain in any language.'

Tsukuru nodded. Coming up with witty sayings about life

seemed, after all, to be a trait shared by all Finns. The long winters might have something to do with it. But she was right. This was a problem that had nothing to do with language. Most likely.

She stood up from the sofa, and Tsukuru stood up too and shook her hand.

'Until tomorrow morning, then,' she said. 'I imagine you're jet-lagged, and with the sun staying out so late at night, people who aren't used to it sometimes have trouble sleeping. It'd be a good idea to ask for a wake-up call.'

'I'll do that,' Tsukuru said. Olga slung her bag over her shoulder and strode off through the lobby and out the entrance. She didn't look back.

Tsukuru folded the paper she'd given him, put it in his wallet, and stuffed the map in his pocket. He left the hotel and wandered around the city.

At least now he knew Eri's address. She was there, along with her husband and two small children. All that remained was whether she would see him. He might have flown halfway around the world to see her, but she might well refuse to meet him. It was entirely possible. According to Ao, it was Kuro who had first taken Shiro's side regarding the rape, the one who'd pushed them to cut off Tsukuru. He couldn't imagine what sort of feelings she had for him after Shiro's murder and the breakup of the group. She might feel totally indifferent toward him. All he could do was go see her and find out.

It was after 8 p.m., but as Olga had said, the sun showed no signs of setting. Many stores were still open, and the streets, still as bright as day, were crowded with pedestrians. People filled the cafés, drinking beer and wine, and chatting. As he walked down the old streets lined with round paving stones, Tsukuru caught a whiff of fish being grilled. It reminded him of grilled mackerel in Japanese diners. Hungry, he followed the smell into a side street but couldn't locate the source. As he searched the streets, the smell grew fainter, and then vanished.

It was too much trouble to search for somewhere to eat, so he went into a nearby pizzeria, sat down at an outdoor table, and ordered iced tea and a margherita pizza. He could hear Sara laughing at him. You flew all the way to Finland, and you ate a margherita pizza? She would definitely be amused by this. But the pizza turned out to be delicious, much better than he'd expected. They'd baked it in a real coal oven, and it was thin and crispy, with fragrant charcoal marks on the crust.

This casual pizzeria was nearly full of families and young couples. There was a group of students, too. Everyone was drinking either beer or wine, and many were puffing away on cigarettes. The only one Tsukuru could see sitting alone, drinking iced tea while he ate his pizza, was himself. Everyone else was talking loudly, boisterously, and the words he overheard were all (he imagined) Finnish. The restaurant seemed to cater to locals, not tourists. It finally struck him: he was far from Japan, in another country. No matter where he was, he almost always ate alone, so that didn't particularly bother him. But here he wasn't simply alone. He was alone in two senses of the word. He was also a foreigner, the people around him speaking a language he couldn't understand.

It was a different sense of isolation from what he normally felt in Japan. And not such a bad feeling, he decided. Being alone in two senses of the word was maybe like a double negation of isolation. In other words, it made perfect sense for him, a foreigner, to feel isolated here. There was nothing odd about it at all. The thought calmed him. He was in exactly the right place. His raised his hand to summon the waiter and ordered a glass of red wine.

A short time after the wine came, an old accordion player strolled by. He had on a worn-out vest and a Panama hat, and was accompanied by a pointy-eared dog. With practiced hands, like tying a horse to a hitching post, he tied the dog's leash to a streetlight and stood there, leaned back against it, and began playing northern European folk melodies. The man was clearly a veteran street musician, his performance practiced and effortless. Some of the customers sang along with the melodies, too, and he took requests, including a Finnish version of Elvis Presley's 'Don't Be Cruel.' His thin black dog sat there, not watching anything around it, its eyes fixed on a spot in the air, as if reminiscing. Its ears didn't twitch or move at all.

Some things in life are too complicated to explain in any language.

Olga was absolutely right, Tsukuru thought as he sipped his wine. Not just to explain to others, but to explain to yourself. Force yourself to try to explain it, and you create lies. At any rate, he knew he should be able to understand things more clearly tomorrow. He just had to wait. And if he didn't find out anything, well, that was okay too. There was nothing he could do about it. Colorless Tsukuru Tazaki would just go on living his colorless life. Not bothering anybody else.

He thought about Sara, her mint-green dress, her cheerful laugh, and the middle-aged man she was walking with, hand in hand. But these thoughts didn't lead him anywhere. The human heart is like a night bird. Silently waiting for something, and when the time comes, it flies straight toward it.

He shut his eyes and gave himself over to the tones of the accordion. The monotonous melody wended its way through the noisy voices and reached him, like a foghorn, nearly drowned out by the crashing of the waves.

He drank only half the wine, left some bills and coins on the table, and got up. He dropped a euro coin in the hat in front of the accordion player and, following what others had done, patted the head of his dog. As if it were pretending to be a figurine, the dog didn't react. Tsukuru took his time walking back to the hotel. He stopped by a kiosk on the way, and bought mineral water and a more detailed map of southern Finland.

In a park in the middle of the main boulevard, people had brought chess sets and were playing the game on raised, built-in stone chessboards. They were all men, most of them elderly. Unlike the people back in the pizzeria, they were totally quiet. The people watching them were taciturn as well. Deep thought required silence. Most of the people passing by on the street had dogs with them. The dogs, too, were taciturn. As he walked down the street, he caught the occasional whiff of grilled fish and kebabs. It was nearly 9 p.m., yet a flower shop was still open, with row upon row of colorful summer flowers. As if night had been forgotten.

At the front desk he asked for a 7 a.m. wake-up call. Then a sudden thought struck him. 'Is there a swimming pool nearby?' he asked.

The desk clerk frowned slightly and thought it over. She then politely shook her head, as if apologizing for some shortcoming in her nation's history. 'I'm very sorry, but I'm afraid there is no swimming pool nearby.'

He went back to his room, drew the heavy drapes to block

out the light, undressed, and lay down in bed. Yet still the light, like an old memory that can't easily be erased, snuck into the room. As he stared at the dim ceiling he thought how strange it was for him to be here in Helsinki, not Nagoya, going to see Kuro. The uniquely bright night of northern Europe made his heart tremble in an odd way. His body needed sleep, but his mind, at least for a while, sought wakefulness.

And he thought of Shiro. He hadn't dreamed of her in a long time. He thought of those erotic dreams, where he came violently inside her. When he woke up afterward and rinsed out his semen-stained underwear in the sink, a complex mix of emotions always struck him. A strange mix of guilt and longing. Special emotions that arise only in a dark corner unknown to other people, where the real and the unreal secretly mingle. Curiously enough, he missed these feelings. He didn't care what kind of dream it was, or how it made him feel. He wanted only to see Shiro once more in his dreams.

Sleep finally took hold of him, but no dreams came.

15.

The wake-up call came at seven, rousing him from sleep. He'd slept long and deeply, and his whole body felt pleasantly numb. He showered, shaved, and brushed his teeth, the numbness still with him. The sky was overcast, with a thin layer of clouds, but rain seemed unlikely. Tsukuru dressed, went down to the hotel restaurant, and had a simple buffet breakfast.

He arrived at Olga's office after nine. It was a cozy little office, halfway up a slope, with only one other person working there, a tall man with bulging, fish-like eyes. The man was on the phone, explaining something. The wall was covered with colorful posters of scenic spots in Finland. Olga had printed out several maps for Tsukuru. The Haatainens' cottage was in a small town a short way down the lake from Hämeenlinna, the location for which she'd marked with an X. Like some long canal, the narrow, meandering lake, gouged out by glaciers tens of thousands of years ago, seemed to go on forever.

'The road should be easy to follow,' Olga said. 'Finland's not like Tokyo or New York. The roads aren't crowded, and as long as you follow the signs and don't hit an elk, you should be able to get there.'

Tsukuru thanked her.

'I reserved a car for you,' she went on. 'A Volkswagen Golf with only two thousand kilometers on it. I was able to get a bit of a discount.'

'Thank you. That's great.'

'I pray everything goes well. You've come all this way, after all.' Olga smiled sweetly. 'If you run into any problems, don't hesitate to call me.'

'I won't,' Tsukuru said.

'Remember to watch out for elk. They're pretty dumb beasts. Be sure not to drive too fast.'

They shook hands again and said goodbye.

At the car rental agency he picked up the new, navy-blue Golf, and the woman there explained how to get from central Helsinki to the highway. It wasn't especially complicated, but you did have to pay attention. Once you got on the highway, it was easy.

Tsukuru listened to music on an FM station as he drove down the highway at about one hundred kilometers an hour, heading west. Most of the other cars passed him, but he didn't mind. He hadn't driven a car for a while, and here the steering wheel was on the left, the opposite of Japan. He was hoping, if possible, to arrive at the Haatainens' house after they'd finished lunch. He still had plenty of time, and there was no need to hurry. The classical music station was playing a gorgeous, lilting trumpet concerto.

There were forests on both sides of the highway. He got the impression that the whole country was covered, from one end to the other, by a rich green. Most of the trees were white birch, with occasional pines, spruce, and maples. The pines were red pines with tall straight trunks, while the branches of the white birch trees drooped way down. Neither was a variety found in

Japan. In between was a sprinkling of broadleaf trees. Huge-winged birds slowly circled on the wind, searching for prey. The occasional farmhouse roof popped into view. Each farm was vast, with cattle grazing behind fences ringing gentle slopes. The grass had been cut and rolled into large round bundles by a machine.

It was just before noon when he arrived in Hämeenlinna. Tsukuru parked his car in a parking lot and strolled for fifteen minutes around the town, then went into a café facing the main square and had coffee and a croissant. The croissant was overly sweet, but the coffee was strong and delicious. The sky in Hämeenlinna was the same as in Helsinki, veiled behind a thin layer of clouds, the sun a blurred orange silhouette halfway up the sky. The wind blowing through the town square was a bit chilly, and he tugged on a thin sweater over his polo shirt.

There were hardly any tourists in Hämeenlinna, just people in ordinary clothes, carrying shopping bags, walking down the road. Even on the main street most of the stores carried food and sundries, the kind of stores that catered to locals or people who lived in summer cottages. On the other side of the square was a large church, a squat structure with a round, green roof. Like waves on the shore, a flock of black birds busily fluttered to and from the church roof. White seagulls, their eyes not missing a thing, strolled along the cobblestones of the square.

Near the square was a line of carts selling vegetables and fruit, and Tsukuru bought a bag of cherries and sat on a bench and ate them. As he was eating, two young girls, around ten or eleven, came by and stared at him from a distance. There probably weren't many Asians who visited this town. One of the girls was tall and lanky, with pale white skin, the other tanned and freckled. Both wore their hair in braids. Tsukuru smiled at them.

Like the cautious seagulls, the girls warily edged closer.

'Are you Chinese?' the tall girl asked in English.

'I'm Japanese,' Tsukuru replied. 'It's nearby, but different.'

The girls didn't look like they understood.

'Are you two Russians?' Tsukuru asked.

They shook their heads emphatically.

'We're Finnish,' the freckled girl said with a serious expression.

'It's the same thing,' Tsukuru said. 'It's nearby, but different.'

The two girls nodded.

'What are you doing here?' the freckled one asked, sounding like she was trying out the English sentence structure. She was probably studying English in school and wanted to try it out on a foreigner.

'I came to see a friend,' Tsukuru said.

'How many hours does it take to get here from Japan?' the tall girl asked.

'By plane, about eleven hours,' Tsukuru said. 'During that time I ate two meals and watched one movie.'

'What movie?'

'*Die Hard* 12.'

This seemed to satisfy them. Hand in hand, they skipped off down the square, skirts fluttering, like little tumbleweeds blown by the wind, leaving no reflections or witticisms about life behind. Tsukuru, relieved, went back to eating his cherries.

It was one thirty when he arrived at the Haatainens' summer cottage. Finding it wasn't as simple as Olga had predicted. The path leading to the cottage could barely be called a road. If a kind old man hadn't passed by, Tsukuru might have wandered forever.

He had stopped his car by the side of the road and, Google map in hand, was unsure how to proceed, when a tiny old man on a bicycle stopped to help. The old man wore a well-worn cloth cap and tall rubber boots. White hair sprouted from his ears, and his eyes were bloodshot. He looked as if he were enraged about something. Tsukuru showed him the map and said he was looking for the Haatainens' cottage.

'It's close by. I'll show you.' The old man spoke first in German, then switched to English. He leaned his heavy-looking bicycle against a nearby tree and, without waiting for a reply, planted himself in the passenger seat of the Golf. With his horny fingers, like old tree stumps, he pointed out the path that Tsukuru had to take. Alongside the lake ran an unpaved road that cut through the forest. It was less a road than a trail carved out by wheel tracks. Green grass grew plentifully between the two ruts. After a while this path came to a fork, and at the intersection there were painted nameplates nailed to a tree. One on the right said *Haatainen*.

They drove down the right-hand path and eventually came to an open space. The lake was visible through the trunks of white birches. There was a small pier and a mustard-colored boat tied up to it, a simple fishing boat. Next to it was a cozy wooden cabin surrounded by a stand of trees, with a square brick chimney jutting out of the cabin roof. A white Renault van was parked next to the cabin.

'That's the Haatainens' cottage,' the old man intoned solemnly. Like a person about to step out into a snowstorm he made sure his cap was on tight, then spit a gob of phlegm onto the ground. Hard-looking phlegm, like a rock.

Tsukuru thanked him. 'Let me drive you back to where you left your bicycle. I know how to get here now.'

'No, no need. I'll walk back,' the old man said, sounding angry. At least that's what Tsukuru imagined he said. He couldn't understand the words. From the sound of it, though, it didn't seem like Finnish. Before Tsukuru could even shake his hand, the man had gotten out of the car and strode away. Like the Grim Reaper having shown a dead person the road to Hades, he never looked back.

Tsukuru sat in the Golf, parked in the grass next to the path, and watched the old man walk away. He then got out of the car and took a deep breath. The air felt purer here than in Helsinki, like it was freshly made. A gentle breeze rustled the leaves of the white birches, and the boat made an occasional clatter as it slapped against the pier. Birds cried out somewhere, with clear, concise calls.

Tsukuru glanced at his watch. Had they finished lunch? He hesitated, but with nothing else to do, he decided it was time to visit the Haatainens. He walked straight toward the cottage, trampling the summer grass as he went. On the porch, a napping dog stood up and stared at him. A little long-haired brown dog. It let out a few barks. It wasn't tied up, but the barks didn't seem menacing so Tsukuru continued his approach.

Probably alerted by the dog, a man opened the door and looked out before Tsukuru arrived. The man had a full, dark blond beard and looked to be in his mid-forties. He was of medium height, with a long neck and shoulders that jutted straight out, like an oversized hanger. His hair was the same dark blond and rose from his head in a tangled brush, and his ears stuck out. He had on a checked short-sleeved shirt and work jeans. With his left hand resting on the doorknob, he looked at Tsukuru as he approached. He called out the dog's name to make it stop barking.

'Hello,' Tsukuru said in English.

'*Konnichi wa*,' the man replied in Japanese.

'*Konnichi wa*,' Tsukuru replied in Japanese. 'Is this the Haatainens' house?'

'It is. I'm Haatainen. Edvard Haatainen,' the man replied, in fluent Japanese.

Tsukuru reached the porch steps and held out his hand. The man held his out, and they shook hands.

'My name is Tsukuru Tazaki.'

'Is that the *tsukuru* that means to make things?'

'It is. The same.'

The man smiled. 'I make things too.'

'That's good,' Tsukuru replied. 'I do too.'

The dog trotted over and rubbed its head against the man's leg, and then, as if it had nothing to lose, did the same to Tsukuru's leg. Its way of greeting people, no doubt. Tsukuru reached out and patted the dog's head.

'What kind of things do you make, Mr. Tazaki?'

'I make railroad stations,' Tsukuru said.

'I see. Did you know that the first railway line in Finland ran between Helsinki and Hämeenlinna? That's why the people here are so proud of their station. As proud as they are that it's the birthplace of Jean Sibelius. You've come to the right place.'

'Really? I wasn't aware of that. What do you make, Edvard?'

'Pottery,' Edvard replied. 'Pretty small scale compared to railroad stations. Why don't you come in, Mr. Tazaki.'

'Aren't I bothering you?'

'Not at all,' Edvard said. He held his hands wide apart. 'We welcome anyone here. People who make things are all my colleagues. They're especially welcome.'

No one else was in the cabin. On the table sat a coffee cup and a Finnish-language paperback left open. He seemed to have been enjoying an after-lunch cup of coffee while he read. He motioned Tsukuru to a chair and sat down across from him. He slid a bookmark into his book, closed it, and pushed it aside.

'Would you care for some coffee?'

'Thank you, I would,' Tsukuru said.

Edvard went over to the coffee maker, poured steaming coffee into a mug, and placed it in front of Tsukuru.

'Would you like some sugar or cream?'

'No, black is fine,' Tsukuru said.

The cream-colored mug was handmade. It was a strange shape, with a distorted handle, but was easy to hold, with a familiar, intimate feel to it, like a family's warm inside joke.

'My oldest daughter made that mug,' Edvard said, smiling broadly. 'Of course, I'm the one who fired it in the kiln.'

His eyes were a gentle light gray, well matched to his dark blond hair and beard. Tsukuru took an immediate liking to him. Edvard looked more suited to the forest and lakeside than to life in the city.

'I'm sure you came here because you needed to see Eri?' Edvard asked.

'That's right, I came to see Eri,' Tsukuru said. 'Is she here now?'

Edvard nodded. 'She took the girls for a walk after lunch, probably along the lake. There's a wonderful walking path there. The dog always beats them home, so they should be back soon.'

'Your Japanese is really good,' Tsukuru said.

'I lived in Japan for five years, in Gifu and Nagoya, studying

Japanese pottery. If you don't learn Japanese, you can't do anything.'

'And that's where you met Eri?'

Edvard laughed cheerfully. 'That's right. I fell in love with her right away. We had a wedding ceremony eight years ago in Nagoya, and then moved back to Finland. I'm making pottery full-time now. After we got back to Finland, I worked for a while for the Arabia Company as a designer, but I really wanted to work on my own, so two years ago I decided to go freelance. I also teach at a college in Helsinki twice a week.'

'Do you spend all your summers here?'

'Yes, we live here from the beginning of July to the middle of August. There's a studio nearby I share with some friends. I work there from early morning, but always come back here for lunch. Most afternoons I spend with my family. Taking walks, reading. Sometimes we go fishing.'

'It's beautiful here.'

Edvard smiled happily. 'Thank you. It's very quiet, and I can get a lot of work done. We live a simple life. The kids love it here too. They enjoy the outdoors.'

Along one of the white stucco walls was a floor-to-ceiling wooden shelf lined with pottery he'd apparently made himself, the only decoration in the room. On another wall hung a plain round clock, a compact audio set and a pile of CDs, and an old, solid-looking wooden cabinet.

'About 30 percent of the pottery on those shelves was made by Eri,' Edvard said. He sounded proud. 'She has a natural talent. Something innate. It shows up in her pottery. We sell our work in some shops in Helsinki, and in some of them, her pottery's more popular than mine.'

221

Tsukuru was a little surprised. This was the first he had ever heard that Kuro was interested in pottery. 'I had no idea she was into pottery,' he said.

'She got interested in it after she turned twenty, and after she graduated from college she went back to school, at the Aichi Arts College, in the industrial arts department.'

'Is that right? I mostly knew her when she was a teenager.'

'You're a friend from high school?'

'Yes.'

'Tsukuru Tazaki.' Edvard repeated the name, and frowned, searching his memory. 'You know, I do remember Eri talking about you. You were a member of that really good group of five friends. Is that right?'

'Yes, that's correct. We all belonged to a group.'

'Three of the people from that group attended our wedding ceremony in Nagoya. Aka, Shiro, and Ao. I believe those were their names? Colorful people.'

'Yes, that's right,' Tsukuru said. 'Unfortunately I wasn't able to attend the wedding.'

'But now we're able to meet like this,' he said with a warm smile. His long beard fluttered on his cheeks like the intimate flickering of a campfire flame. 'Did you come to Finland on a trip, Mr. Tazaki?'

'I did,' Tsukuru replied. Telling the truth would take too long. 'I took a trip to Helsinki and thought I'd take a side trip and see Eri, since I haven't seen her in a long time. I'm sorry I couldn't get in touch ahead of time. I hope I'm not inconveniencing you.'

'No, not at all. You came all this way, and we're happy to have you. It's lucky that I stayed at home. I know Eri will be really happy to see you.'

222

I hope you're right, Tsukuru told himself.

'May I take a look at your work?' Tsukuru said, pointing to the pottery lined up on the shelves.

'Of course. Feel free to touch any of them. Her work and mine are mixed together, but I'm sure you'll figure out which are which without me telling you.'

Tsukuru walked over to the wall shelf and studied the pottery one by one. Most were practical dining ware – plates, bowls, and cups. There were several vases and jars as well.

As Edvard said, Tsukuru could distinguish between his pieces and Eri's at a glance. The ones with a smooth texture and pastel colors were Edvard's. Here and there on the surface, the colors were darker or lighter, a subtle shading like the flow of the wind or water. Not a single one had any added design. The change in colors itself was the pattern, and even Tsukuru, a complete novice when it came to pottery, could tell that coloring like this required a high level of technical skill. The pieces had an intentional absence of any extraneous decoration, and a smooth, refined feel. Though fundamentally northern European, their pared-down simplicity revealed the clear influence of Japanese pottery. They were unexpectedly light to hold, too, and felt natural and right in his hand. Edvard had taken painstaking care with all the details, and they were the kind of work that only the finest craftsman could achieve. He never would have been able to display this kind of talent while working at a large company that dealt in mass production.

Compared to Edvard's style, Eri's was far simpler, hardly reaching the finely wrought subtlety of her husband's creations. Overall there was a lush, fleshy feel to her pieces, the rims slightly warped, and a lack of any refined, focused beauty. But her pottery

223

also had an unusual warmth that brought a sense of comfort and solace. The slight irregularities and rough texture provided a quiet sense of calm, like the feeling of touching natural fabric, or sitting on a porch watching the clouds go by.

In contrast to her husband's work, Eri's pottery featured patterns – like leaves blown on the wind. In some cases the design was scattered over the pottery, in others gathered in one spot, and depending on how the design was distributed, the pieces felt either sad, or brilliant, or even flamboyant. The exquisite designs reminded Tsukuru of fine patterns on an old kimono. He looked closely at each piece, trying to decipher each design, but he couldn't identify what the configurations might signify. They were odd and unique figures. From a slight distance they struck him as leaves scattered on a forest floor. Leaves trampled by anonymous animals who were quietly, secretly, making their way through the woods.

In Eri's works, different again from her husband's, color was simply a backdrop, its purpose to showcase the design, to give it life. The colors lightly, reticently yet effectively, served as background to the design itself.

Tsukuru picked up Edvard's work, then Eri's, comparing them. This couple must live in a nice balance in their real lives as well. The pleasant contrast in their artistic creations hinted at this. Their styles were very different, but each of them seemed to accept the other's distinctive qualities.

'Since I'm her husband, maybe it's not right for me to praise her work so highly,' Edvard said, watching Tsukuru's reaction. 'What do you call that in Japanese? *Favoritism*? Is that the right word?'

Tsukuru smiled but didn't say anything.

'I'm not saying this because we're married, but I really like Eri's work. There are plenty of people in the world who can make better, more beautiful pottery. But her pottery isn't *narrow* in any way. You feel an emotional generosity. I wish I could explain it better.'

'I understand exactly what you mean,' Tsukuru said.

'I think something like that comes from heaven,' Edvard said, pointing to the ceiling. 'It's a gift. I have no doubt she'll only get more skilled as time goes on. Eri still has a lot of room to grow.'

Outside the dog barked, a special, friendly sort of bark.

'Eri and the girls are back,' Edvard said, looking in that direction. He stood up and walked toward the door.

Tsukuru carefully placed Eri's pottery back on the shelf and stood there, waiting for her to arrive.

16.

When Kuro first spotted Tsukuru, she looked as if she couldn't understand what was happening. The expression on her face vanished, replaced by a blank look. She pushed her sunglasses up on her head and gazed at Tsukuru without a word. She'd gone out for an after-lunch walk with her daughters, only to come back and find a man, a Japanese man by the look of him, standing next to her husband. A face she didn't recognize.

She was holding her younger daughter's hand. The little girl looked about three. Next to her stood the older daughter, a little bigger and probably two or three years older than her sister. The girls wore matching flower-print dresses and plastic sandals. The door was still open, and outside the dog was barking noisily. Edvard stuck his head outside and gave the dog a quick scolding. It soon stopped barking and lay down on the porch. The daughters, like their mother, stood there silently, staring at Tsukuru.

Kuro didn't look much different from the last time he'd seen her, sixteen years earlier. The soft, full visage of her teenage years, though, had retreated, filled in now by more straightforward, expressive features. She'd always been robust and sturdy, but now her unwavering, unclouded eyes seemed more introspective. Those eyes had surely seen so many things over the

226

years, things that remained in her heart. Her lips were tight, her forehead and cheeks tanned and healthy-looking. Abundant black hair fell straight to her shoulders, her bangs pinned back with a barrette, and her breasts were fuller than before. She was wearing a plain blue cotton dress, a cream-colored shawl draped around her shoulders, and white tennis shoes.

Kuro turned to her husband as if for an explanation, but Edvard said nothing. He merely shook his head slightly. She turned to look back at Tsukuru, and lightly bit her lip.

What Tsukuru saw in front of him now was the healthy body of a woman who had walked a completely different path in life from the one he'd taken. Seeing her now, the true weight of sixteen years of time struck him with a sudden intensity. There are some things, he concluded, that can only be expressed through a woman's form.

As she gazed at him, Kuro's face was a bit strained. Her lips quivered, as if a ripple had run through them, and one side of her mouth rose. A small dimple appeared on her right cheek – technically not a dimple, but a shallow depression that appeared as her face was filled with a cheerful bitterness. Tsukuru remembered this expression well, the expression that came to her face just before she voiced some sarcastic remark. But now she wasn't going to say something sarcastic. She was simply trying to draw a distant hypothesis closer to her.

'*Tsukuru?*' she said, finally giving the hypothesis a name.

Tsukuru nodded.

The first thing she did was pull her daughter closer, as if protecting her from some threat. The little girl, her face still raised to Tsukuru, clung to her mother's leg. The older daughter stood a bit apart, unmoving. Edvard went over to her and gently patted her hair. The girl's hair was dark blond. The younger girl's was black.

The five of them stayed that way for a while, not speaking a word. Edvard patted the blond daughter's hair, Kuro's arm remained around the shoulder of the black-haired daughter, while Tsukuru stood alone on the other side of the table, as if they were all holding a pose for a painting with this arrangement. And the central figure in this was Kuro. She, or rather her body, was the core of the tableau enclosed by that frame.

Kuro was the first to move. She let go of her little daughter, then took the sunglasses off her forehead and laid them on the table. She picked up the mug her husband had been using and took a drink of the cold, leftover coffee. She frowned, as if she had no idea what it was she'd just drunk.

'Shall I make some coffee?' her husband asked her in Japanese.

'Please,' Kuro said, not looking in his direction. She sat down at the table.

Edvard went over to the coffee maker again and switched it on to reheat the coffee. Following their mother's lead, the two girls sat down side by side on a wooden bench next to the window. They stared at Tsukuru.

'Is that really you, Tsukuru?' Kuro asked in a small voice.

'In the flesh,' Tsukuru replied.

Her eyes narrowed, and she gazed right at him.

'You look like you've seen a ghost,' Tsukuru said. He'd meant it as a joke, though it didn't come out sounding like one.

'You look so different,' Kuro said in a dry tone.

'Everyone who hasn't seen me in a while says that.'

'You're so thin, so . . . grown-up.'

'Maybe that's because I'm a grown-up,' Tsukuru said.

'I guess so,' Kuro said.

'But you've hardly changed at all.'

She gave a small shake of her head but didn't respond.

Her husband brought the coffee over and placed it on the table. A small mug, one she herself had made. She put in a spoonful of sugar, stirred it, and cautiously took a sip of the steaming coffee.

'I'm going to take the kids into town,' Edvard said cheerfully. 'We need groceries, and I have to gas up the car.'

Kuro looked over at him and nodded. 'Okay. Thanks,' she said.

'Do you want anything?' he asked his wife.

She silently shook her head.

Edvard stuck his wallet in his pocket, took down the keys from where they hung on the wall, and said something to his daughters in Finnish. The girls beamed and leaped up from the bench. Tsukuru caught the words 'ice cream.' Edvard had probably promised to buy the girls an ice cream when they went shopping.

Kuro and Tsukuru stood on the porch and watched as Edvard and the girls climbed into the Renault van. Edvard opened the double doors in back, gave a short whistle, and the dog ecstatically barreled toward the van and leaped inside. Edvard looked out from the driver's side, waved, and the white van disappeared beyond the trees. Kuro and Tsukuru stood there, watching the spot where the van had last been.

'You drove that Golf here?' Kuro asked. She pointed to the little navy-blue car parked off a ways.

'I did. From Helsinki.'

'Why did you come all the way to Helsinki?'

'I came to see you.'

Kuro's eyes narrowed, and she stared at him, as if trying to decipher a difficult diagram.

'You came all the way to Finland to see me? Just to see *me*?'

'That's the size of it.'

'After sixteen years, without a word?' she asked, seemingly astonished.

'Actually it was my girlfriend who told me to come. She said it's about time I saw you again.'

The familiar curve came to Kuro's lips. She sounded half joking now. 'I see. Your girlfriend told you it was about time you came to see me. So you jumped on a plane in Narita and flew all the way to Finland. Without contacting me, and with no guarantee that I'd actually be here.'

Tsukuru was silent. The boat went on slapping against the dock, though there wasn't much wind, and just a scattering of waves on the lake.

'I thought if I got in touch before I came, you might not see me.'

'How could you say that?' Kuro said in surprise. 'Come on, we're friends.'

'We used to be. But I don't know anymore.'

She gazed through the trees at the lake and let out a sound-less sigh. 'It'll be two hours before they come back from town. Let's use the time to talk.'

They went inside and sat down across from each other at the table. She removed the barrette and her hair spilled onto her forehead. Now she looked more like the Kuro he remembered.

'There's one thing I'd like you to do,' Kuro said. 'Don't call me Kuro anymore. I'd prefer you call me Eri. And don't refer to

Yuzuki as Shiro. If possible, I don't want you to call us by those names anymore.'

'Those names are finished?'

She nodded.

'But you don't mind still calling me Tsukuru?'

'You're always Tsukuru,' Eri said, and laughed quietly. 'So I don't mind. The Tsukuru who makes things. Colorless Tsukuru Tazaki.'

'In May I went to Nagoya and saw Ao and Aka, one right after the other,' Tsukuru said. 'Is it okay if I keep on using those names?'

'That's fine. But I just want you to use Yuzu's and my real names.'

'I saw them separately, and we talked. Not for very long, though.'

'Are they both okay?'

'It seemed like it,' Tsukuru said. 'And their work seems to be going well, too.'

'So in good old Nagoya, Ao's busy selling Lexuses, one after another, while Aka's training corporate warriors.'

'That about sums it up.'

'And what about you? You've managed to get by?'

'Yes, I've managed,' Tsukuru said. 'I work for a railroad company in Tokyo and build stations.'

'You know, I happened to hear about that not so long ago. That Tsukuru Tazaki was busy building stations in Tokyo,' Eri said. 'And that he had a very clever girlfriend.'

'For the time being.'

'So you're still single?'

'I am.'

'You always did things at your own pace.'

Tsukuru was silent.

'What did you talk about when you met the two of them in Nagoya?' Eri asked.

'We talked about what happened between us,' Tsukuru said. 'About what happened sixteen years ago, and what's happened in the sixteen years since.'

'Was meeting them also, maybe – something your girlfriend told you to do?'

Tsukuru nodded. 'She said there are some things I have to resolve. I have to revisit the past. Otherwise . . . I'll never be free from it.'

'She thinks you have some issues you need to deal with.'

'She does.'

'And she thinks these issues are damaging your relationship.'

'Most likely,' Tsukuru said.

Eri held the mug in both hands, testing how hot it was, and then took another sip of coffee.

'How old is she?'

'She's two years older than me.'

Eri nodded. 'I can see you getting along well with an older woman.'

'Maybe so,' Tsukuru said.

They were quiet for a while.

'There are all kinds of things we have to deal with in life,' Eri finally said. 'And one thing always seems to connect with another. You try to solve one problem, only to find that another one you hadn't anticipated arises instead. It's not that easy to get free of them. That's true for you – and for me, too.'

'You're right, it's not easy to get free of them. But that doesn't mean we should leave them hanging, unresolved,' Tsukuru said. 'You can put a lid on memory, but you can't hide history. That's what my girlfriend said.'

Eri stood up, went over to the window, opened it, then returned to the table. The breeze fluttered the curtain, and the boat slapped sporadically against the dock. She brushed her hair back with her fingers, rested both hands on the tabletop, and looked at Tsukuru, then spoke. 'There could be lids that have gotten so tight you can't pry them off anymore.'

'I'm not trying to force anything. That's not what I'm trying to do. But at least I'd like to see, with my own eyes, what kind of lid it is.'

Eri gazed at her hands on the table. They were larger, and more fleshy, than Tsukuru remembered. Her fingers were long, her nails short. He pictured those hands spinning a potter's wheel.

'You said I look very different,' Tsukuru said. 'I think I've changed, too. Sixteen years ago, after you banished me from the group, all I could think about for five months was dying. Death and nothing else. Not to exaggerate or anything, but I was really teetering on the brink. Standing on the edge, staring down at the abyss, unable to look away. Somehow, I was able to make my way back to the world I came from. But it wouldn't have been surprising if I had actually died then. Something was wrong with me – mentally, I mean. I don't know what would be the correct diagnosis – anxiety, depression. Something like that. But something was definitely abnormal. It wasn't like I was confused, though. My mind was perfectly clear. Utterly still, with no static at all. A very strange condition, now that I think back on it.'

Tsukuru stared at Eri's silent hands and went on.

'After those five months were over, my face was totally transformed. And my body, too. None of my old clothes fit anymore.
When I looked in the mirror, it felt like I'd been put inside a
container that wasn't me. I don't know, maybe my life just
happened to reach that stage – a stage where I had to kind of
lose my mind for a while, where my looks and my body had to
undergo a metamorphosis. But the trigger for this change was
the fact that I had been cut off from our group. That incident
changed me forever.'

Eri listened without a word.

Tsukuru went on. 'How should I put it? It felt like I was on
the deck of a ship at night and was suddenly hurled into the
ocean, all alone.'

After he said this, he suddenly recalled this was the same
description that Aka had used. He paused and continued.

'I don't know if someone pushed me off, or whether I fell
overboard on my own. Either way, the ship sails on and I'm in
the dark, freezing water, watching the lights on deck fade into
the distance. None of the passengers or crew know I've fallen
overboard. There's nothing to cling to. I still have that fear, even
now – that suddenly my very existence will be denied and,
through no fault of my own, I'll be hurled into the night sea
once more. Maybe that's why I haven't been able to form deep
relationships with people. I always keep a distance between me
and others.'

He spread his hands apart on the table, indicating a space of
about twelve inches.

'Maybe it's part of my personality, something I was born with.
Maybe I've always had an instinctive tendency to leave a buffer
zone between me and others. But one thing I do know is that I

234

never thought this when I was with all of you in high school. At least that's how I remember it. Though it seems so long ago.'

Eri put her palms to her cheeks and slowly rubbed them, as if washing herself. 'You want to know what happened sixteen years ago. The whole truth.'

'I do,' Tsukuru said. 'But there's one thing I want to want to make clear. I never, ever did anything to harm Shiro. Yuzu, I mean.'

'I know that,' she said. She stopped rubbing her face. 'You couldn't have raped Yuzu. That's obvious.'

'But you believed her, right from the beginning. Like Ao and Aka did.'

Eri shook her head. 'No, I didn't believe her from the beginning. I don't know what Ao and Aka thought, but I didn't believe it. How could I? There's no way you'd ever do something like that.'

'Then why did you . . . ?'

'Why did I take Yuzu at her word and kick you out of the group? Why didn't I stand up and defend you? Is that what you're asking?'

Tsukuru nodded.

'Because I had to protect her,' Eri said. 'And in order to do that, I had to cut you off. It was impossible to protect you and protect her at the same time. I had to accept one of you completely, and reject the other entirely.'

'Her psychological problems were that severe. Is that what you mean?'

'Yes, they were indeed. Truthfully, she was backed into a corner. Someone had to protect her, and the only person who could possibly do that was me.'

'You could have explained that to me.'

She slowly shook her head a few times. 'There was no room to explain things then. What should I have said? *Tsukuru, would you mind if for a while we say you raped Yuzu? We have to do that now. Something's wrong with her, and we have to take care of the situation. Just be patient, things will settle down later. I don't know, maybe in two years?* I couldn't say something like that. I knew it was wrong, but I had to let you handle it on your own. Things were that tense. You should know, though, that Yuzu actually had been raped.'

Startled, Tsukuru looked at her. 'By who?'

Eri shook her head again. 'I don't know. But someone had forced her to have sex against her will. She was pregnant, after all. And she insisted that it was you who had raped her. She made it very clear that Tsukuru Tazaki was the one who did it. She described it all in depressingly realistic detail. So the rest of us had to accept what she said. Even though we knew in our hearts that you couldn't have done it.'

'She was pregnant?'

'Mmm. There was no doubt about it. I went to the gynecologist's with her. We went to someone far away. Not to her father's clinic, of course.'

Tsukuru sighed. 'And then?'

'All sorts of things happened, and then at the end of the summer, she miscarried. And that was it. It wasn't a phantom pregnancy. She *really* was pregnant, and *really did* have a miscarriage. I guarantee it.'

'Since she miscarried, you mean . . .'

'Yes, she planned to have the baby and raise it herself. She never considered having an abortion. She could never kill a living thing, no matter what the situation. You remember how she was, don't you? She always hated it that her father performed abortions. We often argued about it.'

'Did anyone else know she was pregnant and that she had a miscarriage?'

'I knew. And so did Yuzu's older sister. She was the type who could keep a secret. She got some money together for Yuzu. But that was it – there was nobody else. Her parents didn't know, and neither did Aka or Ao. This was our secret, just the three of us. But I think it's okay, now, to reveal it. Especially to you.'

'And Yuzu kept insisting I was the one who'd gotten her pregnant?'

'She was very insistent about that, yes.'

Tsukuru narrowed his eyes and stared at the coffee cup Eri was holding. 'But why? Why did she say I did it? I can't think of a single reason.'

'I really don't know,' Eri said. 'I can imagine a number of possibilities, none of which are very convincing. I just can't explain it. The only plausible reason I can think of is because I liked you. That might have triggered it.'

Tsukuru looked at her in surprise. '*You* liked me?'

'You didn't know that?'

'Of course not. I had no idea.'

Eri gave a wry smile. 'I guess it's okay to tell you now, but I always liked you. I was really attracted to you. Actually, I was in love with you. I always kept it secret, and never told anyone. I don't think Ao or Aka were aware of it. Yuzu knew, of course. Girls can never hide anything from each other.'

'I never knew,' Tsukuru said.

'That's because you were a moron,' Eri said, pressing an index

237

finger to her temple. 'We were together that long, and I tried sending out *signals*. If you'd had even half a brain, you would have picked up on them.'

Tsukuru pondered these *signals*, but couldn't come up with a thing.

'You remember how you used to tutor me in math after school?' Eri said. 'It made me so happy.'

'You never could grasp the principles of calculus,' Tsukuru said. He suddenly recalled how Eri's cheeks would blush sometimes. 'You're absolutely right. I'm a little slow on the uptake.'

Eri gave a tiny smile. 'About things like that you are. And besides, you were attracted to Yuzu.'

Tsukuru was about to say something, but Eri cut him off. 'No need to explain. You weren't the only one. Everybody was attracted to her. How could they not be? She was so fresh, so beautiful. Like Disney's Snow White. But not me. As long as I was with her, I was always a bit player, like the Seven Dwarves. But that was unavoidable. Yuzu and I had been best friends since junior high. I just had to adapt to that role.'

'Are you saying that Yuzu was jealous? Because you liked me?'

Eri shook her head. 'All I'm saying is that *maybe* that was one latent reason. I'm no psychoanalyst. At any rate, Yuzu insisted to the bitter end that you stole her virginity at your place in Tokyo. For her, this was the definitive version of the truth, and she never wavered. Even now I don't understand where that delusion came from, and why she clung to that distorted version of reality. I don't think anybody can ever explain it. But I do think that sometimes, a certain kind of dream can be even stronger than reality. That's the dream she had. Maybe that's what it was. Please understand, I did feel awful for you.'

238

'Was Yuzu ever attracted to me?'

'No, she wasn't,' Eri said tersely. 'Yuzu was never interested in anyone of the opposite sex.'

Tsukuru frowned. 'She was a lesbian?'

Eri shook her head again. 'No, that's not it. She didn't have those tendencies at all. I'm positive. It's just that Yuzu always had a strong aversion to anything sexual. A fear of sex, you might say. I don't know where those feelings came from. The two of us were very open with each other about almost everything, but we hardly ever talked about sex. I was up-front about sexual things myself, but whenever sex came up, Yuzu quickly changed the subject.'

'What happened to her after the miscarriage?' Tsukuru asked.

'She took a leave of absence from college. In her condition, there was no way she could be around other people. She told them she had health issues, and stayed holed up at home and never went out. Before long, she developed a severe eating disorder. She vomited up almost everything she ate, and gave herself enemas to get rid of the rest. If she'd gone on that way, I don't think she would have survived. I made her see a counsellor, and somehow she was able to get over the eating disorder. It took about a half a year. At one point it was so awful that she was down to under ninety pounds, and she looked like a ghost. But she pulled out of it and reached the point, barely, where she could cling to life. I went to see her almost every day, talking with her, encouraging her, doing whatever I could to keep her going. After a year away from college, she managed to return to school.'

'Why do you think she developed an eating disorder?'

'It's quite simple. She wanted to stop having periods,' Eri said.

239

'Extreme weight loss stops you from having periods. That's what she was hoping for. She didn't want to ever get pregnant again, and probably didn't want to be a woman anymore. She wanted, if possible, to have her womb removed.'

'Sounds pretty serious,' Tsukuru said.

'It was, *very* serious. That's why the only thing I could do was cut you off. I felt really bad for you, and believe me, I knew how cruelly I was treating you. For me it was especially hard not to be able to see you again. It's true. I felt like I was being ripped apart. Like I said before, I really liked you.'

Eri paused, gazing at her hands on the table as if gathering her feelings, and then she went on.

'But I had to help Yuzu recover. That had to be my highest priority. She had life-threatening issues she was dealing with, and she needed my help. So the only thing I could do was make you swim alone through the cold night sea. I knew you could do it. You were strong enough to make it.'

The two of them were silent for a time. The leaves on the trees outside rippled in the wind.

Tsukuru broke the silence. 'So Yuzu recovered and graduated from college. What happened after that?'

'She was still seeing a counselor once a week but was able to pretty much lead a normal life. At least she didn't look like a ghost anymore. But by then she was no longer the Yuzu we used to know.'

Eri took a breath, choosing her words.

'She had changed,' Eri finally said. 'It's like everything had drained out of her heart, like any interest in the outside world had disappeared. She no longer cared much about music. It was painful to see. She still enjoyed teaching music to children, though – that passion never left her. Even when her condition was at its worst, when she was so weak she could barely stand up, she managed to drag herself once a week to the church school where she taught piano to kids. She kept on doing that volunteer work alone. I think the desire to continue that project was what helped her recover. If she hadn't had that work, she might never have made it.'

Eri turned around and gazed out the window at the sky above the trees. She faced forward again and looked directly at Tsukuru. The sky was still covered with a thin layer of clouds.

'By this time, though, Yuzu didn't have that sense of unconditional friendship toward me that she'd had when we were younger. She said she was grateful to me, for everything I'd done for her. And I think she really was. But at the same time, she'd *lost any interest in me.* Like I said, Yuzu had lost interest in *almost everything.* And I was part of this almost everything. It was painful to admit. We'd been best friends for so long, and I really cared about her. But that's the way it was. By then I wasn't indispensable to her anymore.'

Eri stared for a while at an imaginary spot above the table, and then spoke.

'Yuzu wasn't Snow White anymore. Or maybe she was too worn out to be Snow White. And I was a bit tired myself of being the Seven Dwarves.'

Eri half unconsciously picked up her coffee cup, then returned it to the table.

'At any rate, by then our wonderful group – the group of four, minus you – couldn't function the way it had in the past. Everyone had graduated from school and was busy with their own lives. It's an obvious thing to say, but we weren't high school kids anymore. And needless to say, cutting you off left behind emotional scars in all of us. Scars that weren't superficial.'

Tsukuru was silent, listening intently to her words.

'You were gone, but you were always there,' Eri said.

Once more, a short silence.

'Eri, I want to know more about you,' Tsukuru said. 'What brought you to where you are now – that's what I'd first like to know.'

Eri narrowed her eyes and tilted her head slightly. 'From my late teens until my early twenties, Yuzu had me totally under her sway. One day I looked around me and realized I was fading. I'd been hoping to get work as a writer. I always enjoyed writing. I wanted to write novels, poems, things of that nature. You knew about that, right?'

Tsukuru nodded. Eri had carried around a thick notebook, always jotting down ideas when the urge came over her.

'But in college I couldn't manage that. Taking care of Yuzu constantly, it was all I could do to keep up with my schoolwork. I had two boyfriends in college but not much came of it – I was too busy spending time with Yuzu to go on dates very often. Nothing worked out for me. One day I just stopped and asked myself: What in the world are you doing with your life? I had no goals anymore and I was just spinning my wheels, watching my self-confidence disappear. I know things were hard for Yuzu, but you have to understand that they were hard for me, too.'

Eri's eyes narrowed again, as if she were gazing at some distant scene.

'A friend from college asked me to go to a pottery class and I went along, kind of as a lark. And that's where I discovered what I'd been searching for, after so long. Spinning the potter's wheel, I felt like I could be totally honest with myself. Focusing on creating something helped me to forget everything else. From that day on, I've been totally absorbed in pottery. In college it was still just a hobby, but after that, I wanted to become a full-fledged potter. I graduated from college, worked part-time jobs for a year while I studied, then reentered school, this time in the industrial arts department. Goodbye novels, hello pottery. While I was working on my pottery, I met Edvard, who was in Japan as an exchange student. Eventually we got married and moved here. Life is a total surprise sometimes. If my friend hadn't invited me to the pottery class, I'd be living a completely different life now.'

'You really seem to have a talent for it,' Tsukuru said, pointing to the pottery on the shelves. 'I don't know much about pottery, but I get a wonderful feeling when I look at your pieces, and hold them.'

Eri smiled. 'I don't know about talent. But my work sells pretty well here. It doesn't bring in much money, but I'm really happy that other people need what I create.'

'I know what you mean,' Tsukuru said, 'since I make things myself. Very different things from yours, though.'

'As different as stations and plates.'

'We need both in our lives.'

'Of course,' Eri said. She thought about something. The smile gradually faded from her lips. 'I like it here. I imagine I'll stay here for the rest of my life.'

'You won't go back to Japan?'

'I've taken Finnish citizenship now, and have gotten a lot better at speaking the language. The winters are hard to get through, I'll admit that, but then it gives me more time to read.

Maybe I'll find I want to write again. The children are used to Finland now and have friends here. And Edvard is a good man. His family's good to us, too, and my work is going well.'

'And you're needed here.'

Eri raised her head and looked fixedly at Tsukuru.

'It was when I heard that Yuzu had been murdered by somebody that I decided I could stay here the rest of my life. Ao called and told me. I was pregnant with my older girl then and couldn't attend the funeral. It was a terrible thing for me. I felt like my chest was about to be ripped apart. Knowing that Yuzu had been killed like that, in some unknown place, and that she'd been cremated and was nothing more than ash. Knowing that I'd never see her again. I made up my mind then and there that if I had a girl, I'd name her Yuzu. And that I'd never go back to Japan.'

'So your daughter's name is Yuzu?'

'Yuzu Kurono Haatainen,' she said. 'A part of Yuzu lives on, in that name, at least.'

'But why did Yuzu go off by herself to Hamamatsu?'

'She went there soon after I moved to Finland. I don't know why. We wrote letters to each other regularly, but she didn't tell me anything about the reasons behind her move. She simply said it was because of work. But there were any number of jobs she could have had in Nagoya, and for her to move to some place she'd never been before, and live all alone, was the same as committing suicide.'

Yuzu was found inside her apartment in Hamamatsu, strangled to death with a cloth belt. Tsukuru had read the details in old newspapers and magazines. He'd searched online, too, to find out more about the case.

Robbery wasn't involved. Her purse, with cash still in it, was found nearby. And there were no signs she'd been assaulted. Nothing was disturbed in her apartment, and there were no signs of a struggle. Residents on the same floor had heard no suspicious sounds. There were a couple of menthol cigarette butts in an ashtray, but these turned out to be Yuzu's. (Tsukuru had frowned at this. Yuzu smoked?) The estimated time of death was between 10 p.m. and midnight, a night when it rained till dawn, a cold rain for a May night. Her body was discovered in the evening, three days later. She'd lain there, for three days, on the faux tile flooring of her kitchen.

They never discovered the motive for the murder. Someone had come late at night, strangled her without making a sound, not stolen or disturbed anything else, and then left. The door locked automatically. It was unclear whether she had opened it from the inside or if the murderer had a duplicate key. She lived alone in the apartment. Coworkers and neighbors said she didn't seem to have any close friends. Except for her older sister and mother, who occasionally visited from Nagoya, she was always alone. She wore simple clothes and struck everyone who knew her as rather meek and quiet. She was enthusiastic about her job, and was well liked by her students, but outside of work, she seemed to have no friends.

No one had any idea what had led to her death, why she had ended up strangled. The police investigation petered out without any suspects coming to light. Articles about the case grew steadily shorter, and finally vanished altogether. It was a sad, painful case. Like cold rain falling steadily until dawn.

'An evil spirit possessed her,' Eri said softly, as if revealing a secret. 'It clung to her, breathing coldly on her neck, slowly driving her in a corner. That's the only thing that can explain all that happened to her. What happened with you, her eating disorder, what happened in Hamamatsu. I never actually wanted to put it into words. It's like, if I did, it would really exist. So I kept it to myself all this time. I decided to never talk about it, until the day I died. But I don't mind telling you this now, since we'll probably never see each other again. And you need to know this. It was an evil spirit – or something close to it. In the end, Yuzu couldn't escape.'

Eri sighed deeply and stared at her hands on the table. Her hands were visibly shaking, rather severely. Tsukuru turned his gaze away and looked out the window, past the fluttering curtain. The silence that settled on the room was oppressive, full of a deep sadness. Unspoken feelings were as heavy and lonely as the ancient glacier that had carved out the deep lake.

'Do you remember Liszt's *Years of Pilgrimage*? Yuzu used to play one of the pieces a lot,' Tsukuru said after a time to break the silence.

'"Le mal du pays." I remember it well,' Eri said. 'I listen to it sometimes. Would you like to hear it?'

Tsukuru nodded.

Eri stood up, went over to the small stereo set in the cabinet, selected a CD from the pile of discs, and inserted it into the player. 'Le mal du pays' filtered out from the speakers, the simple opening melody, softly played with one hand. Eri sat back down across from him, and the two of them silently listened to the music.

Listening to the music here, next to a lake in Finland, it had a different sort of charm from when he heard it back in his apartment in Tokyo. But no matter where he listened to it, regardless of whether he heard it on a CD or an old LP, the music remained the same, utterly engaging and beautiful. Tsukuru pictured Yuzu at the piano in her parlor, playing the piece, leaning over the keyboard, eyes closed, lips slightly open, searching for words that don't make a sound. She was apart from herself then, in some other place.

The piece ended, there was a pause, then the next piece began. 'The Bells of Geneva.' Eri touched the remote control and lowered the volume.

'It strikes me as different from the performance I always listen to at home,' Tsukuru said.

'Which pianist do you listen to?'

'Lazar Berman.'

Eri shook her head. 'I've never heard his version.'

'It's a little more elegant than this one. I like this performance, it's wonderful, but the style of this version makes it sound more like a Beethoven sonata than Liszt.'

Eri smiled. 'That would be because it's Alfred Brendel. Maybe it's not so elegant, but I like it all the same. I guess I'm used to this version, since it's the one I always listen to.'

'Yuzu played this piece so beautifully. She put so much feeling into it.'

'She really did. She was very good at pieces this length. In longer pieces she sort of ran out of energy halfway through. But everyone has their own special qualities. I always feel like a part of Yuzu lives on in this music. It's so vibrant, so luminous.'

When Yuzu was teaching the children at the school, Tsukuru and Ao usually played soccer with the boys in the small playground outside. They divided into two teams and tried to shoot the ball into the opposite goal (which was usually constructed from a couple of cardboard boxes). As he passed the ball, Tsukuru would half listen to the sound of children playing scales that filtered out the window.

The past became a long, razor-sharp skewer that stabbed right through his heart. Silent silver pain shot through him, transforming his spine to a pillar of ice. The pain remained, unabated. He held his breath, shut his eyes tight, enduring the agony. Alfred Brendel's graceful playing continued. The CD shifted to the second suite, 'Second Year: Italy.'

And in that moment, he was finally able to accept it all. In the deepest recesses of his soul, Tsukuru Tazaki understood. One heart is not connected to another through harmony alone. They are, instead, linked deeply through their wounds. Pain linked to pain, fragility to fragility. There is no silence without a cry of grief, no forgiveness without bloodshed, no acceptance without a passage through acute loss. That is what lies at the root of true harmony.

'Tsukuru, it's true. She lives on in so many ways.' Eri's voice, from the other side of the table, was husky, as if forced from her. 'I can feel it. In all the echoes that surround us, in the light, in shapes, in every single . . .'

Eri covered her face with her hands. No other words came. Tsukuru wasn't sure if she was crying or not. If she was, she did so silently.

While Ao and Tsukuru played soccer, Eri and Aka did their best to keep the other children from interrupting Yuzu's piano lessons. They did whatever they could to occupy the kids – they read books, played games, went outside, and sang songs. Most of the time, though, these attempts failed. The children never tired of trying to disrupt the piano lessons. They found this much more interesting than anything else. Eri and Aka's fruitless struggle to divert them was fun to watch.

Almost without thinking, Tsukuru stood up and went around to the opposite side of the table. Without a word he laid his hand on Eri's shoulder. She still had her face in her hands. As he touched her, he felt her trembling, a trembling the eye couldn't detect.

'Tsukuru?' Eri's voice leaked out from between her fingers. 'Could you do something for me?'

'Of course,' Tsukuru said.

'Could you hold me?'

Tsukuru asked her to stand up, then drew her to him. Her full breasts lay tightly against his chest, as if testimony to something. Her hands were warm where she held his back, her cheek soft and wet as it pressed against his neck.

'I don't think I'll ever go back to Japan again,' Eri murmured. Her warm, damp breath brushed his ear. 'Everything I see would remind me of Yuzu. And of our—'

Tsukuru said nothing, only continued to hold her tightly against him.

Their embrace would be visible through the open window. Someone might pass by and see them. Edvard and his children might be back at any moment. But that didn't matter. They didn't care what others thought. He and Eri had to hold each other now, as much as they wanted. They had to let their skin touch, and drive away the long shadow cast by evil spirits. This was, no doubt, why he'd come here in the first place.

They held each other for a long time – how long he couldn't say. The white curtain at the window went on flapping in the breeze that came from across the lake. Eri's cheeks stayed wet, and Alfred Brendel went on playing the 'Second Year: Italy' suite. 'Petrarch's Sonnet 47,' then 'Petrarch's Sonnet 104.' Tsukuru knew every note. He could have hummed it all if he'd wanted to. For the first time he understood how deeply he'd listened to this music, and how much it meant to him.

They didn't speak. Words were powerless now. Like a pair of dancers who had stopped mid-step, they simply held each other quietly, giving themselves up to the flow of time. Time that encompassed both past and present, and even a portion of the future. Nothing came between their two bodies, as her warm breath brushed his neck. Tsukuru shut his eyes, letting the music wash over him as he listened to Eri's heartbeat. The beating of her heart kept time with the slap of the little boat against the pier.

17.

They sat back down again, across from each other at the table, and took turns opening up about what was in their hearts. Things they had not put into words for ages, things they'd been holding back deep in their souls. Removing the lids on their hearts, pulling open the doors of memory, revealing honest feelings, as the other, all the while, listened quietly.

Eri spoke first.

'In the end I abandoned Yuzu. I had to get away from her. I wanted to get as far away as I could from whatever it was that possessed her. That's why I got into pottery, married Edvard, and moved to Finland. I didn't plan it, of course, it just turned out that way. I did sort of have the feeling that doing so meant I'd never have to take care of Yuzu again. I loved her more than I loved anyone – she was like another self – so I wanted to help her as much as I could. But I was exhausted. Taking care of her for so long had completely worn me out. And no matter how much I tried to help her, I couldn't stop her retreat from reality. It was awful for me. If I'd stayed in Nagoya, I think my mind would have started to go, too. I don't know, maybe I'm just making excuses?'

'You're just saying how you felt. That's different from making excuses.'

Eri bit her lip. 'But the fact remains that I abandoned her. And Yuzu went by herself to Hamamatsu and was murdered. She had the most slender, lovely neck, do you remember? Like a pretty bird, the kind of neck that could snap so easily. If I'd been in Japan that probably would never have happened to her. I would never have let her go off to some town she didn't know, all by herself.'

'Perhaps. But even if it hadn't been then, the same thing might have happened later, in some other place. You weren't Yuzu's guardian. You couldn't keep watch over her every second of every day. You had your own life. There's only so much you could have done.'

Eri shook her head. 'I told myself that, I don't know how many times. But it didn't help. A part of me wanted to get far away from her, to protect myself. I can't deny that. Apart from the question of her being saved or not, I had to deal with my own conflict. And in the process, I lost you, too. In giving priority to the problems Yuzu had, I had to abandon Tsukuru Tazaki, who had done nothing wrong. I wounded you deeply, all because it suited the situation as I saw it. Even though I loved you so much . . .'

Tsukuru didn't say a word.

'But that's not the whole story,' Eri said.

'No?'

'Truthfully, I didn't abandon you just because of Yuzu. That's a superficial justification. I did it because I'm a coward. I didn't have any confidence in myself as a woman. I was sure that no matter how much I loved you, you would never reciprocate. I was sure you were in love with Yuzu. That's why I was able to cut you off so cruelly. I did it to sever my feelings for you.

If I had only had a little more confidence and courage, and no stupid pride, I never would have abandoned you like that, no matter what the circumstances. But something was wrong with me back then. I know I did something terrible. And I am truly sorry for it.'

Silence descended on them.

'I should have apologized to you a long time ago,' Eri finally said. 'I know that very well. But I just couldn't. I was too ashamed of myself.'

'You don't need to worry about me anymore,' Tsukuru said. 'I survived the crisis. Swam through the night sea on my own. Each of us did what we had to do, in order to survive. I get the feeling that, even if we had made different decisions then, even if we had chosen to do things differently, we might have still ended up pretty much where we are now.'

Eri bit her lip and considered this. 'Will you tell me one thing?' she said after a while.

'Name it.'

'If I had come right out then and told you I loved you, would you have gone out with me?'

'Even if you'd said that right to my face, I probably wouldn't have believed it,' Tsukuru said.

'Why not?'

'I couldn't imagine anyone saying they loved me, or wanting to be my girlfriend.'

'But you were kind, cool, and calm, and you'd already figured out your path in life. Plus you were good-looking.'

Tsukuru shook his head. 'I have a really boring face. I've never liked my looks.'

Eri smiled. 'Maybe you're right. Maybe you really do have a

253

very boring face and something was wrong with me. But at least for a silly sixteen-year-old girl, you were handsome enough. I dreamed about how wonderful it would be to have a boyfriend like you.'

'Can't claim to have much of a personality either.'

'Everyone alive has a personality. It's just more obvious with some people than with others.' Eri's eyes narrowed and she looked straight at him. 'So, tell me – how would you have replied? Would you have let me be your girlfriend?'

'Of course I would have,' Tsukuru said. 'I really liked you. I was really attracted to you, in a different way from how I was attracted to Yuzu. If you had told me then how you felt, of course I would have loved for you to be my girlfriend. And I think we would have been happy together.'

The two of them would have likely been a close couple, with a fulfilling love life, Tsukuru decided. There would have been so much they could have shared. On the surface, their personalities seemed so different – Tsukuru introverted and reticent, Eri sociable and talkative – yet they shared a desire to create and build things with their own hands, things that were meaningful. Tsukuru had the feeling, though, that this closeness would have been short-lived. An unavoidable fissure would have grown between what he and Eri wanted from their lives. They were still in their teens then, still discovering their own paths, and eventually they would have reached a fork and gone off in separate directions. Without fighting, without hurting each other, naturally, calmly. And it did turn out that way, didn't it, Tsukuru thought, with him going to Tokyo and building stations, and Eri marrying Edvard and moving to Finland.

It wouldn't have been strange if things had worked out that

way. It was entirely possible. And the experience would never have been a negative one for either of them. Even if they were no longer lovers, they would have remained good friends. *In reality*, though, none of this ever happened. In reality something very different happened. And that fact was more significant now than anything else.

'Even if you're not telling the truth, I'm happy you would say that,' Eri said.

'I am *too* telling the truth,' Tsukuru said. 'I wouldn't joke about something like that. I think we would have had a wonderful time together. And I'm sorry it never happened. I really am.'

Eri smiled, with no trace of sarcasm.

Tsukuru remembered the erotic dream he often had of the two girls. How they were always together, but how it was always Yuzu whose body he came inside. Not once did he ejaculate inside Eri. He wasn't sure of the significance, but he did know he couldn't tell Eri about it. No matter how honestly you open up to someone, there are still things you cannot reveal.

When he thought about those dreams, and Yuzu's insistence that he had raped her (and her insistence that she was carrying his baby), he found he couldn't totally dismiss it out of hand as some made-up story, or say that he had no idea what she was talking about. It might have all been a dream, but he still couldn't escape the feeling that, in some indefinable way, he was responsible. And not just for the rape, but for her murder. On that rainy May night something inside of him, unknown to him, may have slipped away to Hamamatsu and strangled that thin, lovely, fragile neck.

He could see himself knocking on the door of her apartment. 'Can you let me in?' he says, in this vision. 'I have something I need to say.' He's wearing a wet black raincoat, the smell of heavy night rain hovering about him.

'Tsukuru?' Yuzu asks.

'There's something I need to talk with you about,' he says. 'It's very important. That's why I came to Hamamatsu. It won't take long. Please open the door.' He keeps on addressing the closed door. 'I'm sorry about showing up like this, without calling. But if I had contacted you beforehand, you probably wouldn't have seen me.'

Yuzu hesitates, then quietly slips the chain off the lock. His right hand tightly grips the belt inside his pocket.

Tsukuru grimaced. Why did he have to imagine this horrid scene? And why did *he* have to be the one who strangled her?

There were no reasons at all why he would have done that, of course. Tsukuru had never wanted to kill anyone, ever. But maybe he *had* tried to kill Yuzu, in a purely symbolic way. Tsukuru himself had no idea what deep darkness lay hidden in his heart. What he did know was that inside Yuzu, too, lay a deep, inner darkness, and that somewhere, on some subterranean level, her darkness and his may have connected. And being strangled was, perhaps, *exactly* what Yuzu had wanted. In the mingled darkness between them, perhaps he had sensed that desire.

'You're thinking about Yuzu?' Eri asked.

'I've always thought of myself as a victim,' Tsukuru said. 'Forced, for no reason, to suffer cruelly. Deeply wounded emotionally, my life thrown off course. Truthfully, sometimes I hated the four of you, wondering why I was the only one who had to go through that awful experience. But maybe that wasn't the case. Maybe I wasn't simply a victim, but had hurt those around me, too, without realizing it. And wounded myself again in the counterattack.'

Eri gazed at him without a word.

'And maybe I murdered Yuzu,' Tsukuru said honestly. 'Maybe the one who knocked on her door that night was *me*.'

'In a certain sense,' Eri said.

Tsukuru nodded.

'I murdered Yuzu too,' Eri said. 'In a sense.' She looked off to one side. 'Maybe *I* was the one who knocked on her door that night.'

Tsukuru looked at her nicely tanned profile. He'd always liked her slightly upturned nose.

'Each of us has to live with that burden,' Eri said.

The wind had died down for the moment and now the white curtain at the window hung still. The boat had stopped rattling against the pier. The only thing he could hear was the calls of birds, singing a melody he'd never heard before.

Eri listened to the birds for a while, picked up the barrette, pinned her hair back again, and gently pressed her fingertips against her forehead. 'What do you think about the work Aka is doing?' she asked. Like a weight had been removed, the flow of time grew a fraction lighter.

'I don't know,' Tsukuru said. 'The world he lives in is so far removed from mine, it's hard for me to say whether it's good or bad.'

'I certainly don't like what he's doing. But that doesn't mean I can cut him off. He used to be one of my very best friends, and even now I still consider him a good friend. Though I haven't seen him in seven or eight years.'

She put her hand to her hair again. 'Every year Aka donates a large sum of money to that Catholic facility that supported the school where we volunteered. The people there are really grateful for what he does. The school's barely managing financially. But

257

nobody knows he's donating. He insists on remaining anony-mous. I'm probably the only person besides the people who run the school who knows he's donating so much. I found out about it just by chance. You know, Tsukuru, he's not a bad person. I want you to understand that. He just *pretends* to be bad, that's all. I don't know why. He probably has to.'

Tsukuru nodded.

'And the same holds true for Ao,' Eri said. 'He still has a very pure heart. It's just that it's hard to survive in the real world. They've both been more successful than most, in their different fields. They put in a lot of honest, hard work. What I'm trying to say is, it wasn't a waste for us to have been us – the way we were together, as a group. I really believe that. Even if it was only for a few short years.'

Eri held her face in her hands again. She was silent for a time, then looked up and continued.

'We survived. You and I. And those who survive have a duty. Our duty is to do our best to keep on living. Even if our lives are not perfect.'

'The most I can do is keep building railroad stations.'

'That's fine. That's what you should keep doing. I'm sure you build very wonderful, safe stations that people enjoy using.'

'I hope so,' Tsukuru said. 'We're not supposed to do this, but when I'm overseeing construction for one section of a station, I always put my name on it. I write it in the wet concrete with a nail. *Tsukuru Tazaki*. Where you can't see it from the outside.'

Eri laughed. 'So even after you're gone, your wonderful stations remain. Just like me putting my initials on the back of my plates.'

—

258

Tsukuru raised his head and looked at Eri. 'Is it okay if I talk about my girlfriend?'

'Of course,' Eri said. A charming smile rose to her lips. 'I'd love to hear all about this wise, older girlfriend of yours.'

Tsukuru told her about Sara. How he had found her strangely attractive from the first time he saw her, and how they made love on their third date. How she had wanted to know everything about the group of friends he'd had in Nagoya. How when he saw her the last time, he'd been impotent. Tsukuru told Eri about it all, hiding nothing. About how Sara had pushed him to visit his former friends in Nagoya and to travel to Finland. She'd told him that unless he did so, he'd never overcome the emotional baggage he still carried. Tsukuru felt he loved Sara. And he thought he would like to marry her. This was probably the first time he'd ever felt such strong emotions about someone. But she seemed to have an older boyfriend. When he saw her walking with him on the street she had looked so happy, so content, and he wasn't sure he could ever make her that happy.

Eri listened intently, and didn't interrupt. Finally, she spoke.

'You know, Tsukuru, you need to hang on to her. No matter what. I really believe that. If you let her go now, you might not ever have anyone else in your life.'

'But I don't have any confidence.'

'Why not?'

'Because I have no sense of self. I have no personality, no brilliant color. I have nothing to offer. That's always been my problem. I feel like an empty vessel. I have a shape, I guess, as a container, but there's nothing inside. I just can't see myself as the right person for her. I think that the more time passes, and the more she knows about me, the more disappointed Sara will be, and the more she'll choose to distance herself from me.'

'You need to have courage, and be confident in yourself. I mean – I used to love you, right? At one time I would have given myself to you. I would have done whatever you wanted me to do. An actual, hot-blooded woman felt that strongly about you once. That's how valuable you are. You're not empty – not at all.'

'I appreciate you saying that,' Tsukuru said. 'I really do. But that was then. What about *now*? I'm thirty-six, but when I think about who I am, I'm as confused – or maybe *more* confused – than I've ever been. I can't figure out what I should do. I've never felt this strongly about anybody before.'

'Let's say you *are* an empty vessel. So what? What's wrong with that?' Eri said. 'You're still a wonderful, attractive vessel. And really, does *anybody* know who they are? So why not be a completely beautiful vessel? The kind people feel good about, the kind people want to entrust with precious belongings.'

Tsukuru understood what she was getting at. But whether or not this applied to him was another question.

'When you get back to Tokyo,' Eri said, 'tell her everything. Being open and honest is always the best way to go. But don't tell her you saw her with that other man. Keep that to yourself. There are some things women don't want other people to see. Besides that, tell her everything you're feeling.'

'I'm scared, Eri. If I do something wrong, or say something wrong, I'm scared it will wreck everything and our relationship will vanish forever.'

Eri slowly shook her head. 'It's no different from building stations. If something is important enough, a little mistake isn't going to ruin it all, or make it vanish. It might not be perfect, but the first step is actually building the station. Right? Other-wise trains won't stop there. And you can't meet the person who means so much to you. If you find some defect, you can adjust it later, as needed. First things first. Build the station. A special station just for her. The kind of station where trains want to stop, even if they have no reason to do so. Imagine that kind of station, and give it actual color and shape. Write your name on the foundation with a nail, and breathe life into it. I know you have the power to do that. Don't forget – you're the one who swam across the freezing sea at night.'

Eri asked him to stay for dinner.

'They catch big, fresh trout around here. We just fry them up with herbs in a frying pan, but they taste wonderful. We'd love to have you stay and eat with us.'

'Thank you, but I'd better be getting back. I want to get to Helsinki while it's still light out.'

Eri laughed. 'Still light out? This is summer in Finland. It's light out almost the whole night.'

'I know, but still,' Tsukuru averred.

Eri understood how he felt.

'Thank you for coming all this way to see me,' she said. 'I can't tell you how happy I am that we could talk like this. I really feel like a great burden has been lifted, something that's been weighing me down forever. I'm not saying this solves everything, but it's been a huge relief.'

'I feel the same way,' Tsukuru said. 'Talking with you has helped a lot. And I'm happy I could meet your husband and daughters, and see what sort of life you're living here. That alone made the trip worthwhile.'

They left the cabin and walked over to where his Volkswagen Golf was parked. Slowly, deliberately, as if weighing the significance of each step. They hugged each other once more, and this time, she didn't cry. He felt her gentle smile on his neck, her full breasts pressed against him, filled with the vitality to keep on living. Her fingers against his back were strong and real.

Tsukuru suddenly remembered the presents he'd brought from Japan for her and the children. He took them out from his shoulder bag in the car and handed them to her, a boxwood barrette for Eri and Japanese picture books for the children.

'Thank you, Tsukuru,' Eri said. 'You haven't changed at all. You were always so kind.'

'It's nothing,' Tsukuru said. And he remembered the evening when he bought the presents, seeing Sara walking down Omotesando with that other man. If he hadn't thought to buy the presents, he wouldn't have witnessed that scene. It was a strange thing.

'Farewell, Tsukuru Tazaki. Have a safe trip home,' Eri said as they said goodbye. 'Don't let the bad elves get you.'

'Bad elves?'

Eri's eyes narrowed, her lips curling mischievously like in the old days. 'It's a saying we use a lot here. Don't let the bad elves get you. So many creatures have lived in these forests since olden times.'

'Understood,' Tsukuru laughed. 'I'll keep an eye out for them.'

'If you get a chance,' Eris said, 'let Ao and Aka know that I'm doing well here.'

'I will.'

'I think you should go see them sometimes. Or get together, all three of you. For your sake. And for theirs.'

'I agree. That might be a good idea,' Tsukuru said.

'It'd be good for me, too,' Eri said. 'Even though I can't be with you.'

Tsukuru nodded. 'Once things settle down, I'll make sure to do that. For your sake, too.'

'But it's strange, isn't it?' Eri said.

'What is?'

'That amazing time in our lives is gone, and will never return. All the beautiful possibilities we had then have been swallowed up in the flow of time.'

Tsukuru nodded silently. He thought he should say something, but no words came.

'Winter here is really long,' Eri said, gazing out at the lake, sounding as if she were addressing herself far away. 'The nights are so long and it seems never-ending. Everything freezes solid, like spring will never come. All sorts of dark thoughts come to me. No matter how much I try to avoid them.'

Still no words came to him. Tsukuru silently followed her gaze to the surface of the lake. It was only later, after he boarded the direct flight back to Narita and had buckled his seat belt, that the words came, the words he should have said. The right words always seemed to come too late.

He turned the key and started the engine. The four-cylinder Golf engine awoke from its short sleep and slowly found its rhythm.

'Goodbye,' Eri said. 'Be well. And make sure you hang on to Sara. You really need her.'

'I'll try.'

'Tsukuru, there's one thing I want you to remember. You aren't colorless. Those were just names. I know we often teased you about it, but it was just a stupid joke. Tsukuru Tazaki is a wonderful, colorful person. A person who builds fantastic stations. A healthy thirty-six-year-old citizen, a voter, a taxpayer – someone who could fly all the way to Finland just to see me. You don't lack anything. Be confident and be bold. That's all you need. Never let fear and stupid pride make you lose someone who's precious to you.'

He put the car into drive and stepped on the gas. He stuck a hand out the open window and waved. Eri waved back. She kept on waving, her hand held high.

Finally she disappeared in the trees. All he saw in the rearview mirror now was the deep green of a Finnish summer. The wind seemed to have picked up again, and small waves rippled on the surface of the lake. A tall young man in a kayak appeared on the water, slowly and silently slipping through the water like some gigantic whirligig.

I'll probably never be back here again, Tsukuru thought. And never see Eri again. We each have our paths to follow, in our places. Like Ao said, *There's no going back*. Sorrow surged then, silently, like water inside him. A formless, transparent sorrow. A sorrow he could touch, yet something that was also far away, out of reach. Pain struck him, as if gouging out his chest, and he could barely breathe.

When he reached the paved road, he steered the car to the side, switched off the engine, leaned against the steering wheel, and closed his eyes. His heart was racing and he took slow, deep breaths. And as he inhaled, he suddenly noticed a cold, hard object near the center of his body – like a hard core of earth

264

that remains frozen all year long. This was the source of the pain in his chest, and the difficulty breathing. He had never known, until this moment, that such a thing existed inside him.

Yet it was this pain, and this sense of being choked, that he needed. It was exactly what he had to acknowledge, what he had to confront. From now on, he had to make that cold core melt, bit by bit. It might take time, but it was what he had to do. But his own body heat wasn't enough to melt that frozen soil. He needed someone else's warmth.

First he had to get back to Tokyo. That was the first step. He turned the key and started the engine again.

On the road to Helsinki, Tsukuru prayed that Eri wouldn't be caught by any bad elves of the forest. All he could do at this point was pray.

18.

Tsukuru spent the remaining two days of his trip wandering the streets of Helsinki. It rained occasionally, just a light sprinkle that didn't bother him. As he walked, he thought of many things. There was much he needed to consider, and he wanted to gather his thoughts before he returned to Tokyo. When he got tired of walking, or of thinking, he'd stop by a café and have a coffee and a sandwich. He got lost, not knowing where he was, but that didn't bother him either. Helsinki wasn't a huge city, and streetcars ran everywhere. And for him right now, losing sight of where he actually was felt good. On his last afternoon in the city he went to Helsinki Central Station, sat on a bench, and watched the trains come and go.

From the station he called Olga on his cell phone to thank her. I found the Haatainens' house all right, he told her, and my friend was definitely surprised to see me. And Hämeenlinna was a beautiful town. That's great, Olga replied. Wonderful. She seemed genuinely happy for him. I'd like to take you out to dinner to thank you, he said. I appreciate the invitation, Olga said, but today is my mother's birthday and I'm having dinner with my parents at home. But please be sure to tell Sara hello from me. I will, Tsukuru replied. And thank you for everything.

In the evening he had seafood and half a glass of chilled Chablis at a restaurant that Olga had recommended near the harbor. As he sat there, he thought about the Haatainens. Right now the four of them must be seated around their table. Was the wind still blowing on the lake? And what was Eri thinking about, at this very moment? The warmth of her breath still grazed his ear.

He arrived back in Tokyo on a Saturday morning. He unpacked, took a leisurely bath, and spent the rest of the day busy with random tasks. As soon as he got back, he thought of calling Sara, and had actually picked up the phone and dialed her number. But then he put the phone down. He needed more time to think. It had been a short trip, but so many things had happened. It still felt unreal to be back in the middle of Tokyo. It felt like just a short time ago he'd been beside the lake in Hämeenlinna, listening to the transparent sound of the wind. No matter what he said to Sara, he needed to choose his words carefully.

He did the laundry, glanced through the newspapers that had piled up, then went out before evening to shop for food, though he had no appetite. Probably because of jet lag, he got terribly sleepy while it was still light out, lay down in bed at eight thirty, and fell asleep, only to wake up before midnight. He tried reading the book he'd started on the plane, but his mind was still a blur, so he got up and cleaned the apartment. Just before dawn, he returned to bed, and when he awoke it was almost noon on Sunday. It looked like it was going to be a hot day. He switched on the AC, made coffee, and had a cup with a slice of toast and melted cheese.

After he took a shower, he phoned Sara's home. The phone

went to voicemail. *Please leave a message after the beep,* the message said. He hesitated, then hung up without saying anything. The clock on the wall showed that it was just after one. He was about to call her cell phone, but thought better of it.

She might be having lunch on her day off with her boyfriend. It was a little early for them to be making love. Tsukuru recalled the man he'd seen her with, walking down Omotesando hand in hand. He couldn't wipe the picture from his mind. He lay down on the sofa, images buzzing through his head, when suddenly it felt as if a sharp needle had stabbed him in the back. A thin, invisible needle. The pain was minimal, and there was no blood. Probably. Still, it hurt.

He pedaled his bike to the gym and swam his usual distance in the pool. His body remained oddly numb, and as he swam he felt like he fell asleep a couple of times. Of course no one can swim and sleep at the same time. It just seemed that way. Even so, as he swam, his body moved on autopilot, and he was able to finish without any further thoughts of Sara, or of that man, going through his mind. For that, he was thankful.

He came home from the pool and took a thirty-minute nap. It was a deep, dreamless sleep, his consciousness switching off as soon as his head hit the pillow. Afterward he ironed a few shirts and handkerchiefs and made dinner. He grilled salmon with herbs in the oven, drizzled lemon over it, and ate it with potato salad. Tofu and scallion miso soup rounded out the meal. He had half a cold beer and watched the news on TV. Then he lay down on the sofa and read.

It was just before 9 p.m. when Sara phoned.

'How's the jet lag?' she asked.

'My sleep cycle's messed up, but otherwise I feel fine,' Tsukuru said.

'Can you talk now? Or are you sleepy?'

'I'm sleepy, but I can hold out another hour before I go to bed. I have to go to work tomorrow and can't very well take a nap at the office.'

'That's good,' Sara said. 'Someone called my home around one this afternoon. That was you, right? I keep forgetting to check my messages and just noticed I missed a call.'

'That was me.'

'I was out shopping in the neighborhood.'

'Um,' Tsukuru said.

'But you didn't leave a message.'

'I'm not very good at leaving phone messages. I get kind of nervous and don't know what to say.'

'You could have at least said your name.'

'You're right. I should have at least done that.'

She paused for a moment. 'I was quite worried about you, you know. Whether your trip went well. You should have left a short message.'

'I'm sorry. I know, I should have,' Tsukuru apologized. 'By the way, what did you do today?'

'I did the laundry and went shopping. Cooked, cleaned the kitchen and the bathroom. Sometimes I need that kind of quiet day off.' She fell silent for a while. 'So, were you able to take care of everything in Finland?'

'I got to see Kuro,' Tsukuru said. 'The two of us had a good long talk. Olga really helped me out.'

'I'm glad. She's a nice girl, isn't she?'

'She really is.' He told her about driving an hour and a half

269

out of Helsinki to a beautiful lakeside town to see Eri (or, Kuro). How she lived in a summer cottage there with her husband, her two young daughters, and a dog. How she and her husband made pottery in a small studio nearby.

'She looked happy,' Tsukuru said. 'Life in Finland seems to agree with her.' Except for some nights during the long dark winter – but he didn't say this.

'Was it worth going all the way to Finland?' Sara asked.

'I think so. There are some things you can only talk about face-to-face. It cleared up a lot of things for me. Not that I've found all the answers, but it was definitely worthwhile. On an emotional level, I mean.'

'That's wonderful. I'm very happy to hear it.'

A short silence followed. A suggestive silence, as if it were measuring the direction of the wind. Then Sara spoke.

'Your voice sounds different. Or am I just imagining things?'

'I don't know. Maybe it's because I'm tired. I've never been on a plane for that long before.'

'But there were no problems?'

'No, no real problems. There's so much I need to tell you, but once I start, I know it's going to take a long time. I'd like to see you soon and tell you the whole story, from start to finish.'

'That sounds good. Let's get together. Anyway, I'm glad your trip to Finland wasn't a waste of time.'

'Thank you for all your help. I really appreciate it.'

'You're quite welcome.'

Another short silence followed. Tsukuru listened carefully. The sense of something unspoken still hung in the air.

'There's something I'd like to ask you,' Tsukuru said, deciding to take the plunge. 'Maybe it would be better not to, but I think I should go with what I'm feeling.'

'Certainly, go ahead,' Sara said. 'It's best to go with your feelings. Ask me anything.'

'I can't find the right words, exactly, but I get the sense that – you're seeing someone else, besides me. It's been bothering me for a while.'

Sara didn't respond right away. 'You get that sense?' she finally asked. 'Are you saying that, for whatever reason, you get that *sort of feeling*?'

'That's right. For whatever reason, I do,' Tsukuru said. 'But like I've said before, I'm not the most intuitive person in the world. My brain's basically set up to make things, tangible things, like my name implies. My mind has a very straightforward structure. The complex workings of other people's minds are beyond me. Or even my own mind. I'm often totally wrong when it comes to subtle things like this, so I try to avoid thinking about anything too complex. But this has been weighing on me for a while. And I thought I should ask you, instead of pointlessly brooding over it.'

'I see,' Sara said.

'So, is there someone else?'

She was silent.

'Please understand,' Tsukuru said, 'if there is someone else, I'm not criticizing you. I should probably mind my own business. You have no obligation to me, and I have no right to demand anything of you. I simply want to know – whether what I'm feeling is wrong or not.'

Sara sighed. 'I'd prefer you didn't use words like "obligation" and "rights." Makes it sound like you're debating the revision of the constitution or something.'

'Okay,' Tsukuru said. 'I didn't put it well. Like I said, I'm a very simple person. And I don't think I can handle things while I feel this way.'

Sara was silent for a moment. He could clearly picture her, phone in hand, lips pursed tight.

Her voice was soft when she finally spoke. 'You're not a simple person. You just try to think you are.'

'Maybe, if you say so. I don't really know. But a simple life suits me best, I do know that. The thing is, I've been hurt in my relationships with others, hurt deeply, and I never want to go through that again.'

'I know,' Sara said. 'You've been honest with me, so I'd like to be honest with you. But can I have a little time before I respond?'

'How much time?'

'How about – three days? Today's Sunday, so I think I can talk on Wednesday. I can answer your question then. Are you free Wednesday night?'

'Wednesday night's open,' Tsukuru said. He didn't have to check his schedule. Once night fell, he seldom had plans.

'Let's have dinner together. We can discuss things then. Honestly. Does that sound good?'

'Sounds good,' Tsukuru said.

They hung up.

That night Tsukuru had a long, bizarre dream. He was seated at a piano, playing a sonata – a huge, brand-new grand piano, the white keys utterly white, the black keys utterly black. An oversized score lay open on the music stand. Beside him stood a woman, dressed in a tight, subdued black dress, swiftly turning the pages for him with her long pale fingers. Her timing was impeccable.

Her jet-black hair hung to her waist. Everything in the scene appeared in gradations of white and black. There were no other colors.

He had no idea who had composed the sonata. It was a lengthy piece, though, with a score as thick as a phone book. The pages were filled with notes, literally covered in black. It was a challenging composition, with a complex structure, and required a superior technique. And he had never seen it before. Still, he was able to sight-read it, instantly grasping the world expressed there, and transforming this vision into sound. Just like being able to visualize a complicated blueprint in 3D. He had this special ability. His ten practiced fingers raced over the keyboard like a whirlwind. It was a dazzling, invigorating experience – accurately decoding this enormous sea of ciphers more quickly than anyone else, and instantaneously giving them form and substance.

Absorbed in his playing, his body was pierced by a flash of inspiration, like a bolt of lightning on a summer afternoon. The music had an ambitious, virtuoso structure, but at the same time it was beautifully introspective. It honestly and delicately expressed, in a full, tangible way, what it meant to be alive. A crucial aspect of the world that could only be expressed through the medium of music. His spine tingled with the sheer joy and pride of performing this music himself.

Sadly, though, the people seated before him seemed to feel otherwise. They fidgeted in their seats, bored and irritated. He could hear the scraping of chairs, and people coughing. For some reason, they were oblivious to the music's value.

He was performing in the grand hall of a royal court. The floor was smooth marble, the ceiling vaulted, with a lovely skylight in the middle. The members of the audience – there must have been about fifty people – were seated on elegant chairs as they listened to the music. Well-dressed, refined, no doubt cultured individuals, but unfortunately they were unable to appreciate this marvelous music.

As time passed, the clamor they made grew louder, even more grating. There was no stopping it now, as it overwhelmed the music. By now even he could no longer hear the music he was playing. What he heard instead was a grotesquely amplified and exaggerated noise, the sounds of coughs and groans of discontent. Still, his eyes remained glued to the score, his fingers racing over the keyboard, as if he were possessed.

He had a sudden realization. The woman in black, turning the pages of the score for him, had six fingers. The sixth finger was about the same size as her little finger. He gasped, and felt a shudder run through his chest. He wanted to look up at the woman standing beside him. Who was she? Did he know her? But until that movement of the score was over, he couldn't spare a moment's glance away. Even if there wasn't a single person now who was still listening.

At this point Tsukuru awoke. The green numbers on his bedside clock read 2:35. His body was covered in sweat, his heart still beating out the dry cadence of time passing. He got up, tugged off his pajamas, wiped himself down with a towel, put on a new T-shirt and boxers, and sat down on the sofa in the living room. In the darkness, he thought about Sara. He agonized over every word he'd spoken to her earlier on the phone. He should never have said what he did.

He wanted to call her and take back everything that he'd said.

But he couldn't call anyone at nearly 3 a.m. And asking her to forget what he'd already said was all the more impossible. At this rate I might well lose her, he thought.

His thoughts turned to Eri. Eri Kurono Haatainen. The mother of two small girls. He pictured the blue lake beyond the stand of white birch trees, and the little boat slapping against the pier. The pottery with its lovely designs, the chirps of the birds, the dog barking. And Alfred Brendel's meticulous rendition of *Years of Pilgrimage*. The feel of Eri's breasts pressed against him. Her warm breath, her cheeks wet with tears. All the lost possibilities, all the time that was never to return.

At one point, seated across from each other at the table, they were silent, not even searching for words, their ears drawn to the sounds of the birds outside the window. The cries of the birds made for an unusual melody. The same melody pierced the woods, over and over.

'The parent birds are teaching their babies how to chirp,' Eri said. And she smiled. 'Until I came here I never knew that. That birds have to be taught how to chirp.'

Our lives are like a complex musical score, Tsukuru thought. Filled with all sorts of cryptic writing, sixteenth and thirty-second notes and other strange signs. It's next to impossible to correctly interpret these, and even if you could, and then could transpose them into the correct sounds, there's no guarantee that people would correctly understand, or appreciate, the meaning therein. No guarantee it would make people happy. Why must the workings of people's lives be so convoluted?

Make sure you hang on to Sara, Eri had told him. *You really need her. You don't lack anything. Be confident and be bold. That's all you need.*

And don't let the bad elves get you.

He thought of Sara, imagined her lying naked in someone else's arms. No, not *someone*. He'd actually seen the man. Sara had looked so very happy then, her beautiful white teeth showing in a broad smile. He closed his eyes in the darkness and pressed his fingertips against his temples. He couldn't go on feeling this way, he decided. Even if it was only for three more days.

Tsukuru picked up the phone and dialed Sara's number. It was just before four. The phone rang a dozen times before Sara picked up.

'I'm really sorry to call you at this hour,' Tsukuru said. 'But I had to talk to you.'

'*This hour*? What time *is* it?'

'Almost 4 a.m.'

'Goodness, I'd forgotten such a time actually existed,' Sara said. Her voice sounded still half awake. 'So, who died?'

'Nobody died,' Tsukuru said. 'Nobody's died yet. But I just have something I need to tell you tonight.'

'What sort of thing?'

'I love you, Sara, and I want you more than anything.'

Over the phone he heard a rustling sound, as if she were fumbling for something. She gave a small cough, then made a sound he took to be an exhalation.

'Is it okay to talk with you about it now?' Tsukuru asked.

'Of course,' Sara said. 'I mean, it's not even four yet. You can say whatever you want. Nobody's listening in. They're all sound asleep.'

'I truly love you, and I want you,' Tsukuru repeated.

'That's what you wanted to call me at not-quite-4-a.m. to tell me?'

'That's right.'

'Have you been drinking?'

'No, not a drop.'

'I see,' Sara said. 'For a science type, you certainly can get pretty passionate.'

'It's the same as building a station.'

'How so?'

'It's simple. If there's no station, no trains will stop there. The first thing I have to do is picture a station in my mind, and give it actual color and substance. That comes first. Even if I find a defect, that can be corrected later on. And I'm used to that kind of work.'

'Because you're an outstanding engineer.'

'I'd like to be.'

'And you're building a specially made station, just for me, until nearly dawn?'

'That's right,' Tsukuru said. 'Because I love you, and I want you.'

'I'm fond of you, too, very much. I'm more attracted to you each time we meet,' Sara said. Then she paused, as if leaving a space on the page. 'But it's nearly 4 a.m. now. Even the birds aren't up yet. It's too early to think straight. So can you wait three more days?'

'All right. But only three,' Tsukuru said. 'I think that's my limit. That's why I called you at this hour.'

'Three days is plenty, Tsukuru. I'll keep to the construction completion date, don't worry. I'll see you on Wednesday evening.'

'I'm sorry to have woken you.'

'It's all right. I'm glad to know that time still keeps on flowing at four in the morning. Is it light out yet?'

'Not yet. But it will be in a little while. The birds will start chirping.'

'The early bird catches the worm.'

'In theory.'

'But I don't think I'll be able to stay up to see that.'

'Goodnight,' he said.

'Tsukuru?' Sara said.

'Mmm?'

'Goodnight,' Sara said. 'Relax, and get some rest.'

And with that, she hung up.

Shinjuku Station is enormous. Every day nearly 3.5 million people pass through it, so many that the *Guinness Book of World Records* officially lists JR Shinjuku Station as the station with the 'Most Passengers in the World.' A number of railroad lines cross there, the main ones being the Chuo line, Sobu line, Yamanote line, Saikyo line, Shonan–Shinjuku line, and the Narita Express. The rails intersect and combine in complex and convoluted ways. There are sixteen platforms in total. In addition, there are two private rail lines, the Odakyu line and the Keio line, and three subway lines plugged in, as it were, from the side. It is a total maze. During rush hour, that maze transforms into a sea of humanity, a sea that foams up, rages, and roars as it surges toward the entrances and exits. Streams of people changing trains become entangled, giving rise to dangerous, swirling whirlpools. No prophet, no matter how righteous, could part that fierce, turbulent sea.

It's hard to believe that every morning and evening, five days a week, this overwhelming crush of human beings is dealt with efficiently, without any major problems, by a staff of station employees that no one would ever accuse of being adequate, in terms of numbers, to the task. The morning rush hour is particularly problematic. Everyone is scurrying to get to where they need to be, to punch their time clock, and no one's in a great mood. They're still tired, half asleep, and riding the bursting-at-the-seams trains is physically and emotionally draining. Only the very lucky manage to find a seat. Tsukuru was always amazed that riots don't break out, that there are no tragic, bloody disasters. If a fanatical band of terrorists did happen to target one of these jam-packed stations or trains, it would be lethal, with a horrific loss of life. For the people working on the rail lines, and the police, and, of course, the passengers, this remained the one unimaginable, nightmare scenario. And there was no way to prevent it, even now, after such a nightmare *actually did* take place in Tokyo in the spring of 1995.

Station employees bark out endless announcements over the loudspeakers, a repetitious tune marking train departures plays constantly, the automated wickets silently input a huge amount of information from all the rail cards, tickets, and train passes they scan. The long trains, their arrivals and departures timed down to the second, are like long-suffering, well-trained farm animals, systematically exhaling and inhaling people, impatiently closing their doors as they rush off toward the next station. The crowds surge up and down the stairs, but if someone steps on your foot from behind and your shoe comes off, good luck ever retrieving it. The shoe is sucked into the intense rush-hour quicksand, where it vanishes forever. The person who suffers this fate has a long day ahead, clomping around on one shoe.

In the early 1990s, before Japan's bubble economy burst, a leading newspaper in the U.S. published a large photo taken on a winter's morning of rush-hour commuters in Shinjuku Station (or possibly Tokyo Station – the same applies to both) heading down the stairs. As if by agreement, all the commuters were gazing downward, their expressions strained and unhappy, looking more like lifeless fish packed in a can than people. The article said, 'Japan may be affluent, but most Japanese look like this, heads downcast and unhappy-looking.' The photo became famous.

Tsukuru had no idea if most Japanese were, as the article claimed, unhappy. But the real reason that most passengers descending the stairs at Shinjuku Station during their packed morning commute were looking down was less that they were unhappy than that they were concerned about their footing. Don't slip on the stairs, don't lose a shoe – these are the major issues on the minds of the commuters in the mammoth station during rush hour. There was no explanation of this, no context for the photograph. Certainly it was hard to view this mass of people, clad in dark overcoats, their heads down, as happy. And of course it's logical to see a country where people can't commute in the morning without fear of losing their shoes as an unhappy society.

Tsukuru wondered how much time people spend simply commuting to work every day. Say the average commute was between an hour and an hour and a half. That sounded about right. If your typical office worker, working in Tokyo, married with a child or two, wanted to own his own house, the only choice was to live in the suburbs and spend that much time getting to work and back. So two to three hours out of every twenty-four would be spent simply in the act of commuting. If you were lucky, you might be able to read the newspaper or a paperback in the train. Maybe you could listen to your iPod, to a Haydn symphony or a conversational Spanish lesson. Some people might even close their eyes, lost in deep metaphysical speculation. Still, it would be hard to call these two or three hours rewarding, quality time. How much of one's life was snatched away to simply vanish as a result of this (most likely) pointless movement from point A to point B? And how much did this effort exhaust people, and wear them down?

But these were not issues that Tsukuru Tazaki, a railroad company employee tasked with designing stations, needed to worry about. It wasn't his life. Let people live their own lives. Each person should decide for himself how happy, or unhappy, our society might be. All Tsukuru had to think about was what might be the safest and most efficient way to keep this massive flow of people moving. For a job like this, reflection is not required, as it simply calls for accurate, tested, best practices. He was no thinker or sociologist, but a mere engineer.

Tsukuru Tazaki loved to watch JR Shinjuku Station.

When he went to the station he would buy a platform ticket from the machine and go upstairs to the platform between Tracks 9 and 10. This is where express trains on the Chuo line came and went, long-distance trains to places like Matsumoto and Kofu. Compared to the platform for commuters, there were far fewer passengers, fewer trains arriving and departing. He could sit on a bench and leisurely observe what went on in the station.

Tsukuru visited railroad stations like other people enjoy attending concerts, watching movies, dancing in clubs, watching sports, and window shopping. When he was at a loose end, with nothing to do, he headed to a station. When he felt anxious or needed to think, his feet carried him, once again of their own accord, to a station. He'd sit quietly on a bench on the platform, sip coffee he bought at a kiosk, and check the arrival and departure times against the pocket-sized timetable he always carried in his briefcase. He could spend hours doing this. Back when he was a college student he used to examine the station's layout, the passenger flow, the movements of the station staff, writing detailed observations in his notebook, but he was beyond that now.

An express train slows down as it pulls up to the platform. The doors open and passengers alight, one after another. Just watching this made him feel calm and content. When trains arrived and departed right on schedule, he felt proud, even if the station wasn't one his company had helped to construct. A quiet, simple sense of pride. A cleaning team quickly boards the train, collecting trash and turning the swivel seats around so they all neatly face forward. A new crew, wearing hats and uniforms, boards and briskly runs through a checklist. The destination sign is replaced, along with the train's designated number. Everything proceeds smoothly, efficiently, without a hitch, down to the second. This is Tsukuru Tazaki's world.

At Helsinki Central Station he had done the same thing. He got a simple train schedule, sat down on a bench, and, sipping hot coffee from a paper cup, watched the long-distance trains arrive and depart. He checked their destinations on a map, and where they'd come from. He observed the passengers getting off the trains, watched others rushing toward their respective plat- forms to board more trains, and followed the movements of the uniformed station employees and train crews. As always, doing this calmed him. Time passed, smoothly, homogeneously. Other than not being able to understand the PA announcements, it was no different from being in Shinjuku Station. The protocol for operating a railway station was pretty much the same throughout the world, the whole operation reliant on precise, skillful professionalism. This aroused a natural response in him, a sure sense that he was in the right place.

On Tuesday when Tsukuru finished work it was after eight. At this time of night he was the only one left in his office. The work he had left to do wasn't so urgent that he needed to stay late to finish it, but he was meeting Sara on Wednesday evening and he wanted to complete any leftover tasks before then.

He decided to call it a day, switched off his computer, locked up important disks and documents in a drawer, and turned off the light. He left though the company's rear entrance, saying goodnight to the security guard he knew by sight.

'Have a good night, sir,' the guard said to him.

He thought of having dinner somewhere but wasn't hungry. Still, he didn't feel like going straight home, so he headed for JR Shinjuku Station. This evening, too, he bought coffee at a kiosk. It was a typical muggy Tokyo summer night, and his back was sweaty, but still he preferred hot black coffee, the steam rising off it, to a cold drink. It was just a habit.

As always, on Platform 9 the final night train bound for Matsumoto was preparing for departure. The crew walked the length of the train, checking with practiced, diligent eyes that everything was in order. The train was not as sleek as a Shinkansen bullet train, but Tsukuru liked the plain no-nonsense trains, these familiar E257 models. The train would proceed to Shiojiri along the Chuo line, then run on the Shinonoi line to Matsumoto, and arrive in Matsumoto at five minutes till midnight. Until Hachioji it was still in an urban area and had to keep the noise down, but after that it ran through the mountains, where there were many curves, so it never could get up to the maximum speed. For the distance involved, the trip took a long time.

There was still some time before the train opened its doors for boarding, yet passengers were hurriedly buying boxed dinners, snacks, cans of beer, and magazines at the kiosk. Some had white iPod headphones in their ears, already off in their own little worlds. Others palmed smartphones, thumbing out texts, some talking so loudly into their phones that their voices rose above the blaring PA announcements. Tsukuru spotted a young couple, seated close together on a bench, happily sharing secrets. A pair of sleepy-looking five- or six-year-old twin boys, with their mother and father dragging them along by their hands, were whisked past where Tsukuru sat. The boys clutched small game devices. Two young foreign men hefted heavy-looking backpacks, while a young woman was lugging a cello case. A woman with a stunning profile passed by. Everyone was boarding a night train, heading to a far-off destination. Tsukuru envied them. At least they had a place they needed to go to.

Tsukuru Tazaki had no place he needed to go.

He realized that he had never actually been to Matsumoto, or Kofu. Or Shiojiri. Not even to the much closer town of Hachioji. He had watched countless express trains for Matsumoto depart from this platform, but it had never occurred to him that there was a possibility he could board one. Until now he had never thought of it. Why is that? he wondered.

Tsukuru imagined himself boarding this train and heading for Matsumoto. It wasn't exactly impossible. And it didn't seem like such a terrible idea. He'd suddenly gotten it into his head, after all, to take off for Finland, so why not Matsumoto? What sort of town was it? he wondered. What kind of lives did people lead there? But he shook his head and erased these thoughts. Tomorrow morning it would be impossible to get back to Tokyo in time for work. He knew that much without consulting the timetable. And he was meeting Sara tomorrow night. It was a very important day for him. He couldn't just take off for Matsumoto on a whim.

He drank the rest of his now-lukewarm coffee and tossed the paper cup into a nearby garbage bin.

Tsukuru Tazaki had nowhere he had to go. This was like a running theme of his life. He had no place he had to go to, no place to come back to. He never did, and he didn't now. The only place for him was *where he was now.*

No, he thought. That's not entirely true.

At one point in his life he did have a place he needed to go to. In high school, he had his heart set on going to an engineering college in Tokyo and majoring in railroad station design. That was *the place he needed to go.* And he studied hard to make sure he could do so. His academic advisor had coolly warned him that with his grades, he had only a 20 percent chance of getting into that school, but he'd done his best and somehow surmounted that hurdle. He had never studied so hard in his life. He wasn't cut out for competing with others for rank and grades, but given a set goal he put his heart and soul into it. He exerted himself beyond anything he'd ever imagined, and the experience was a new, and precious, discovery for him of his own capabilities.

As a result, Tsukuru left Nagoya and ended up living alone in Tokyo. In Tokyo he longed to return to his hometown as soon as he could, even if only for a short time, to see his friends again. At that point Nagoya was the place he *needed to go back to*. He shuttled back and forth between two different places for a little over a year. But then, without warning, the cycle was broken.

After this, he no longer had a place to go, or a place to which he could return. His house was still in Nagoya, his mother and eldest sister still living there, his room the same as he'd left it. His other older sister was also living in the city. Once or twice a year he made an obligatory visit and was always warmly received, but there was nothing he needed to talk to his mother or sister about, and being with them never brought back any nostalgic feelings. What they sought from him was the *Tsukuru of old*, a person he had left behind and no longer needed. To revive that person, and present him to his family, necessitated that he play a role that made him uncomfortable. The streets of Nagoya now felt remote and dreary. There was nothing there he wanted, nothing that called up even a hint of warmth.

Tokyo, meanwhile, was just the place he *happened* to end up. It was where he had attended school, where his job was located. Professionally it was the place he belonged, but beyond that, the city meant nothing to him. In Tokyo he lived a well-ordered, quiet life. Like a refugee in a foreign land, not making waves, not causing any trouble, being ever cautious so that his residence permit was not revoked. He lived there as if he were a refugee from his own life. And Tokyo was the ideal place for someone seeking a life of anonymity.

He had no one he could call a close friend. A few girlfriends entered his life along the way, but they hadn't stayed together. Peaceful relationships followed by amicable breakups. Not a single person had really climbed inside his heart. He had not been seeking that sort of relationship, and most likely the women he went out with hadn't desired him that much either. So they were even.

It's like my life came to a halt at age twenty, Tsukuru Tazaki thought, as he sat on the bench in Shinjuku Station. The days that came afterward had no real weight or substance. The years passed by, quietly, like a gentle breeze. Leaving no scars behind, no sorrow, rousing no strong emotions, leaving no happiness or memories worth mentioning. And now he was entering middle age. No – he still had a few years to go before that. But it was true that he was no longer young.

In a sense, Eri was a refugee from life as well. She too carried emotional scars, scars that had led her to leave everything behind and abandon her country. She had chosen a new world, Finland, on her own. And now she had a husband and two daughters, as well as her work making pottery, work in which she completely immersed herself. She had a summer cottage by the lake, and a chipper small dog. She'd learned Finnish, and was steadily constructing her own little universe. That makes her different from me, Tsukuru thought.

He glanced at the Heuer watch on his left wrist. It was 8:50. Passengers had begun boarding the express train. One after another, people dragged their luggage aboard, plunking themselves down in their designated seats, stowing their bags in the overhead racks, settling down in the air-conditioned cars, sipping cold drinks. He could see them through the windows of the train.

He'd inherited the watch from his father. One of the few tangible things he'd received. It was a beautiful antique, from the early 1960s. If you didn't wear it for three days, the mechanism would wind down and the hands would stop. An inconvenience, but that's what Tsukuru liked about it. It was a purely mechanical device, a piece of craftsmanship. No quartz or a single microchip inside, everything operated by delicate springs and gears. It had been working faithfully, without a rest, for a half century and was, even now, surprisingly accurate.

Tsukuru had never bought a watch himself, not once in his whole life. When he was young, someone inevitably gave him a cheap one, which he used without much thought. As long as it kept the right time, he didn't care what he wore. That was the extent of his feelings for watches. A simple Casio digital watch did the trick. So when his father died, and he was given this expensive wristwatch as a keepsake, again it aroused no special feelings one way or the other. He had to make sure to wear it regularly so it didn't wind down, but once he got used to this, he found that he had a great fondness for the watch. He enjoyed the weight and heft of it, the faint mechanical whir it made. He found himself checking the time more often than before, and each time he did, his father's shadow passed, faintly, through his mind.

Truth be told, he didn't remember his father all that well, nor did he have particularly warm memories of him. He could not recall ever going anywhere with his father, from the time he was small until he was grown up, or even having a friendly talk, just the two of them. His father was basically an uncommunicative person (at least, at home, he barely spoke), and besides, work kept him so busy that he was rarely around. Only now did Tsukuru realize that his father might have been keeping a mistress somewhere.

To Tsukuru he felt less like his real father than some well-placed relative who often visited. Tsukuru was essentially raised by his mother and his two older sisters. He knew next to nothing about what sort of life his father had led, his thoughts and values, and what he actually did day to day. What he did know was that his father had been born in Gifu, had lost both parents while still a boy, was taken in by a paternal uncle who was a Buddhist priest, managed to graduate from high school, started a company from scratch, had tremendous success, and ultimately built up a substantial fortune. Unlike most people who had struggled in life, he preferred not to dwell on the trials he'd gone through, perhaps not wishing to relive the hard times. At any rate, it was clear that his father had an extraordinary head for business, the talent to immediately obtain what he needed, and jettison everything he didn't. Tsukuru's oldest sister had, in part, inherited this talent for business from her father, while the younger sister had also, in part, inherited her mother's cheerful sociability. Neither of these qualities had been passed on to Tsukuru.

His father had smoked over fifty cigarettes a day, and had died of lung cancer. When Tsukuru went to visit him at the hospital in Nagoya, he could no longer speak. His father seemed to want to tell him something, but couldn't do so. A month later he died in his hospital bed. His father left him the one-bedroom condo in Jiyugaoka, a bank account with a fair amount of money in his name, and this Heuer self-winding wristwatch.

No, there *was* one other thing his father had left him. His name – Tsukuru Tazaki.

When Tsukuru announced that he wanted to study at an engineering college in Tokyo, his father seemed deeply disappointed that his only son had no interest in taking over the real estate business he had worked so hard to build. Still, he fully supported Tsukuru's desire to become an engineer. 'If that's what you want,' his father had told him, 'then you should go to the college in Tokyo, and I'll be happy to pay for it. Learning a technical skill and building real objects is a good thing. It contributes to society. Study hard,' he'd said, 'and build as many stations as you like.' His father seemed pleased that the name he'd chosen – Tsukuru – had turned out to be so appropriate. This was probably the first and last time Tsukuru had made his father happy, certainly the only time he had seen his father so openly pleased.

At exactly 9 p.m., right on schedule, the express train for Matsumoto pulled away from the platform. Seated on the bench, Tsukuru watched as its lights faded down the tracks, as the train sped up and finally disappeared into the summer night. Once the last car was no longer visible, everything around him felt suddenly deserted. Even the lights of the city seemed to have faded a notch, like when a play is over and the lights go out after the last act. He got up from the bench and slowly made his way down the stairs.

He left Shinjuku Station, went into a nearby restaurant, sat at the counter, and ordered meatloaf and potato salad. He barely finished half of each. Not that the food tasted bad. This restaurant was famous for its delicious meatloaf. He just had no appetite. As always, he only finished half his beer.

He rode the train home and took a shower, and carefully scrubbed his whole body with soap. He then put on an olive-green bathrobe (a gift from a girlfriend back on his thirtieth birthday) and sat down on a chair on the balcony, letting the night breeze waft over him as he listened to the muffled din of the city. It was nearly 11 p.m., but he wasn't tired.

Tsukuru remembered those days in college when all he'd thought about was dying. Already sixteen years ago. Back then he was convinced that if he merely focused on what was going on inside of him, his heart would finally stop of its own accord. That if he intensely concentrated his feelings on one fixed point, like a lens focused on paper, bursting it into flames, his heart would suffer a fatal blow. More than anything he hoped for this. But months passed, and contrary to his expectation, his heart didn't stop. The heart apparently doesn't stop that easily.

From far off in the distance, he heard a helicopter. It seemed to be getting nearer, the sound growing louder. He looked up at the sky, trying to catch sight of it. It felt like a messenger bringing some vital news. But he never saw it, the sound of the propellers fading, then disappearing completely to the west, leaving behind only the soft, vague hum of the city at night.

Maybe back then Shiro had been hoping to break up their group. This possibility suddenly struck him. Seated on a chair on the balcony, he slowly filled out this hypothesis.

Their group in high school had been so close, so very tight. They accepted each other as they were, understood each other, and each of them found a deep contentment and happiness in their relationship, their little group. But such bliss couldn't last forever. At some point paradise would be lost. They would each mature at different rates, take different paths in life. As time passed, an unavoidable sense of unease would develop among them, a subtle fault line, no doubt turning into something less than *subtle*.

Shiro's nerves might not have been able to stand the pressure of *what had to come*, the trauma of the inevitable end of this tight-knit group of friends. She may have felt she had to unravel the emotional bonds of the group herself or else be caught up, fatally, in its collapse, like a castaway sucked down into the abyss by the whirlpool of a sinking ship.

Tsukuru could, to an extent, understand that feeling. Now he could, that is. The tension of suppressed sexual feelings began to take on greater significance than Tsukuru could imagine. The graphic sexual dreams he had later were probably an extension of that tension. And that tension must have had some effect – what, exactly, he had no idea – on the other four as well.

Shiro had wanted to escape from that situation. Maybe she couldn't stand that kind of relationship anymore, the close relationship that required constant maintenance of one's feelings. Shiro was, unquestionably, the most sensitive of the five, so she must have picked up on that friction before anyone else. But she was unable, at least on her own, to escape outside that circle. She didn't possess the strength. So she set Tsukuru up as the apostate. At that point, Tsukuru was the first member to step outside the circle, the weakest link in the community. To put it another way, he deserved to be punished. So when someone raped her (who did it and what the circumstances were behind her rape and subsequent pregnancy would remain eternal mysteries), in the midst of the hysteric confusion brought on by shock, she ripped away that weakest link, like yanking the emergency cord to stop a train.

Viewed in this way, many things fell into place. Back then Shiro followed her instincts and chose Tsukuru as a stepping stone, a way for her to reach outside the walls of their group. Shiro must have had a gut feeling that Tsukuru, even put in that awful position, would be able to survive – just as Eri, too, had arrived at the same conclusion.

Tsukuru Tazaki, always cool and collected, always doing things at his own pace.

Tsukuru got up from the chair on the balcony and went inside. He took a bottle of Cutty Sark from a shelf, poured some into a glass, then carried it back out to the porch. He sat down again and, for a time, pressed the fingers of his right hand against his temple.

No, he thought, I'm not cool and collected, and I'm not always doing things at my own pace. It's just a question of balance. I'm just good at habitually shifting the weight I carry around from one side of the fulcrum to the other, distributing it. Maybe this strikes others as cool. But it isn't an easy operation. It takes more time than it seems. And even if I do find the right balance, that doesn't lessen the total weight one bit.

And yet he was able to forgive Shiro, or Yuzu. She carried within her a deep wound and had only been trying, desperately, to protect herself. She was a weak person, someone who lacked the hard, tough exterior with which to guard herself. It was all she could do to find a safe refuge when danger came, and she couldn't be particular about the methods. Who could blame her? But in the end, no matter how far she ran, she couldn't escape, for the dark shadow of violence followed her relentlessly. What Eri dubbed an *evil spirit*. And on a quiet, cold, and rainy May night, *it* knocked at her door, and strangled her lovely slim throat. In a place, and time, that had, most likely, already been decided.

Tsukuru went back inside, picked up the phone, and without thinking much about what he was doing, pushed the speed-dial number for Sara. The phone rang three times before he thought better of it and hung up. It was already late. And he would be seeing her tomorrow. Then he would see her and talk to her in person. He shouldn't short-circuit the process before he saw her. He knew that. Still, he wanted to hear Sara's voice, right now. The feeling welled up inside him so overwhelmingly that it was hard to suppress the urge.

He placed the record of Lazar Berman's performance of *Years of Pilgrimage* on the turntable, and lowered the needle. He turned his attention to the music. The scene of the lakeside at Hämeenlinna came to him. The white lace curtain rustling in the breeze, the sound of the little boat rocked by the waves, slapping against the pier. The birds in the forest patiently teaching their tiny bird babies how to chirp. The citrusy smell Eri's shampoo had left on her hair. The dense weight of the life force, the will to survive, within the ample softness of her breasts. The hard phlegm spat out in the weeds by the dour old man who'd shown him the way. The dog wagging its tail excitedly as it leaped into the back of the Renault. As he traced memories of these scenes, the pain in his chest that he'd felt returned once more.

Tsukuru drank the Cutty Sark, savoring the fragrance. His stomach grew faintly warm. From the summer of his sophomore year in college until the following winter, when every day brought thoughts of dying and nothing else, he'd had one small glass of whiskey at night like this. Without it, he hadn't been able to sleep.

The phone suddenly rang. He stood up from the sofa, gently raised the needle from the record, and stood in front of the phone. It had to be Sara. No one else would call him at this hour of night. She knew he'd called and was calling him back. As the phone rang a dozen times Tsukuru hesitated, unsure if he should answer. He bit his lip hard, held his breath, and stared intently at the phone, like a person standing far away, off studying the details of a difficult formula on a blackboard, trying to puzzle it out. But he could find no clues. The phone stopped ringing, followed by silence. A deep, suggestive silence.

To fill in the silence Tsukuru lowered the needle onto the record again, went back to the sofa, and settled in to listen to the music. This time he tried his best not to think of anything in particular. With his eyes closed and his mind a blank, he focused solely on the music. Finally, as if lured in by the melody, images flashed behind his eyelids, one after the next, appearing, then disappearing. A series of images without concrete form or meaning, rising up from the dark margins of consciousness, soundlessly crossing into the visible realm, only to be sucked back into the margins on the other side and vanish once again. Like the mysterious outline of microorganisms swimming across the circular field of vision of a microscope.

Fifteen minutes later the phone rang again, and again he did not answer it. This time he stayed seated, listening to the music, gazing at the black phone. He didn't count how many times it rang. Eventually it stopped, and all he could hear was the music.

Sara, he thought. I want to hear your voice. I want to hear it more than anything. But right now I can't talk.

Tomorrow Sara may choose that other man, not me, Tsukuru thought as he lay down on the sofa and closed his eyes. It's entirely possible, and for her it may well be the right choice.

What kind of person this other man was, what sort of relationship they had, how long they'd been seeing each other – all of this Tsukuru had no way of knowing. And he didn't want to know, either. One thing he could say at this point was this: he had very little he could give her. Limited in amount, and in kind, the contents negligible. Would anybody really want the little he had to give?

Sara said she has feelings for me. He had no reason to doubt it. But there are countless things in the world for which affection is not enough. Life is long, and sometimes cruel. Sometimes victims are needed. Someone has to take on that role. And human bodies are fragile, easily damaged. Cut them, and they bleed.

If Sara doesn't choose me tomorrow, he thought, I may *really* die. Die in reality, or die figuratively – there isn't much difference between the two. But this time I definitely will take my last breath. Colorless Tsukuru Tazaki will lose any last hint of color and quietly exit the world. All will become a void, the only thing that remains a hard, frozen clump of dirt.

It doesn't matter. The same thing has nearly happened a few times already, and it wouldn't be strange if it actually did this time. It's just a physical phenomenon, no more. The spring on a wound watch gets steadily looser, the torque grows closer and closer to zero, until the gears stop altogether and the hands come to rest at a set position. Silence descends. Isn't that all it is?

He slipped into bed just before the date changed, and switched off the bedside lamp. How nice it would be to dream of Sara, Tsukuru thought. An erotic dream. Or one that wasn't – either would be good. If possible, though, a dream that wasn't too sad. A dream in which he could touch her body would be more than he could ask for. It was, after all, just a dream.

He longed for her more than he could say. It was a wonderful thing to be able to truly want someone like this – the feeling was so real, so overpowering. He hadn't felt this way in ages.

Maybe he never had before. Not that everything about it was wonderful: his chest ached, he found it hard to breathe, and a fear, a dark oscillation, had hold of him. But now even that kind of ache had become an important part of the affection he felt. He didn't want to let that feeling slip from his grasp. Once lost, he might never happen across that warmth again. If he had to lose it, he would rather lose himself.

Tsukuru, you need to hang on to her. No matter what. If you let her go now, you might not ever have anyone else in your life.

Eri was right. No matter what, he had to make Sara his. But this wasn't something he could decide on his own. It was a question decided by two people, between one heart and another. Something had to be given, and something had to be accepted. Everything depends on tomorrow. If Sara chooses me, accepts me, he thought, I'm going to propose to her right away. And give her everything I'm capable of giving – every single thing. Before I get lost in a dark forest. Before the bad elves grab me.

Not everything was lost in the flow of time. That's what Tsukuru should have said to Eri when he said goodbye at the lakeside in Finland. But at that point, he couldn't put it into words.

We truly believed in something back then, and we knew we were the kind of people capable of believing in something – with all our hearts. And that kind of hope will never simply vanish.

He calmed himself, shut his eyes, and fell asleep. The rear light of consciousness, like the last express train of the night, began to fade into the distance, gradually speeding up, growing smaller until it was, finally, sucked into the depths of the night, where it disappeared. All that remained was the sound of the wind slipping through a stand of white birch trees.